Sunshine &
SHADOWS

Sunshine &
SHADOWS

Emily Sage

POOLBEG

This novel is entirely a work of fiction. The names, characters and incidents portrayed in it are the work of the author's imagination. Any resemblance to actual persons, living or dead, events or localities is entirely coincidental.

Published 2005
by Poolbeg Press Ltd
123 Grange Hill, Baldoyle
Dublin 13, Ireland
E-mail: poolbeg@poolbeg.com

© Emily Sage 2005

The moral right of the author has been asserted.

Typesetting, layout, design © Poolbeg Press Ltd.

1 3 5 7 9 10 8 6 4 2

A catalogue record for this book is available from the British Library.

ISBN 1-84223-117-0

Typeset by Patricia Hope in Palatino 10.5/15
Printed by Nørhaven Paperback A/S, Denmark

www.poolbeg.com

About the Author

Born in Ireland, Emily Sage now lives in Ramsgate, Kent, with her two teenage sons and cat, Lizzie. She is currently working on her fourth novel.

Acknowledgements

No man is an island and at no time does this become more obvious than when you are writing a book, because it's then that the influences of the many people you've met throughout your life come to bear. And so I would like to take this opportunity to thank all of you who lent (quite unwittingly) your voices and mannerisms, sayings and stories, to the characters that make up *Sunshine & Shadows*. Neither Eileen nor Paddy are real, yet they, their family and the characters surrounding them live and breathe just as surely as if they had flesh to their bones and blood in their veins and I have come to love them as I would my nearest and dearest.

So thank you, Frances Finneran McBride – for the stories we shared during many a long evening, when you spoke about your life as a young girl growing up in Galway, for making me laugh and for providing more than a dollop of inspiration.

To Dan Fox, late of Rosemount, Co Westmeath – to you I owe the voice of Paddy, the wisdom, the generosity of spirit and Paddy's love of books. Some people will never be forgotten, and you are one of them!

To my mother and father and the whole of the Manning family, thanks, as always, for your unstinting belief in me. Ditto for my best friend in the whole world, Susan Cummins.

The biggest thanks of all, I reserve for Gaye Shortland, editor sublime and the only one I know who can take a pig's ear and turn it into something closely approximating a silk purse.

Thank you too to Paula Campbell and all at Poolbeg, as well as to all the readers who make writing worthwhile. I hope you enjoy this book.

Finally, I would like to apologise if I have missed anybody out. It was not intentional and should be put down to my being another year older and a few brain cells shorter.

PROLOGUE

It seemed inappropriate, a mockery almost, for the sun to shine on a day so full of despair. Rain would have been better. Teeming rain, like angels weeping at the death of one of their own. And wind. Howling keening wind to catch and blow away the words of the priest below, who in a voice sonorous as a tolling bell, intoned the requiem over a freshly dug grave. But shine the sun did, a bright golden penny etched against the unseasonable blue of the sky, while undisturbed by any breath of air the priest prayed on.

A safe distance away, perched atop an ancient headstone, a crow kept vigil, head cocked and bright-eyed, biding his time till the mourners went away and the fresh-turned earth gave up its wealth of insect life. Patient, he let the priest's voice wash over him, rising and dipping like notes on a scale, angling his gaze to watch as, bending down, the man hefted a handful of soft earth, and tossed it into the gaping hole. *"In nomine Patris, et Filii et Spiritus Sancti . . ."* His right hand, the palm stigmata'd with rusty earth, rose in benediction, but just as he reached the "Amen", and the congregation opened their mouths in preparation for the response, a young woman sprang forward, almost knocking him off balance.

"No!" With a scream dredged up from the primordial depths of her soul, she threw herself headlong down beside the grave, scrabbling frantically with her bare hands and sending the crow into a mad panic of black wings that lifted him, flapping crossly, into the sanctuary of the church eaves. *"No! No! No!"* The scream rose, became a shriek, an obscenity, a howl of pure untethered agony that ripped and stripped and plundered the consecrated air of the churchyard, ricocheting off gravestones and walls and the shocked bone-white faces of the black-clad mourners. "Not my baby! Give him back to me!" Wild-eyed, her long hair breaking free from the black lace mantilla that covered her head, she fought like a spirit possessed as a flurry of arms reached out to hold her back. "Oh, God, give him back! Give him back!"

Hopping irritably from leg to leg, the crow chattered his displeasure at the drama unfolding below, falling silent again as a man, young, handsome despite the sorrow so clearly etched on his face, barged forward. "Leave her be!" Sharp-voiced and commanding, he stooped down, caught the woman by her wrists and pulled her gently, but firmly, to her feet. "There now, my love," he crooned, cradling her safely against him. "There now, my darling. It'll be all right. Really, it will." But, tossing and turning within the circle of his arms, the woman refused to be restrained. Throwing her head back, she bawled her pain, teeth bared, at the sky above, flailing and battering at his chest as the mantilla slid to the ground and her hair uncoiled itself all the way down past her waist, red as a river of blood. Close by, three little girls stood, hand in hand, and wept.

After they had all gone away and the gravedigger had filled in the grave, carelessly heaping the earth into a lopsided pyramid, the bird ventured hopefully closer to the edge, sticking out his long neck, then retreating like a shot as, below, a solitary figure emerged from behind a nearby yew tree. Picking his way almost stealthily over to the grave, the man stood there for a while, head bent well forward in silent contemplation, shoulders jerking spasmodically. A black curl tumbled across his forehead and, impatient, he swiped it away.

"I'm sorry . . ." The words came out on a groan, so low as to be barely audible. "I'm sorry!" he said again and this time there was no mistaking either the words or the anguish behind them. "As God is my judge, I'd swop places with you if I could." Falling to his knees, he covered his face with his hands, unaware that the sun had moved slowly across the sky and now stood directly above him like an artfully placed spotlight highlighting his shame. After a while, willed on by the bird, he rose unsteadily to his feet and with a last sorrowful look at the grave, turned his back and walked away. Squawking in triumph, the crow launched himself victoriously into the air.

CHAPTER ONE

Paddy McNab smacked his fist down with such fury his tea slopped over the edge of the mug and formed a rough map of Ireland on the table.

"They're going and that's all there's to it!" Mutinous, he stuck his bottom lip out, head jutting forward in aggression. "No one's making little of my girls. Good as the rest they are. Aye, and better than most!"

"Well, if you say so, Paddy." Dubious, his wife grabbed hold of a dishcloth and with an expert flick arrested the spillage before it dripped onto the floor. "But Mother Benignus said –"

"Mother Benignus, is it? Mother Benignus!" Whiplashing through the air, his hand cut her off. "Frustrated that one is, just like the rest of them.

Some fella gave her the elbow, no doubt, and away with her to lick her wounds up at the convent and torment the life out of the poor kids she's supposed to be teaching." Snorting, he shot her a look that could dissolve marble. "I'll tell you this, Eily, the day that one gets into Heaven will be the day I buy a ticket for hell because, as God's my witness, if it comes to a contest, I'll take Lucifer over that one, any day. Aye, the devil *and* all his legions!"

Narrowing her eyes, Eileen sent a warning look to where her three young daughters were playing at babby-houses in the corner. "Ssh, now! Mind how you talk in front of the children. They'll grow up with respect for neither God nor man if you continue like that."

"Respect has to be earned," he reminded her darkly, dropping his voice all the same. "In any case, it's a done deed. They're going and that's that! Mother Benignus or no bloody Mother Benignus!"

Dabbing at the table, Eileen didn't even attempt to argue further and truth to tell she was glad at the stance he'd taken. Paddy McNab was not a man to let his bone go with any dog. As he said himself, they might not have tuppence to jingle on a tombstone, but, by God, they had their pride and plenty of it.

Scraping his chair back from the table, he sketched a hurried Sign of the Cross, rose and dropped a light kiss on her cheek, wrinkling his nose in appreciation at the fresh clean soap-and-water smell of her. "That was a grand bit of bacon, Eileen." He patted his stomach, a twinkle in his eye. "All it needs now is a drop of the black to wash it down."

Indulgent, she flapped him away with the dishcloth. "Go on with you then. But don't spend all night down the pub and watch you don't go falling in any ditches on the way home!"

Not that there was any danger of that, she thought, watching a little sadly as tousling the heads of each of his three daughters he disappeared out the door. A pint of Guinness, two at the most and his pockets would be as empty as a politician's promise on the eve of a general election. Occasionally, mind, he struck gold. There would be a celebration or a wake and then she would be awakened in the small hours of the morning by 'The Auld Triangle' or 'Kevin Barry' belted out in the rich baritone voice some compared to John McCormack, the great Irish tenor. Still, drunk or sober, Paddy McNab was a gentle man with a heart as big as himself and not a day went by that she didn't thank God for him.

Leaning against the door frame, she followed his progress up the road, watching till he disappeared round a sudden bend, lifting his hand in a kind of backward wave. Eleven years on and four children later and she still found him as hard to resist as the first time he'd caught her eye at a *Feis Ceoil* over in Galway.

Gazing into the middle distance, Eileen thought back to that day with a good deal of satisfaction. It had been one of those rare days, the kind that made you feel good from the first moment you opened your eyes, where there was a sense of anticipation that anything might happen and where everything seemed to be melded in harmony, from the sun, bright as a button of gold in the cloudless sky, to the sky itself, smooth and blue, a bolt of satin that unravelled all the way into infinity. And down below, the sea, holding up a silver-tinged mirror to the glory of both. Putting on her best frock, a full-skirted summer dress, the green of fresh spring grass and dotted about with white daisies, Eileen experienced a flash of happiness so intense that even after all these years it still had the power to bring a smile to her face. Oh, but she'd been pretty back then, even though she hadn't known it. Tall and slender with that wonderful pennant of fiery hair, which, for years, had been the bane of her life as people teased her with names that ranged from 'carrot-head' to 'copper-nob'. But then, Paddy McNab had come along and with the wand of mere words, gleaned from the books he so loved to read, completely transformed her appearance, so that her hair suddenly became 'Titian' and her blue eyes took on the hue of a bluebell field, whilst her skin, lightly spattered with the freckles so often found on and detested by people that shared her colouring, became 'kissed by the sun'. Paddy had a different way of looking at things, all right. He should have been a poet or an artist or even a great writer. But, as he said himself, professions like that were for the privileged few, the ones with money behind them, the ones with back doors to their houses where the tradesmen came to call. There was no back door to their cottage. The tradesman lived inside! Nevertheless, Paddy had the soul of an artist and the mind of a philosopher and, most important of all, his heart was in the right place.

Smoothing her hands down over her hips, shapely still, but not quite so slender these days since the birth of her children, her thoughts turned back to the first time she'd laid eyes on him.

The *Feis Ceoil* was a big event, one of the biggest music festivals in all Ireland. Held annually, it was an opportunity for people to come from miles around, even from neighbouring counties, to meet and greet and renew old acquaintances. Some even came to find love. But not her. Eileen had no intention of marrying, not for ages yet, but then, as her mother was fond of pointing out, the road to hell was paved with good intentions and Eileen hadn't bargained on meeting Paddy McNab. And she certainly hadn't bargained on him turning all her carefully laid plans for the future on their heads. From the first moment she'd caught sight of him up on the stage, all of that had paled into insignificance. Neither had she been the only one smitten – not by a long chalk. Oh, there'd been many the lassie sending out smoke signals as, clearly dressed in his Sunday best – a dark suit and a shirt so white you nearly had to shade your eyes from the dazzle – he'd serenaded them all with one of the best renditions of 'Danny Boy' she'd heard either before or since. But small luck to them! For all that they'd stood there primping and preening and peering coyly out from under their fluttering lashes, hers was the eye he caught and within six months the banns were called and by the time the *Feis Ceoil* came round again, they were already married in the sight of man and God.

Not that it had been as easy as all that. Life seldom was, Eileen had long since learned. Some poet fella Paddy told her about had put it well. The road less travelled, he called it, the road she and Paddy had inadvertently set out upon the day they fell for each other. It was a road strewn with obstacles and pitfalls, the very first of which had been her own father whose reaction had been firstly one of pure disbelief, and then real anger or 'incandescence' as Paddy put it – another favourite jawbreaker word he'd picked up from some book or other and to this day whenever he had a free moment, that's where you'd find him, with his head stuck in a book. All kinds of books. Everything from James Joyce to that American fella . . . drawing a blank for a moment, Eileen sought inspiration from the heavens and a passing wraith of opaque cloud. Steinbeck! John Steinbeck. Just recently he'd finished reading *The Grapes of Wrath* to her at night while she did the ironing or caught up on a bit of sewing and she'd really enjoyed it, which was as much down to the way he read it, putting his heart and soul into it, as to the content itself. And her father had had the cheek, the pure gall, to call him a big uneducated, gormless galoot and threaten to set the dogs on him!

"You will not!" Eileen had faced him out, which took some courage as Richie Brady had the devil's own temper when roused and even her soft-hearted mother couldn't shift him on this point.

"He's no good, I'm telling you, Eileen. Marry that fella and you'll repent at leisure all right. Sure what is he?" Bewildered, his glance ranged wildly around the room, seeking answers from the walls and ceiling, the floor, the window, even the picture of St Martin de Porres that hung over the mantelpiece, before finally honing in on her own mutinous face. "A blacksmith! I ask ye! A common blacksmith! And where will he find work? Eh? Where will he find work? There's hardly a working forge left in the country. It's all factories now that do the ironmongery and little one-man-band outfits that can hardly keep body and soul together, let alone employ a big hulking gom like Paddy McNab!" Black as thunder, he'd reached out, jabbing at the air with a calloused finger. "Oh, I grant you, he's a good-looking blackguard all right, but looks don't last forever. They go off the boil sooner or later, Eily, just like that pot on the stove over there and they certainly won't put a roof over your head or keep the bailiffs from the door." His voice rose in direct proportion to the heat of his anger. "Go ahead and marry him, my girl, and I guarantee you'll be storing up a lifetime of poverty for yourself. Poverty and misery, for you and yours!" He jerked his head floorwards. "And when you're in the poverty trap, when you're down the well and the water's closing over your head, you need one hell of a big rope to climb back out of it again." He gave a half stamp of his foot. "Aye, and the services of a saint to throw it to you!"

It still hurt to remember his fury, the way he'd used his finger like a baton, swishing it backwards and forwards beneath her nose, then up and down, slicing through the air.

"And don't think you can come running to me or your mother. When you make your bed, you'd better learn to settle on it, lumps, bumps, fleas and all!"

"There's nothing wrong with being a blacksmith. It's an honest occupation." Trembling, Eileen stood her ground. "He could have gone on to secondary school, you know. He won a scholarship to the Brothers in Galway. And who knows, after that, he could have gone off to university in Dublin or somewhere and really made something of himself. But he didn't!" Her voice shook. "And do you know why he didn't? Because his family needed him, that's why. They needed whatever bit of money he could add to the pot and so he was apprenticed at a smithy when he was only twelve, because his family were hungry and next to that his own dreams didn't seem that important!" Her bright blue eyes, made brighter by the tears that stood in them, had pleaded, if not for his blessing, then at least for understanding. "And I love him for that, Da. I *really* love him." Dramatically she'd banged her hand against her heart. "There's times I love him so much, my heart hurts."

But her father had no truck with sentimentality, or 'that ould rubbish' as he called it. Life was a school for hard knocks and every dog and devil in the street could tell you a story that would take a tear from your eye. Tales a hell of a lot worse than anything McNab had had to go through and, fair enough, while he could sympathise with him, he wanted more for his daughter. He'd spent his own life running just to stand still, and while love might be a word that tripped easily from Eileen's lips, experience had shown him that it really didn't have much to do with the real world. Not their world, anyway.

Knitting his brow fiercely, he looked her straight in the eye, pinioning her in a way that made Eileen feel that she couldn't move, even if she'd wanted to and no matter how hard she tried. "Aye, well, if your heart hurts now, my girl, it's nothing to what it's going to hurt like when you're living hand to mouth with a posse of snotty-nosed kids looking up in your face begging for a crust." Grabbing his blackthorn stick, he'd stormed for the back door. "And remember this, Eileen. When poverty comes in the door, love flies out the window. That's a true saying. None truer. You'd do well to heed it!"

He left the house with a slam of the door that set the very windows to rattling and every utensil on the rickety shelves and, all these years on, Eileen still recalled hearing the sharp-pitched whistle that called for Con the sheepdog and the way it echoed and reverberated round and round in her head like the voice of doom.

Above her the evening sun moved slowly towards the west, but, intent on looking inward at the past, Eileen never even noticed, no more than she noticed the gentle breeze that had sprung up suddenly, gently teasing red strands of hair out of the loose bun

14

she habitually wore, and chivvying the tide on the beach below.

Always the peacemaker, her mother had tried pouring oil on troubled waters. "I know he sounds harsh, Eily, but he means it for the best, you know. And he does know what he's talking about." With a jerk of her head, she invited her daughter to take stock of the poorly furnished room around them. "Not much to show for twenty-five years, is it? A few sticks of furniture, most of it riddled with the woodworm, and not much else. And that's why he wants more than this for you. *No*, Eily!" Her voice grew urgent as Eileen made to walk away. "*No!* You stay here and listen, because me and your father *know* what it's like to struggle. We've done it all our lives. Oh, we might have hid it well from you and your brother, but many's the night found us lying wakeful and fearful, dreading the knock on the door in the morning that might have seen us all turfed out onto the street." Tenderly she reached up and brushed a wayward strand of burnished hair back from where it had fallen across Eileen's forehead. It was a tender gesture and one she had made countless times down through the years. Her eyes, two deep pools of honesty, pinned themselves on her daughter's. "God knows, there were times when I didn't think we'd make it. And there were times when I would cheerfully have lain down, shut my eyes and never woken up again. But the life force is very strong and somehow the dawn came up again each morning and somehow I struggled on. But it's not a life I would recommend." Coaxing, she'd taken Eileen by the hand, led her to an armchair, perching on the arm herself. "Why do you think I took on all those midwifery and laying-out jobs, Eily? Not for the pleasure of it, I can assure you, although I'll be the first to admit that there's nothing quite as amazing as seeing a new life enter the world. Hearing the first cry! Being there to witness the sheer joy, the wonder on the face of the mother! Now that, I grant you, is truly priceless! But then, on the other hand, there's nothing quite so heart-rending as laying out a dead body, particularly when it's that of a friend or neighbour, someone you've known and cared about, exchanged pleasantries over the garden fence with, as well as hopes and dreams. To see them with all the life drained out of them, cold and dead as a side of beef and already beginning to reek. It's horrible, Eileen. Undignified. More than that, it's frightening! And those are the pictures I carry in my head at night. Those are the ones that have me up and walking the floors at all hours, those dark, deadly hours before dawn when life is at its lowest ebb and hope is a thing for other people." Slipping off the arm of the chair, she got down on her knees in front of her daughter, clasped both her hands in her own, leaning in so close they were almost chin to chin. "But, like I said, *I* had no choice but to take whatever work I could. You *have*! And I'm not too proud to beg you, Eily. Don't throw your life away for a mess of pottage dressed up as love. Go to Dublin, like you'd planned. Spread your wings. Get away from here and give yourself the chance of something better. It's not all that long ago you were hopping up and down with excitement when you got that letter from McVeigh's. Surely you can't have forgotten that already?"

Forgotten it? Eileen remembered it well, the mingled sense of dread and anticipation as she held the letter with the Dublin postmark in her hand, turning it over and back as though at any moment it would explode and burst into flames, while her parents and elder brother, Dick, his three young children trick-acting round his feet, seethed with frustration. Three weeks since the interview, three long weeks during which time she'd waited and prayed for this letter, waylaying old Packy-the-Post every morning till finally he'd begged her to "lave off damming him – if a letter was coming for her, it wouldn't go past her". And when finally it did come, importantly enclosed in a manila envelope and regally franked with McVeigh's insignia, she'd been too frightened to open it. Eventually, to put them all out of their misery, she'd handed it over to Dick, who, knowing she was on tenterhooks, left off his normal teasing, ripped it open, scanned the contents and a moment later waved the letter like some sort of victory banner over his head.

"You've done it, Eily! You've bleddy done it!" With a whoop he scanned it again, reading selected passages aloud. *"Dear Miss Brady, it is with much pleasure that McVeigh's invites you to take up the post of junior seamstress at our Dublin premises in Mary Street. The position carries . . . to be remunerated . . . commencing . . ."* Eyes shining, Dick broke off. "Imagine it. Dublin! You lucky little devil! Here I am, a full ten years older than you, and I've never even been within an ass's roar of Dublin and there's yourself, Lady Godiva, beating me to the post." Mock-annoyed, he smote his forehead, although those watching sensed that his frustration was only too real, because, since Nancy had run off to God-knows-where, leaving him to raise their young family alone, Dick had little chance of seeing anything past the last acre of the small farm he owned. For him, Dublin might as well have been the capital city of Mars! Still, he put a good face on it, and beaming round declared, much to his children's delight, "Did you hear that, you three? Your Aunty Eily is going to Dublin. Well, I'll be a monkey's uncle!"

"Did you hear that, Aunty Eily?" Dick's eight-year-old son, John-Joe, Eileen's pet, echoed, bounding over with all the effervescence of a young puppy, wrapping his arms around her middle and squeezing the life out of her. "Daddy's a monkey's uncle!"

"Ah, you're a bit of a monkey yourself, John-Joe Brady," Eileen declared, loosening his grip, turning round and bending over so that he could climb on her back. "And I think it's time you went back to the jungle. So, climb up here and I'll give you a lift."

"And us, Aunty Eily! Don't forget us!" In hot pursuit, Nuala and Mary, John-Joe's ten-year-old twin sisters hurtled after them, as Eileen pelted up the back garden with John-Joe holding on for dear life and laughing like a maniac all the way. Collapsing into an exhausted and undignified heap beneath the horse-chestnut tree at the end of the garden, Eileen chuckled as they piled on top of her. "Oh, you'd better make hay while the sun shines," she'd told them. "You'd better make the most of your old aunty, all right, because I might develop notions up in Dublin, fierce airs and graces altogether, and not know you at all when I come back."

The following weekend, she had gone to the *Feis Ceoil.*

With a long-drawn-out sigh for old memories, Eileen turned away from the door and set about the business of clearing the table, re-emerging a short time later with the carefully wrapped remains of the bacon and stowing it in the cool press attached to the outside of the cottage wall. Tomorrow she would fry it up with maybe a potato cake or two and that would be another meal taken care of.

Despite its shortcomings, the lack of space, the creeping damp, the mould in the rafters and the thatch that looked like an untidy fringe, Eileen loved every inch of the cottage. Built in the traditional style, it was a long low building, perched high on a promontory overlooking a great expanse of ever-changing Atlantic Ocean. To anyone looking landward from a boat, it must have looked pretty much picture perfect, white and sparkling in the sunlight like an iced ornament on the top tier of a wedding cake. On evenings such as this with the hint of summer in the air, she could sit for hours and watch the waves below, curtseying back and forth in a curious old-fashioned minuet, each one scalloped with an edging of the finest lace like a courtesan's ball-gown. When winter prevailed, however, when both sky and sea were clad in full mourning and the wind was keening a requiem, she was glad to seek the sanctuary of its four walls and to turn her back on the tumultuous breakers below, fighting to the death in a spray of fury.

Sometimes, though, she was lonely, especially for

the company of other women. The Mackeys, their nearest neighbours, lived a good mile away and, although people did make the long trek to the cottage and she herself went visiting on occasion, it wasn't quite the same as being able to pop next door when the mood took you for a cup of tea and a good old chinwag. Mind you, there was talk recently that Donal Flynn had been approached about selling the land next to their cottage, but Paddy had shrugged it off, saying that if he'd had a penny for every time he'd heard that particular rumour, he'd be living in *Áras an Uachtaráin* right alongside of the President. And Eileen suspected he was right. It took a certain kind of character to bury yourself this far out in the sticks. Years ago when old Jack McNab, from whom Paddy had inherited the cottage, had approached Donal Flynn's father about buying the land, it was said Donal Senior, unable to believe his luck at finding such a big eejit, had been drunk for a week and had practically given it away. And, fair enough, there was no real value in the land. The salty winds blowing in from the sea saw to it that not much grew, just a bit of scutch grass and a few trees dotted here and there, stunted misshapen skeletons in grotesque balletic poses. But old Jack had been something of a hermit and the solitude suited him well. He had also, some of the old-timers had it, been something of a rogue and being far away from the long arm of the law also suited him well. But that, as far as Eileen knew, was simply conjecture and if Jack had hidden any ill-gotten gains anywhere, she had yet to find them. Which thought brought her straight back to her immediate problems. If only Paddy could get a job. It was hard trying to raise a family with no idea where the next penny was coming from. Still, she would manage, she supposed, frowning into the distance. She would have to. Just like her mother.

"You should have listened!" a seagull seemed to taunt, flashing past her suddenly in a blur of white wings and yellow beak, the air around it shattering like crystal at the harshness of his cry. "You should have listened!"

Deep in thought she watched as, reaching its final destination and weary of the day, the sun began its descent, easing itself slowly out of the jaded sky and deep down into its own reflection. Then, making sure the mesh door on the cool press was securely hooked, she turned and went back inside where it was warm and smoky and where the light from the oil-lamp threw giant picture-shadows across walls and ceiling. On nights when she couldn't sleep, and there had been a lot of those lately, she liked to lie there and watch the shadows, now looming as the lamp gave a sudden splutter that set the wick to dancing, now shrinking back as the flame died down again. Rabbits, mermaids, fantastical monsters with any amount of heads and legs and once, she could have sworn, the outline of the Virgin Mary with the Holy Child in her arms. That had been on a night when she'd felt particularly low, when the loss of Liam was at its keenest and her arms felt empty and aching.

Inside, the cottage was divided into two rooms, the first of which provided both kitchen and living-room and, indeed, bedroom too for herself and Paddy. The other was a much smaller room altogether, partitioned off by an old curtain, behind which the girls slept. Once the curtain had bloomed with flowers, great yellow and red cabbage-roses that swayed and danced as the material caught a breeze. Now, it hung limp and lifeless, the colours sad ghosts of their former glory through time and constant washing with soda. The bed too had been grand in its day, having once stood centre stage in the master bedroom at Beehive Hall, and had been acquired only by default after it had been unceremoniously dumped in a field and Paddy, out on one of his rambles, had spotted the potential in it.

"There's life in the ould dog yet! One man's junk is another man's treasure!" he'd remarked cheerfully to young John-Joe Brady, as they'd hoiked and pulled the mattress two miles home and then gone back for the base which, though rusty, was strong and built to last.

"Aye," John-Joe had remarked sourly, having almost slipped his entire set of vertebrae shifting the damn thing. "And one man's philosophy is another man's load of gobbledegook, so would you shut up outta that, Uncle Paddy, and put your back into it!"

The same passage of years that had faded the curtain had also left the mattress as flat as a pancake, the original blue and white ticking stained with the unmistakable pale yellow of children's urine, which no amount of washing-soda or scrubbing could erase. Aged ten, nine and eight now – steps on a stairs – the girls had, thankfully, gained control over their bladders and wet, smelly patches were a thing of the past. Quarrels weren't, however, and later that night as on most nights a fight broke out between Mollie and Daisy.

"Stop poking me!" Red hair swinging indignantly, Mollie shot up in the bed, elbowing her sister sharply in the ribs. "You're always taking over the bed, big bum!"

"I'm telling Mammy!" Insulted, Daisy hoisted herself up into a sitting position, then tried to clamber across a furious Mollie, who yanked her viciously back by her hair.

"Tell-tale tattle, buy a penny rattle!"

"*Ow!* That hurt!" Her eyes filling with easy tears, Daisy's lower lip trembled ominously. "You're a bitch, so you are, Mollie McNab. A big bitch!"

"Mammy!" Triumphantly pucking her sister in the soft part of the arm, Mollie's voice rose to ear-splitting levels. "Daisy called me a swear-word! Twice!"

Dragging a weary hand through her hair, Eileen erupted around the curtain, before Mollie could gather enough breath for a second shriek. "For the love of God, what's going on in here? Is a person to have no peace, at all?"

"It's that one!" Mollie hoisted an injured look on her face. "She called me the 'B' word!" Blue eyes, innocent as forget-me-nots raked her mother's face for sympathy. "You know the word that rhymes with itch?"

"Only because she called me big bum first!" Bridling, Daisy's small face suffused with self-righteous ire.

"I did not!" Outraged, Mollie exuded innocence from every pore. "She's a liar, Mammy. Honest to God! Is it any wonder the priest has a headache for a fortnight when that one goes to confession!" Slipping a surreptitious hand beneath the bedclothes, she pinched her sister's thigh, squeezing the plump flesh hard between thumb and first finger. Later there would be a bruise.

"*Ouch!*" At this final insult the threatened tears spilled over, cascading wetly down Daisy's cheeks. Frantically she searched around for and found, without too much trouble, the worst word she knew. "You're a big hoor, Mollie McNab!" she shouted, arms flailing wildly at Mollie's head. "I wish you were dead! So I do! I wish you were dead right now!"

"Enough!" With a crack like a rifle-shot, Eileen McNab's hand snaked out and lashed across Daisy's face. "Never ever say that!" Two bright patches of angry colour crept up her cheeks, in stark almost deadly contrast to the whiteness of her skin. "Never ever say that again! Do you hear me?" Her glance bounced from one to the other as, terrified of the fury they had unwittingly unleashed, both children quailed back against the bed. "You've got me heart-scalded, the pair of you! Why can't you be like Rose?" Her voice was shaking, her eyes wet with imminent tears. "Why can't you take a leaf out of Rose's book?" Despite her anger, her look softened as it veered away to where her youngest daughter lay sleeping on the far side of the bed, a cloud of black hair spread out about her like an ebony halo. She had always said that Rose could sleep through the bugles on Judgment Day and the fact that she'd slept through all this commotion bore her out.

Guiltily, both girls hung their heads. It was unknown for their mother to actually hit them, although she could on occasion give them a good shaking and threatened them with fire and brimstone a hundred times a day. "Get in here at once, or I'll beat the living daylights out of you!" Or, "I'll murder you if you don't cut that out!" Or the one that far from reducing them to jelly made them shriek with laughter: "Don't come bawling to me when I've killed you stone dead!"

The fact that between them they had upset her to the point where she had actually struck Daisy was shocking indeed and Mollie felt a stinging at the back of her own eyes.

"Sorry, Mammy!" Her apology was small, almost inaudible, a far cry from the boisterous Mollie of only moments before.

Equally cowed, Daisy echoed the apology. "Sorry, Mam. I didn't mean it. Really I didn't."

"Enough said then!" Wheeling about, Eileen made her way round the curtain. "Not another word out of either one of you, mind!" Spinning sharply on her heel and pulling back the curtain, she wagged a threatening finger. "Not *one* word – do you hear me?"

Far too subdued to even think about carrying on their feud, the girls nodded. Then, as the curtain twitched back into place, Mollie silently turned on her side, her body forming a U-shape around which her sister curled.

"Mollie?" The whisper was tentative. "What does 'hoor' mean?"

Her sister shook her head. "I don't know, Daise, but it must be pretty bad or Mammy wouldn't have walloped you." Yawning widely she felt about for Daisy's small hand, drawing it comfortingly about her own waist. "Now whisht, would you, or we'll both be throttled." But her warning fell on deaf ears for Daisy was already treading the fine line between wakefulness and dreams, the finger-marks on her cheek growing fainter by the minute.

With shaking fingers Eileen McNab poured herself a strong cup of tea, and carried it over to the mantelpiece, where she stood gazing unseeingly into the blue-edged flames thrown up by the peat fire. Poor little Daisy! She hadn't really wished her sister dead, but with Liam's death still fresh in her mind, Eileen had felt like it was tempting fate. No mother expected to have to bury her own child. That wasn't the natural order of things. But then there hadn't been anything natural in Liam's death. Wasn't it strange though, how he'd talked of Heaven all that week before he died? She could see him as though it were only yesterday, with the golden-red locks he had inherited from her own people, small, grimy hands plucking at the buttons on her cardigan, chubby face alight with questions.

"What's Heaven like, Mammy?"

"Heaven?" She'd lifted him onto her lap, loving the little-boy smell of him, warm hay and dandelions, her chin resting lightly on his soft baby hair. "Heaven is like Dublin. Do you know where that is?" Liam shook his head. "Well, Dublin is the capital city of Ireland, so it is. There's beautiful big houses there where lords and ladies lived in the olden days and street upon street of shops where they sell every kind of knick-knack under the sun."

"Do they sell bull's-eyes, Mammy?"

Eileen had laughed at that. "They do, indeed. Barrels of bull's-eyes. Acid drops and toffee. Enough to rot every tooth in your head."

"And what else is there?"

God, she could feel the soft weight of him still, nestled in against her chest. For a moment she closed her eyes, warming her soul on the memory. If only she'd realised at the time how special it would become! How often she would come to rely on it to comfort her when the grief, like tonight, threatened to rip the heart right out of her chest and trample it underfoot.

"Oh, great big cathedrals with bells that ring out morning, noon and night, and fancy hotels where rich people can stay and have the time of Riley. There's a great big river that runs right through the heart of Dublin too. That's the River Liffey." She tweaked his nose. "And there's a load of bridges crossing over it from one side to the other but my favourite is the Ha'penny Bridge."

"That's a funny name – the Ha'penny Bridge," Liam said, rolling it around on his tongue. "I like that! Have you ever been to Dublin, Mammy?"

"Once," she said, thinking of the day she had travelled there for her interview with McVeigh's. "But I hardly spent any time there at all, so most of what I know is what your father told me and he got it mainly from books." Idly, she played piggy-went-to-market on his still-chubby fingers, gently squeezing each perfect pearly nail in passing. "And once your daddy went to an All-Ireland hurling match at Croke Park. Galway were playing Kilkenny and do you know what they call the Kilkenny players?" She'd dropped a kiss on his head. "The Kilkenny Cats! That's because of the colours they wear. Black and amber."

Liam had looked considering then, his small face so serious that for a moment she'd felt a distinct chill of fear.

"I think I'd like Dublin, Mammy," he'd said, "and I think I'd like Heaven."

Within the week he was dead. To her dying day Eileen would take with her the memory of her five-year-old son's body crushed beneath the wheels of Devlin's truck and Paddy, a man demented, half-running, half-staggering down the road, his hands held out imploring the sky. "Why?" he'd screamed. *"Whyyy?"* And people who saw him had turned away, ashamed to witness this outpouring of raw primeval grief and sent up a silent prayer that they would never have to walk a mile in that poor man's shoes. But if God had been listening, he'd kept his own counsel and the broken father on the earth below was left to gather up the shattered pieces of his heart and go on surviving as best he might. Her mother had been right about the life force being very strong, because if ever there was a case for ending it all, Liam's death was it.

Placing her cup on the mantelpiece, Eileen crossed over to the rickety old dresser with its odd assortment of mismatched china and crockery. Stretching up she felt about on the very top till her fingers closed over and grasped the small brown-paper-wrapped package she'd hidden there. Liam's old gumboot, the shine long gone off it. She pressed it tenderly against her lips. Next week spring would turn to summer, April would turn to May, and the flowers so lovingly planted on her small son's grave would commence their first ever blooming. May, the month of Mary, when Catholics all over Ireland dressed in their Sunday best and formed processions in honour of the Blessed Virgin. Out they'd stream from the schools and churches, with banners and statues, the children in front scattering rose-petals from straw baskets with blue and white ribbons, the colours of Our Lady, fluttering from their handles. Following a prescribed route they would parade through the town, eyes meekly downcast, voices raised in song and prayer.

Even if they hadn't been in the back door of a church since they were baptised, Eileen thought sourly. Then she softened as she thought of how, despite the objections of Mother Benignus, her three daughters would march at the head of the procession this year. In memory of Liam, as was right and fitting! A tear slipped down her face and dropped onto Liam's old boot, one more mosaic in the pattern of older tearstains already scattered upon its once bright surface. Sighing, Eileen kissed the little boot as tenderly as though it were the face of her small son, then carefully placed it back in its wrapping before returning it to its place of safety on top of the dresser. Paddy would be home soon. He didn't know about the boot, would be upset if he found her crying. It was true that Liam's death had all but destroyed him. Like her, his hair was prematurely streaked by the hand of sorrow and there was an underlying sadness in his eyes, where once there had been only laughter. Eyes, the colour of the sea on a storm-tossed day, green-grey eyes that had once turned the heads of girls all over the West of Ireland, but which had settled on Eileen Brady that day at the

Feis Ceoil. A lot of water had flowed under the bridge since that time but their devotion to each other had never wavered. In sunshine or in shadow. No matter what God had thrown at them! Eileen thought angrily, then was immediately guiltily contrite. As a good Catholic, she had been raised to count her blessings. And she did try. Really, she did! But nevertheless there was a great, black hole in her heart and, though she might learn to walk around it one day, she knew as clearly as she knew her own name that it was destined to remain unfilled forever more.

CHAPTER TWO

"Eileen! Eileen!"

Startled, Eileen awoke to find dawn busy painting the sky with shades of sunrise and her limbs cramped and sore from where she had fallen asleep in her chair whilst waiting for Paddy to return from O'Dwyer's the night before.

"Eileen! Eileen!"

"What? What is it?" Heart pounding, she jumped up as quickly as her stiff legs would allow, turning to face Paddy just as he came bursting through the door.

"Eileen, come here!" His face white with a mixture of despair and anger, her husband caught her by the arm, part-pushing, part-pulling her over to the small, cubed window, down the centre of which a wooden cross marched, dividing it into four equal squares.

"What do you see?" he demanded, a note of hysteria in his voice, his hand gesturing vaguely towards the outside. "Well, what do you see?"

"Nothing," she replied, dismayed and frightened by his odd behaviour.

"Aye!" He nodded vigorously. "Nothing at all, unless you count the sea, the scutch grass, the rock wall and that biteen of a tree over there." His hand fell away from her arm. There was a hopelessness about the gesture. "Enjoy the view, Eileen girl! Look at it as though you've never seen it before and burn the image well into your mind, for soon the memory will be all you've got. All we've got!" he amended, voice suddenly low and bitter.

Eileen felt the sudden, cold claw of fear clutch at her heart, felt its fingers opening and closing relentlessly, squeezing the bruised flesh, weakening her so that she had to grip the narrow windowsill to prevent herself from falling. "Why? W-what do you mean, Paddy? What on earth are you talking about?"

"Devlin!" Paddy McNab spat out the name as though the saying of the word contaminated his mouth.

"Devlin?" Eileen knitted her brow. "Mick Devlin, you mean? What's he got to do with it?"

"Of course, Mick Devlin," Paddy snarled. "Who else? And he's got everything to do with it, because if what I heard in O'Dwyer's last night is anything to go by, he's only gone and bought the land!" He curled his lip. "Mind you, when I say *heard* it, let's just say a little bird made a point of telling me, although 'twas only a matter of time before I got wind of it anyway. It's not as if you can avoid noticing a house being thrown up not fifty foot away from your door!"

"Devlin's building a house next to us?" Incredulous, Eileen's gaze never left her husband's mouth as though she couldn't believe that the words coming from it matched those she was hearing.

"Aye, the bastard! It seems the rumours were true after all. Someone was after the land all right – Devlin!" Viciously Paddy slammed his right fist into the palm of his left hand. "It wasn't enough for him to murder our Liam, it seems. Now he wants to rub our faces in it every time we look out the bloody window. And I can't believe Donal Flynn was that hard up that he had to sell it to him. Oh, it's true what they say. With friends like that, who needs enemies?"

"Oh, dear God!" Stricken, Eileen groped for a chair. Paddy was right. It was as though Devlin was sneering at them. He had murdered their son. Yes, murder wasn't too strong a word for it! Sure wasn't it an ill-kept secret that he was reeking of whisky when his truck went out of control and the accident happened? Of course, there was a school of thought that queried if it were an accident at all. Wasn't it strange, people mused, that on a barely used stretch of country road two miles long, that the truck should just happen to mount the bank at the very place on which young McNab was standing? They scratched their heads and pondered over their pints at the strangeness of it all but, as they said in their summing up, there were no witnesses. It was Devlin's word against that of a dead child. No contest!

Whatever the ins and outs, Devlin's life continued, untrammelled apparently by any guilt, and those who spoke behind his back spoke to his face only to ask for jobs and favours – for Mick Devlin, a building contractor, was both wealthy and influential. And what Devlin wanted, Devlin got! And now he'd got the land, right next to them! Though why he should want to go on crucifying them was anyone's guess.

"What are we going to do?"

"I'm going to kill him, that's what I'm going to do!" Like a caged lion, Paddy had begun pacing the length of the small room, turning as he reached each end and pacing back again. "I'm going to tear him apart with my bare hands and scatter his limbs to the four Provinces of Ireland!"

"Daddy?" Awakened by all the commotion, Mollie appeared suddenly by the curtain, a much-patched nightdress Eileen had run up out of an old flour-sack bagging round her ankles, sleep-tousled red hair wild about her shoulders. "Why are you shouting? Is it because me and Daisy were fighting last night?"

"Aw no, pet!" Breaking off his pacing, Paddy immediately came to kneel before the little girl, encircling her childish waist with his large calloused hands. "Nothing to do with you and Daisy. I'm sorry I woke you."

"What then?" Vivid blue Mediterranean eyes clashed with Atlantic greeny-grey.

"Nothing that need concern you, miss," her mother interrupted sharply. "It's almost time you were up anyway. Daisy! Rose!" she called. "Rise and shine!" A look passed between her husband and herself. They would talk later. "Why don't you lie down for a bit!" she suggested, guessing that he had spent the better part of the night walking out his anger. He had been the same after Liam had died, walking always walking, almost as though he were afraid that if he were to stand still for a minute, his sorrow would rise up and drown him where he stood.

"All right," he nodded. "Not that I'm likely to sleep for thinking about that ba–.!"

"Later, Paddy, later!" She cut him off with a look, her eyes veering to where the curious Mollie, despite her apparent absorption in studying the floor, was undoubtedly all ears.

He nodded again, then disappeared behind the

curtain where he routed a reluctant Daisy and Rose and, much to their annoyance, lay down in their place, letting the warmth left over from their small bodies envelop him like a comfort blanket. Despite Devlin and the cacophony of female voices on the other side of the curtain, he was almost immediately soundly and dreamlessly asleep.

"I hate school! *Why* do we have to go to school?" Daisy, dribbling porridge down her chin, fixed eyes the mirror-image of her father's on her mother who was buttering doorsteps of bread with a miserly hand. Show it to the bread and take it away again, that was her motto!

Eileen sighed. She had this argument with one or other of her daughters virtually every morning and it really browned her off. "You go to school for an education, Daisy, something your father and me never had much of and not through choice, let me tell you."

"Well, it hasn't stopped you from doing anything, has it?" Mollie joined in belligerently.

Slicing the doorsteps, Eileen folded them over into sandwiches, which she wrapped in brown paper for their lunches. She wished she could put a bit of bacon between them, but yesterday's leftovers were the makings of today's dinner. Lifting the heavy enamel milk-jug she commenced pouring a quarter pint of milk or so into three small glass bottles that had once respectively held Milk of Magnesia, cod liver oil and calamine lotion, deftly corking them with tightly screwed pieces of brown paper as the tops had long since disappeared. "It stopped us from doing a lot," she said quietly, turning her attention full on her daughters. "It stopped us from having a decent roof over our heads, decent food on the table, decent clothes on your backs. It stopped your father, God help him, from having a decent job." Her voice rose suddenly, became angry. "Instead he has to go cap in hand to any Tom, Dick or Harry that will give him a bit of work, be it digging ditches or kissing their arses." Breaking off abruptly, a red blush stained her cheeks. She seldom swore in front of the children, having drummed it into them that, although they might be poor, good manners cost nothing.

"Daddy's educ – educ . . . Daddy can read." Rose piped up.

"That's right!" Mollie nodded vigorously. "Daddy can read as good as Mother Big-Knickers, so he can. Can't he, Daise?"

"I hate school. I hate Mother Big-Knickers!" Daisy said glumly, ignoring the question and bringing the conversation round full circle. "*Why* do we have to go to school?"

Eileen snapped, all attempts at reasoning flying out the window. "Because I say so, that's why! And

41

how many times have I told you not to call Mother Benignus that?"

"What?" Mollie used her innocent, blue, forget-me-not look. "Mother Big-Knickers?" Daisy and Rose started to giggle, knowing what was coming next. "Because she has!" Ignoring her mother's frown of disapproval, Mollie continued unabashed. "Assumpta Riley was sent round to the nun's quarters with a message one day for one of the nuns. Anyway she had to pass the clothes-line and there right in the middle of it was a great big black knickers, as big as the Twelve Bens, and Mother Benignus' name was embroidered on the ar – bottom of them," she amended hastily.

"Get ready for school, Mollie McNab," her mother gritted, "before I kill you stone dead." Rightly or wrongly she had great respect for the religious, though it must be said she had strong reservations about that Mother Benignus up at St Joseph's. Still, for the most part, nuns and priests were a cut above everyone else. Why otherwise would God have chosen them, given them a vocation like? They were leaders in the community, people educated to dispense advice, wisdom and charity to those in need. Maybe she should visit Father Clarke about Devlin. He would be able to advise Paddy and herself, might even be able to get Devlin to change his mind and build somewhere else. Yes, that's exactly what she would do. The thought of positive action made Eileen feel a little better and it was with a somewhat lighter heart that she waved the girls off to school.

"Come on, slow coach!" Mollie turned and beckoned to Rose, who was trailing behind, boots scuffling in the dust of the road. "The Inspector is coming this morning and we'll be murdered if we're late."

"What's a inspector?" Rose panted, catching up with her sisters.

"He's a VIP," Daisy said grandly. "At least that's what Sister Imelda said."

"Huh!" Mollie was unimpressed. "You don't want to be mindin' what that one says. Sure didn't she say we could lead the Procession this year and all, and now them other scutters, Nancy Doyle, Helen Maher and Majella McBride, are doing it instead." Moodily she kicked a loose stone out of her way, looking around to ensure that no adults were in earshot. "That lot thinks their pee doesn't smell."

Her sisters giggled.

"Still, it's not Sister Imelda's fault." Daisy liked the young nun, who was kind to all her pupils rich and poor alike, and jumped rapidly to her defence. "It's ould Mother Big-Knickers who doesn't think we're good enough. Daddy said she's always sucking up to the ones with money just because she needs a new roof on the convent or something."

"Well, she's not likely to suck up to us so."

Spinning round, Daisy grabbed Rose by the arm as she started to lag behind again. "We can't even afford a new thatch for our cottage and that's just an ould bit of straw."

"What's a VIP?" Rose asked again, as if the intervening conversation had never taken place. Daisy shrugged.

"Very Ignorant Pig!" Mollie grunted out the words and the girls laughed again, then broke into a run as the tinny bell of St Joseph's sounded on the nippy morning air. "Janey! We'll be massacred. Hurry up, Rose!"

"I am! I am!" Rose gasped then found herself swept up between her two sisters and practically run into the playground where pupils of various ages and sizes were forming their unruly selves into arrow-straight lines. Relieved not to be late, the McNab girls split up and joined the ranks of classmates who in another minute or so would be swallowed up by the great maw of St Joseph's.

"Girls!" Mother Benignus clapped her hands as though it were necessary to bring order to a room already as silent as the grave. "This is Mr Manning, our School Inspector."

An unusually tall, cadaverous man of indeterminable age unfurled himself from somewhere behind her, eyes two burnt holes in a blanket, sweeping over the rows of girls who were sitting in the prescribed manner at their desks, hands folded neatly one over the other, ankles crossed in a ladylike fashion.

"Say good morning to Mr Manning, girls."

"Good morning, Mr Manning," the pupils chorused dutifully in the curious, flat monotone particular to schoolchildren speaking in assembly.

Gracious, Mr Manning inclined his head.

"Mr Manning will be examining you on your Catechism and I'm sure you will all be a credit to St Joseph's."

The pupils, including Mollie McNab, were not fooled by Mother Benignus's attempt to look playful as she spoke. To a child, they recognised the threat implicit at the end of her sentence. God help anyone who proved not to be a credit to St Joseph's was the real subtext. More than one young girl felt her palms begin to grow damp and the blouse on her back begin to stick uncomfortably to the soft flesh beneath. "I'll just sit over here by Sister Imelda." Mother Benignus tried her best to simper, blissfully unaware that a face whose normal expression ranged somewhere between tortured and martyred could not easily be made to look coy.

Inclining his head again, the Inspector cleared his throat and when he opened his mouth Mollie fully expected to see moths fly out, or dust at the very least, so dry was his voice.

"Now," his eyes ranged around the room, "let's start with an easy question. Who made the world? You!" A long finger like a gnarled map-pointer shot out towards a large untidy girl who was desperately trying to make herself invisible at the back of the room.

"Stand up, Mary Ryan!" Mother Benignus hissed, turning her eyes up to heaven as the girl, who had the misfortune to be built like a Donegal heifer, scrambled to her ungainly feet, knocking a pile of books to the floor as she did so.

"God, sir."

"Speak up!" Another hiss from Mother Benignus, followed by a roll of the eyes.

"God made the world, sir!"

"Aye, so he did." Mr Manning, assented with a nod of his skull-like head. "But what did he make it out of, eh?" His head swivelled round again. "You!"

Mother Benignus groaned inwardly as the large map-pointer finger shot out and landed on Bridie McNamara. Bridie, it had to be said, was not one of the leading lights of St Joseph's. Bridie, it had to be said, was as thick as two short planks.

"Was it sticks, sir?" True to form, Bridie, a frown of intense concentration on a face as vapid as a blank page, came up with the most stupid answer imaginable.

"No! No, it was not!" Apparently grieved to the core, Mr Manning shook his large head, stretching his lips across his wide mouth and furthering the skeletal illusion as large yellow teeth were displayed in a deadly grimace. "Nor was it bricks or straw, in case any of yis were wondering." His voice rose suddenly, came out in a bellow, so that even the two nuns almost leapt out of their chairs. *"But I might turn into the Big Bad Wolf and blow St Joseph's down if I get any more eejity answers, so I might!"* Instantly his manner changed again, became almost placatory. Confiding. "I suppose I'd better tell ye the way ye won't embarrass yerselves if ever ye're asked again. He made it out of *nothing*."

He made a great show of dusting his hands, finishing off with a snap of the fingers. "Nothing entirely! Wasn't he the great man all the same?" Suitably impressed, the children nodded. "Will we do some more?" Having no real choice in the matter the pupils nodded again leaving Mother Benignus and Sister Imelda to exchange puzzled glances with one another. Mr Manning was certainly not in the usual mould of school inspectors, most of whom asked tried and trusted questions such as 'What is nine times nine?' or 'What is the spelling of "blackboard"?' or, if on religion, 'What is the fourth Commandment?'.

"When Jesus was crucified, there was how many boyos decorating crosses alongside of him? You!"

47

To Mother Benignus' relief, this time the questing digit found a target worthy of its quest, coming to land on Majella McBride, a grand respectable girl, daughter of Dr McBride, pillar of society and generous benefactor to the convent roof fund.

"Two, sir!" Majella's voice was low and well-modulated as befitted her status.

Mother Benignus smiled beatifically. You could always tell breeding.

"There *was* two right enough," Mr. Manning agreed heartily. "But they weren't up there for the good of their health now, were they? So what were they doing up there, eh? Was it out of sympathy for Jesus? Did they join his political party, do ye think? Were they comrades in arms?"

Majella shook her head, her long blonde hair arcing out about her like a halo. "No, sir! They were thieves, sir!"

"Thieves? Is that a fact?" Stroking his chin, Mr Manning endeavoured to look as interested as a skull possibly could. "What did they steal, I wonder? Eh?"

Frantically the young girl racked her brains but drew a blank. "I don't know, sir."

"She doesn't know, sir!" the Inspector mocked, screwing up his mouth in a vicious, but accurate, parody. "Can you credit that? She doesn't know. Do any of yis know?"

"Was it hens, sir?"

This time Mother Benignus failed to suppress a groan as Sheila Connolly, of even less promising material than Bridie McNamara, scrambled to her feet. "We had some hens stole last night, but 'twas a fox as done it. There was blood and feathers all over the yard." Excited, she looked around at the rest of the class as Mother Benignus felt her own blood rushing to her head and dancing in front of her eyes. "Da said he'd crucify the bugger if ever he caught up with him!"

With a roar that put the heart across both children and nuns, Mr Manning leapt suddenly to his feet, crossed the room in two strides and delivered a resounding slap to Sheila's right ear. "Get thee behind me, Satan!" he shouted, waving his fist in the poor girl's face and causing her to lose all control of her bladder. "And the meek shall inherit the earth!"

As Mother Benignus watched in a kind of fascinated horror the pool of urine trickling slowly out across the floor, she found her hand itching in sympathy. Later, she promised it. Later! Fortunately, Sheila Connolly had a left ear too.

"Now then." Equanimity, for everyone apart from poor Sheila, restored, the Inspector cleared the moths from his throat and once more took up his position at the front of the class. "When Jesus was nailed up on the cross and dying with the thirst, the soldiers gave him a sponge on the top of a spear. Who can tell me what was on the sponge? You!"

Panicking, Mollie McNab shot up out of her seat, wild red hair escaping from the plait that tried its ineffectual best to keep it under control. What in the name of God was on the sponge? She knew it wasn't water. Grown-ups didn't like water. Inspiration hit her. She had it! "Poteen!" Triumphant, Mollie leaned across her desk, fixing him with an earnest and educating eye. "They gave him a drop of poteen like Mammy gives me if I have an earache or toothache or something." Like a moth blundering helplessly into a naked flame, she innocently continued, completely oblivious of the shocked silence that had fallen over the room and which hung in the ether like the pall over a funeral bier. "My da has an awful lot of earaches and toothaches, so he does. My da drinks an awful lot of poteen." Mollie was proud of her knowledge and anxious to share it with her companions, so it came as a horrible shock to find Mother Benignus looming over her like the dragon over St George.

"You ignorant scut, you!" Catching Mollie by the front of her Fair Isle cardigan, the Head Nun rhythmically pulled and pushed her to and fro, causing the buttons to pop off one by one and roll like shiny mother-of-pearl tears across the floor. "You no-good, impudent brat!" Momentarily she released one of her hands to send it cracking across Mollie's cheek so that her head rocked flowerlike on the stem of her neck. "For two pins I'd – I'd –"

Thankfully, Sister Imelda, who up till that point had been suffering from a bad case of paralysis, staged a sudden and miraculous recovery. Throwing herself into the fray, she commenced with some difficulty to haul the older, far heavier nun off the cowering and frightened Mollie. "That's enough, Mother! Do you want to kill the child? Here, Mr Manning! Give me a hand!"

Running a lascivious eye over her black-clad body, the Inspector completely ignored her, choosing instead to hone in on her bosom, tossing and heaving with the exertion of restraining the Reverend Mother.

"By God but you're a grand woman, Sister!" He made a smacking noise with his lips. "I haven't seen a chest like that since me grandfather came home from the sea!"

Stunned, Sister Imelda released her grip on Mother Benignus, who immediately slipped to the floor banging her head, which luckily enough did more to bring her to her senses than anything that had happened previously.

"You could do a lot worse than me, so you could!"

Sister Imelda flinched, then screamed, as lunging forward the Inspector clamped a hand over her right breast and began to sing, bastardising the words of an old music hall song: "*'Tis true 'pon my word, you're a nice little bird, Imelda, my darling . . .*" his voice tailed off into a squeaky reed, "*I . . . love . . . youuu . . .*", as with a sudden almighty crash, Sergeant O'Shea, flanked by two burly men in white coats burst through the classroom door.

"What the hell is going on here?" Almost starting from their sockets, the sergeant's eyes flew to where Mr Manning, hand still making pincer motions on Sister Imelda's breast, stood like one turned to stone. "Jaysus!" he muttered, suitably awed as the full impact hit him. "Do something, would ya!"

Dutifully one of the other men approached the Inspector, softly, as you might approach a nervous thoroughbred. "Ah! There ye are, Frankie!" he said conversationally, making a pantomime of blowing on his hands and stamping his feet. "God but 'tis cold outside. Cold enough to turn your vomit to cake, so 'tis."

"Aye, 'tis that!" The other man attested, his movements echoing that of his colleague. "Look, we brought you your cardigan." Shaking out a peculiar white garment with very long sleeves, out of which a variety of tapes dangled, he attempted to look playful. "There you go. This'll keep you nice and cosy, you poor ould divil! Come on! I'll give ye a hand to put it on."

Like Lot's wife, Mr Manning stood for a moment, seemingly rooted to the spot. Then a most peculiar thing happened. His skull-like face seemed to crumple inward till, losing all resemblance to an adult, it took on instead the caricature appearance of a young child. To add to the illusion, a trickle of drool appeared at the corner of his mouth and ran unchecked down his chin. Even his gait changed as, freeing Sister Imelda, he shambled forward arms outstretched, standing obediently as the two burly men eased his arms into the sleeves of the straitjacket. Then crisscrossing them neatly around his body, they led him outside to a white van with bars on the window.

"Is that how they make Egyptian mummies?" One child was heard to ask, as with a rattle and a bang, the van accelerated and sped away with the inspector gazing forlornly through the back window.

"Fair play to yis, Sisters!" Sergeant O'Shea tipped his peaked Guard's hat to where Mother Benignus and Sister Imelda stood pale-faced and aghast. "'Tis not everyone who could subdue an escaped lunatic. You deserve a medal, so you do, the pair of you, or a great big cup."

"E-escaped lunatic?" Stammering, Mother Benignus felt vainly around for some support. "We thought he was from the Board of Education." Then for the first and last time in her life she fainted. When she came round some time later, it was to find Sister Imelda slapping her face, harder than was warranted, although the younger nun would never admit it, not even to herself. And never in a thousand years, in the confessional!

"Escaped lunatic, says she, flinging up her arms and screaming like a mad thing!" Sergeant O'Shea embellished the story in O'Dwyer's later that night, aware that the telling of such a good tale was worth a good deal of free lubrication. "We thought he was from the Board of Edjication!" Roaring with delight, his audience hung on his every word, and whenever it looked like the policeman might have hit a dry spell, instructed the publican to "Put your knittin' down, O'Dwyer, and pull the Sergeant here another pint!"

CHAPTER THREE

When Paddy McNab finally awoke it was to the sound of a male voice on the other side of the curtain which, after a moment of two, became identifiable as that of Father Clarke. Struggling out of bed he pulled on his trousers which he had cast over the back of a chair, straightened the gallowses over his shoulders, then with a quick lick of the palm of his hand over his hair, went to investigate.

"Ah, there you are now, Paddy." Pouring tea from an enamel pot, Eileen glanced up briefly, but not so briefly that her husband couldn't detect a trace of guilt in her expression. "I was just going to wake you. Father Clarke's here!"

"So I see!" Striding over, Paddy shook the outstretched hand of the priest who had half risen to his feet upon his entrance. "And to what do I owe the honour, Father?"

Blushing, Eileen intervened before the priest could reply. "It was my idea, Paddy. I thought maybe Father Clarke could give us a bit of advice – concerning Devlin, like."

"Oh, aye?" Paddy quirked an eyebrow in the direction of the priest, who having reseated himself, was in the process of appropriating one of Eileen's scones from the cooling-rack in the centre of the table.

"Manna from heaven!" he proclaimed, finishing the entire scone in just one bite. "You've a hand as light as the Angel Gabriel, so you have, Eileen. Your pastry's the talk of all Galway. You should think about opening a bakery." Gratified, Eileen refilled the priest's cup before sliding one across the table to Paddy. "Well, man, are you just going to stand around making the place untidy? Sit down, for heaven's sake!"

As Father Clarke gestured him into the chair opposite, Paddy felt a huge flash of irritation. Wasn't it just like a priest to give orders in someone's own house?

"Now what's all this I hear about Devlin? Is it true he's building outside?"

Paddy took a long slurp of his tea and, fanning his mouth, reached for the milk jug. "True enough by all accounts." He slopped the milk into his cup, picked up a teaspoon and gave his tea a stir. "Though I don't know how the bastard has the brass nerve." Challenging, his chin came up.

"Paddy!" Shocked and apologetic, Eileen stole a worried glance at the priest, but he waved a placatory hand.

"Now, now, Eileen! There's times when a man has every right to swear and I'd say this is one of them." Father Clarke nodded his bull-like head. A fair man, he tempered religion with common sense, as a result of which he had become the most popular Parish Priest since poor Father O'Malley, who was murdered by the Black and Tans many years before.

"I'm going to kill him, Father!" Losing his temper, Paddy roughly pushed his chair away from the table and leaping to his feet stormed over to the little window, superimposed upon the panes of which he could see Devlin staggering three-sheets-to-the-wind out of O'Dwyer's only hours after he, Paddy McNab, had buried his only son. "I'm going to batter him senseless, the rotten sod, and then I'm going to kill him, the way he killed our Liam." Turning on his heel, Paddy glared at the priest, as if daring him to argue. "A life for a life! Isn't that what they say, Father?"

"Some do all right!" the priest returned mildly. "Then others say the moon is made of green cheese, whilst even more claim that 'tis the height of bad luck to see a priest or red-haired woman whilst putting to sea or even going to the races. Indeed my own father used to turn back from the Derby, if ever he'd the misfortune to meet a red-haired woman on the way – no offence intended, Eileen." Fishing in his pocket he extracted a blackthorn pipe which he proceeded to fill with tobacco, expertly tamping it down with a thumb the size of a garden hoe. "Then there's another class entirely who claim the Devil is dead and buried in Killarney, would you credit it? But are they right?" With that, he lit up and drew the sweet smoke deep into his lungs.

Turning round, Paddy waved a dismissive hand. "Sure that's not the same thing at all, Father. There's no comparison."

Shrugging his shoulders, Father Clarke eased his chair further back from the table the way it didn't cut into his belly. "Isn't it? Well, let me put it another way so. Just supposing you were to knock seven bells out of Devlin, as is your inclination, then finish the blackguard off so that his toes are pointing skywards – where would be the benefit?"

"Where would be the benefit?" Challenging, the younger man marched back over to the table where, hands clenching the back of a chair, he stood glowering over the priest. "He'd be dead, and I'd be happy. I'd call that some benefit, wouldn't you?"

Father Clarke exhaled on the pipe, the bluish smoke rising like ectoplasm between them. "Would it bring young Liam back?" He issued a challenge of his own. "And what about Eileen there, and them three little cailíns of yours? Of what benefit to them would it be to have their father locked up in Mountjoy jail or the likes for the rest of his natural?" Standing up, he placed a hand on Paddy's shoulder. "Haven't they suffered enough? Haven't you suffered enough?"

"But I can't just let him away with it, Father." Paddy's shoulders drooped, his face twisting, suffused with misery. "What sort of a man would I be?"

"A real man! A man who puts the welfare of his family before personal vengeance." Extinguishing his pipe, the priest reached for his coat which immediately sent up a strong stink of camphor, thanks to the mothballs his housekeeper insisted on stuffing in the pockets. "Now I want you to promise me, Paddy, that you'll do nothing rash. Will you promise me that?"

Struggling to master his baser instincts, Paddy McNab looked candidly into the other man's eyes. "All right, Father. I promise, though I'm not sure you understand what a terrible hard thing you're asking of me and the way it sticks in me craw."

"I do understand. But understand this, Paddy McNab, the tide goes out and the tide comes in, and whatever you send out on the tide will eventually roll back the way it came and likely more along with it. In other words, bide your time, watch, wait, and eventually Devlin will get what's coming to him." Inserting a finger beneath his collar, he pulled it free from where it was digging into the fat folds of his neck. "Just remember, God has a plan for us all. At first sight, it might appear like something of a jigsaw, an almighty mess, with some of the bits missing." Pleased with his analogy, the priest nodded with satisfaction. "But, mark my words, when He's ready – Him, the Man Upstairs – the pieces will all slot together and the picture become plain."

"Thanks, Father." Eileen saw the priest to the door, knowing her husband was too full to speak but also knowing that the storm was past, at least for the moment. The wise old priest had got through. Nonetheless she was human enough to hope that both she and Paddy would be around to witness the tide come in and the man who had killed her child get his just comeuppance.

"We thought he was from the Board of Edjikayshun!" Mollie mimicked Mother Benignus's cultured tones as she regaled her family with the tale of the bogus School Inspector.

"God, that's a good one!" Wiping his streaming

eyes, Paddy looked over to where his wife was practically bent double, her arm across her middle as though the force of her laughter would tear her apart. "She must've felt an awful eejit!"

"Well, not straight away she didn't." Mollie was enjoying the effect her story was having upon her family, embroidering it freely as she went. "Because she fainted just then and Sister Imelda had to give her a ferocious clatter to bring her around. Honestly, she was sitting on top of her, belting her round the head and strangling her and everything." There were fresh gales of laughter as everyone imagined Mother Benignus measuring her full length on the floor and Sister Imelda taking advantage of the situation to get a bit of her own back. "And then they put this thing they called a cardigan on him, but later we found out it was a straitjacket, and then they took him back to the asylum."

"B-back to the asylum!" her mother spluttered, bent so far forward now that her head was almost touching her knees. "The poor ould divil!" She struggled for control. "But what happened to the real inspector?"

Mollie giggled. "Ah, he showed up a few hours later. He said his car had broken down, but I overheard Sister Imelda saying that if it did, it must have broken down inside Guinness's brewery, because the stink of booze from him would take your life!"

This further revelation brought fresh hoots of laughter and as Eileen looked round at the bright eyes and smiling faces of her husband and daughters, she couldn't help but reflect on what a difference a few hours could make. This Paddy, with his eyes creased up in merriment and shaking shoulders, was a different man entirely from the one who had faced Father Clarke earlier on. Then, those same eyes had been sunken mirror-images of hell, shoulders drooping like a sapling that has stood up to the wind only to find it has confused bravery with sheer brute strength and come out the loser. Something of her thoughts must have transmitted themselves to him as for a split second his eyes met hers, all laughter gone. Then he closed one eye in a huge wink, and a moment later she was joining in the hilarity once more as Mollie, delighted to be taking centre stage, decided to milk the story for all it was worth and tell it all over again.

A few days later, Eileen was thrilled to receive a parcel from her Aunty Kay in America. Kay, her mother's younger sister, had emigrated years before, starting as a lowly shop girl and working up to the position of manageress in a big department store in New York. Bloomingdales, Eileen thought it was called. Consequently she was able to send the odd parcel of clothes and bits and pieces over to Eileen and her three grand-nieces. Judging from its size this was a particularly interesting parcel and Eileen could hardly wait to get shot of Packy-the-Post so that she could open it in peace. Easier said than done! Packy overlooked the fact that he was paid to deliver the mail, preferring to think he was doing it from the goodness of his heart and therefore entitled to cadge freebees en route in the form of tea, gossip or what have you.

"You'll have a cup of tea, Packy?" Reluctantly putting the parcel to one side, Eileen took the hint.

"Arrah, I will so, Mrs McNab." Full of importance the postman made a great show of checking his watch, despite the fact that it hadn't worked for years on account of having no hands, no dial and no glass. "But it'll have to be quick, mind. I'm a terrible busy man, you know. It's not everyone who could do my job." His voice was weary, defeated, as if he'd just spent half an hour arguing the toss with her and been coerced against his better judgment.

Eileen nodded. She had heard it all before. A hundred and one times!

Propping his High-Nelly bicycle against the cottage wall, his mail-sack thrown over the cross-bar, he followed her inside, rubbing his hands together in anticipation of one the scones for which Eileen McNab was justifiably renowned. "You heard about the hoo-ha up at St Joseph's, I suppose?"

"I did!" Eileen cast a last longing look at the package before turning her attention to the teapot. She couldn't wait to be alone to savour the parcel's contents.

"They say Mother Benignus is going round with an eye as black as the ace of spades because of the trouncing Sister Imelda gave her."

Spooning tea into the pot, Eileen suppressed a giggle. At the rate the story was doing the rounds and growing with each telling and retelling, poor old Sister Imelda would be lucky not to find herself up in court soon on a charge of attempted manslaughter. Or nunslaughter, come to that! Pouring on the hot water, she gave it a stir, covered it with a tea-cosy, and left it to draw. Then going to the cupboard she took down a large biscuit tin, opened it up, extracted a couple of scones and placed them on a plate in the centre of the table.

"Mind you, it could have been a different story entirely." Reaching out a none-too-clean hand, Packy helped himself to a scone, as Eileen poured a generous mug of tea and pushed it across the table. "Sure, isn't it common knowledge that that Manning fella killed six people over at Oughterard a few year ago? Carved them up with a garden shears is what I heard, then took a match to the remains. We're all lucky not to have been murdered in our beds, if you ask me."

This time Eileen did giggle. "Ah would you go 'way outta that, Packy. The poor divil is as harmless as they come."

Sticking out a lugubrious lower lip, he cradled the mug between his arthritic fingers, enjoyed the heat seeping into his swollen knuckles. "Try telling that to Sister Imelda. The poor woman is in an awful state."

An irrepressible imp of mischief rose in Eileen's bosom. "Ah, for all you know she might have enjoyed it, Packy!"

"Well, may God forgive you, Mrs McNab!" Jumping to his seemingly outraged feet, Packy drained the remainder of his mug in one gulp, simultaneously managing to secrete the other scone in his pocket. "Is that any way to talk about a nun, I ask ye? Have you no respect?"

"Ah, it was just a joke." A little ashamed, Eileen attempted to soothe his ruffled feathers as huffily he headed for the door. "Sure I didn't mean a bit of it."

But Packy was made of self-righteous stuff and not easily appeased, and besides Eileen showed no signs of getting any more scones out. "Yes, well, I'd better be getting on anyways. Time and tide waits for no man, you know. And the post must get through!" As an afterthought he thanked her for the tea then almost caused her to jump out of her skin as, sticking his nose out the door, he emitted a roar loud enough to wake all the dead that had ever died.

"Jumpin Jaysus! Me mailbag! Would you look at what the fecker's done!"

Hurrying after him, Eileen was bemused to find a rather large billy-goat with its head buried deep inside the mailbag Packy had left outside.

"Clear off, ye bugger!" Shaking a futile fist, Packy advanced warily, but, removing its head from the mailbag, the goat merely fixed him with a baleful amber eye, continuing to masticate a letter, out of the corner of which a pound note was clearly peeking. "I'll have yer guts for garters!" Packy yelled, jumping up and down on legs so bandy you could drive a wheelbarrow through them. "So help me I'll swing for ye, ye hairy bastard!"

Eileen, for the second time in a couple of days, found herself giggling away. Wait till she told Paddy. Oh but he'd be sorry to have missed this!

Awestruck, Mollie, Daisy and Rose gazed at the sherbet-coloured dresses laid out on the bed, each frock cleverly designed so that the colours faded each into the other: peppermint green shading into lemon, then lemon blending seamlessly into a pale rose-pink around the full-skirted poplin hem, each dress being finished off at the waist by a broad blue sash. All of which, according to the edicts of fashion, should have clashed horribly, but which somehow came together in a perfectly miraculous symphony of colour.

"Oooh, they're lovely, Mammy! Where did you get them from?" Almost beside herself with excitement, Mollie reached across and gently, almost reverently, stroked the soft poplin of one of the frocks.

Their delighted reaction was all that Eileen could have wished for. It wasn't often they had new clothes, God help them! And certainly not clothes of this quality. For the most part they had to make do with bits and pieces she ran up herself and though she was still a fair needlewoman – the best in the county, some said – her efforts were as nothing in comparison to these. "Aunty Kay sent them. All the way from America! Aren't you the lucky girls all the same? Aren't you the Yankee Doodle Dandies?"

"Can we try them on now?" Jigging about with impatience, Daisy grabbed one of the dresses and held it up against herself.

"No!" Eileen was firm. "Not till you've had a bit of a wash. By the looks of those hands I'd say you must have been out digging potatoes all day. Anyway, that's not all your fairy godmother sent. What do you think of these?" Triumphantly she delved below the bed and brought out three pairs of Shirley Temple, black-patent leather shoes with the narrowest ankle straps the girls had ever seen.

The girls gasped in delight. Then, glumly, Mollie said, "They're gorgeous, Mammy." Her hand rose to touch them, fell away again before she could make contact. "But we can't wear them! It's not allowed."

"What?" Eileen rounded on her as if she had suddenly grown horns and a tail. "What do you mean, you can't wear them? Of course you can wear them! Who said it's not allowed?"

Stubbornly Mollie shook her head. "No, we can't. Mother Benignus says black-patent shoes are a sin because boys can see the reflection of your knickers in them and it might give them ideas."

"That's right!" Daisy nodded importantly. "And then you might get a baby like Breda Corcoran. Only she got hers sitting on a bus."

"What?" Eileen repeated, her head bouncing in astonishment between the pair of them.

"She sat on a seat after a man got up, you see?" Daisy elaborated with a blush.

"Sat on a seat? What do you mean she sat on a seat?" Eileen could feel a distinct note of hysteria creeping into her voice. "What on earth are you talking about, child?"

Sending an entreating look to her sister, Daisy scuffled the toe of her shoe into the ground. "You tell her, Moll."

Mollie could feel an identical flush creeping up her own face. Oh, why couldn't Daisy have kept her big gob shut? "It's Mother Benignus, you see . . ." she said at last. And as her mother plainly didn't, continued in a rush. "She says you should never sit on a seat a man has just sat on or you'll get a baby."

Astounded, Eileen didn't know whether to laugh, cry or get angry. One thing she did know was that nuns must have been in terrible short supply the day that one got her vocation. Either that, or the Man Upstairs must have been half-tanked and asleep on the job. Placing indignant hands on her hips, she bent a stern look on the three girls who had suddenly become interested in looking anywhere but at her.

"Well, I've heard it all now. And there was I thinking that there was not much else left in the world that could surprise me. But I have to hand it to you. You've taken the wind out of my sails all right. Because, honest to God, I never heard such a load of old rubbish in all my born days! Look –" her voice grew kind, confiding, "there's a bit more to getting a baby than that and one day when you're old enough I promise I'll tell you. In the meantime don't be paying any attention to that old nonsense. If you sit on a seat after a man, the worst that can happen is that you'll get a warm bum from the heat from his backside. Do you believe me?"

"Yes, Mammy," Mollie said, while Daisy and Rose nodded.

"Good!" It was time to have a little talk with

Molly about the matter, she thought, and the sooner the better. Satisfied for the moment, she returned her attention to the question of the shoes. "Here, Mollie, slip these on like a good girl." Obediently, Mollie kicked off her boots, took the shoes from her mother and slipped her feet into them. "Now, Daisy, Rose, bend forward. Can you see her drawers in their reflection? No? Well, then!" Pleased that that objection too had been overcome, Eileen bustled them out to the kitchen where their attention was immediately diverted by the enticing smell of cabbage and bacon bubbling away on the range. It was only an end of bacon she'd got cheap from the butcher, who had a bit of a thing for her, and the cabbage was on the stalky side, but still, beggars couldn't be choosers.

"The three flowers of Salthill, that's what you are!" Paddy McNab surveyed his young daughters who, fed, watered and washed, were parading their new finery for their father's inspection. "Amn't I the great man all the same to have three such beautiful cailíns?"

"And didn't I have something to do with it and all, Paddy McNab?" Eileen demanded, on her way to refill the teapot and having no intention of letting him take all the credit.

"You did! You did!" Playfully he reached out and

smacked her rump. "And I'll tell you something else, girls – " he paused to light a Sweet Afton cigarette, flicked the match with practised ease into the fireplace, "beautiful and all as you are, there's not one of you can hold a candle to your mother."

"Ah, would you don't be talking nonsense!" Dismissive, Eileen chucked a dishcloth at his head, but he could tell she was pleased by the two bright spots of colour that appeared high up on her cheekbones. "Mind you, there was a time when I *could* have put you all in the shade. Yes, indeed!" She wagged her head. "Sure wasn't the whole of Galway and the half of Clare throwing me the glad eye at one time or another!"

"Aye! Including meself," her husband interrupted, a broad smile on his face. "And then I chased her till she caught me!" The children laughed, delighted by their parents' banter. "Now would you shift with that tea, woman, before the tongue dries up in my head." He paused dramatically, slid a sly look across at Mollie. "And then, who'll keep the home fires burning?"

Just as he'd bargained for, Mollie's ears pricked up. "Are you going to the woods tonight, Daddy?"

"And what if I am?" Knowing what was coming next, Paddy feigned ignorance.

"Well, can I come with you?"

His eyebrows shot up. "You? Come with me?"

Teasing, his fingers, yellowed at the tips from years of smoking, drummed against his chin. "Ah, I don't know about that so much, Moll. The woods at night is no place for a young girl. Besides, isn't your place at home with your mother, helping her wash the dishes and the likes and learning to be a lady?"

Predictably Mollie, who had she lived in earlier times would surely have been on first-name terms with Emmeline Pankhurst, was unimpressed with this line of reasoning. "It is not! I hate housework and I'm *never* going to be a lady. Besides, I bet John-Joe is going with you! And Cathal Power. I bet he's going too."

"And, so what if they are?" Paddy blew an unintentional smoke ring, which Rosie immediately dived on and dispersed with a wildly waving hand, looking hopefully up in his face for another. "Sure aren't John-Joe and Cathal both boys?"

Mollie sniffed. "So what? I'm as good as them and I want to go too."

"And would you not be afraid we might see a big white ghost up in the trees with the moon shining full on its head," Paddy asked in a sepulchral voice, "only it wouldn't be a head, but a skull?"

"I would not!" Mollie was indignant. "I'm not afraid of anything, so I'm not!"

"Oh well, all right, so!" Throwing up his hands in mock surrender her father capitulated. "Be it on your own head, but you'd better go and change out of your fine feathers then, unless you want the lads to get the wrong idea and think you fancy them."

"You can't marry your first cousin!" Daisy piped up knowledgeably as, wasting no time, Mollie scuttled off to change. "Besides, John-Joe's courting! And Cathal Power's going to marry me."

"Courting? John-Joe?" This was news to her parents. "Who? And how do you know anyway?" Eileen asked, wondering how it was that Daisy always seemed to have information before any one else.

"He's courting Majella McBride's sister, Bernie." Daisy blushed importantly.

"The doctor's daughter?" Pursing his lips, Paddy gave a low whistle. "You're mistaken, surely, Daisy?"

"I am not!" Annoyed, Daisy kicked the table leg. "I saw them kissing round the back of the church only yesterday." She wrinkled her nose. "Yeuch! It was disgusting!"

"Well, if that's true, McBride'll kill him!" Worried, Eileen tucked a strand of hair behind her ear. Over the years, John-Joe had become more like a son than a nephew and had been a great comfort to her after Liam was killed. His own mother, Nancy, had walked out on the family when he was only six and his sisters, Mary and Nuala, only eight. Small wonder then that he spent so much time at the

McNab's place. He missed having a mother, she supposed, and though Dick tried his hardest to be all things to his children, there were certain times when a child needed a mother figure in its life, someone to kiss all his hurts away and show that she cared. And care about John-Joe, Eileen certainly did, almost to distraction, but even her jaundiced eye couldn't pretend that he was of the same social standing as the McBride girl. And for all that Oscar McBride's job was geared towards saving life, it was common knowledge that when his dander was up, he'd a temper on him like Beelzebub. As for those daughters of his! Majella and Bernie! Everyone knew he doted on them, especially since their mother had haemorrhaged to death from a miscarriage some years earlier.

Sharing none of her fears, Paddy, much to her annoyance, seemed to think the whole thing a great joke entirely. Slapping his thigh he emitted another low, admiring whistle. "The young scut! I never thought he had it in him. Young McBride, eh? Well, well! You live and learn! And there was I thinking he wouldn't say boo to a goose. It just goes to show, you can never judge a book by its cover."

"John-Joe Brady is a big pig," Rose interjected huffily, her eight-year-old face red as a beet. "He said he was going to marry me when I grow up."

Rolling her eyes, Daisy gave an exaggerated sigh.

"What's the matter with you, Rosie McNab? Didn't I just say you can't marry your first cousin, because you'll be – you'll be," she struggled to recall a word she'd heard recently, "ex – ex-decapitated by the Pope!"

Paddy winked. "I suppose that's why he's called the 'head off' the Catholic Church, eh, Eileen?"

Half-heartedly, because her mind was still very much on John-Joe, his wife picked up and brandished a metal ladle in his direction. "Would you get out, you big galoot, before I brain you!"

"Don't worry. I'm going." Rising from his chair, he shrugged himself into the old tweed hacking-jacket he wore for dirty work and made for the door, with Mollie, a foreshortened shadow, trailing at his heels. "Come on, Moll. Your mother's finally gone off her rocker!"

CHAPTER FOUR

It was dark in Friar's Copse, except for odd patches of luminescence where the moon peeped down between the treetops – but then, darkness was a primary requisite for the appropriation of trees that did not belong to you. Despite her brave words of earlier, Mollie kept close to her father, grateful for his large presence and that of John-Joe and his friend, Cathal, who had met them en route, handcart at the ready. With its odd rustling noises, unidentifiable squeaks, and sighs, Friar's Copse at night was completely unrecognisable as the place where she, her sisters and friends often played by day.

"It's a grand night for it, Uncle Paddy, all the same!" John-Joe set down the handcart beside a likely-looking tree and rubbed his hands together.

"That would depend, of course, on what you're

talking about." Paddy McNab decided the time was ripe for a bit of teasing. "To tell the truth, I'm surprised you turned up at all the night. The way I heard it, you've got better fish to fry nowadays."

"What on earth are you talking about?" John-Joe pretended ignorance but, despite being unable to see him clearly in the dark, everyone could tell he was blushing. "Have you been at the hard stuff, Uncle Paddy? Is that what it is?" He enlisted his friend's support. "Hey, Cathal, do you think my Uncle Paddy's been on the drink?"

Well used to their banter and loving it, Cathal laughed softly. On nights like this, he felt like a real member of the McNab family, accepted and wanted, in on all the jokes, and not at all like the stranger he felt with his own family. Not that his family were bad people. They weren't. They just had high expectations, especially his mother, and now that Finn was a fully-ordained priest and Lorcan had left home to study medicine at the College of Surgeons in Dublin, the focus had turned full on him and his mother's disappointment rolled over him in waves.

Crumpling suddenly to his knees, Paddy clutched melodramatically at his heart. "Ooh, the pain!" he groaned. "You wouldn't happen to know a doctor, would you, John-Joe? Or you, Cathal?" He groaned louder, enjoying the pantomime. "Or a doctor's daughter might do!"

Picking up an axe from the handcart, John-Joe brandished it threateningly. "Ah, would you get up, you ould eejit, or it's an undertaker you'll be looking for!"

Laughing, Paddy struggled to his feet, brushing his trousers down with the flat of his hand. "Ah, sure that would be grand," he chortled. "I wouldn't object to that at all, so I wouldn't!"

"Why would it be grand, Daddy?" Mollie was puzzled. "That would mean you were dead. It wouldn't be grand to be dead! It would be horrible."

Her father tapped his nose, though again she sensed rather than saw the gesture. "Because, Moll darlin', an undertaker is always the last man to let you down."

Careful to keep the noise down, John-Joe and Cathal chuckled appreciatively, but, failing to get the joke, Mollie bit her lip.

"Ah, stop talking rubbish, Daddy," she said, leaving him to reflect ruefully on her uncanny resemblance to his wife. Honest to God, Eileen could have spit her out, so alike were they.

"Would you get a move on, Uncle Paddy," John-Joe urged, spitting on his hand and taking a firmer grip on the axe, "unless you want Sergeant O'Shea breathing down our necks. Time's getting on, you know."

"And time and tide wait for no man." Paddy

picked up his own axe. "But doctors' daughters? Now they're a different kettle of fish entirely, wouldn't you say? Isn't that right, Cathal?"

"All right! All right!" Wielding the axe with fervour, John-Joe made the first cut in the tree. "You've had your fun. Now !et me show you what a real man is capable of."

"Real man, is it? I'll show you a real man, you impudent scut! It's chopping trees I was before you were even born." Pausing to make sure Mollie was standing well clear, he swung the handle and matched his nephew swing for swing, while Cathal stood patiently by, waiting to chop the fallen timber into blocks.

Letting their low-pitched chatter pass over her head, Mollie went and sat on a tree stump, content to wait till such time as the men judged they had enough firewood to be going on with. Later when Cathal had finished chopping the blocks she would help rub clay into the fresh-cut wood. That way, if anyone chanced to remark on the recent theft of trees from Friar's Copse, the McNabs' wood-pile would look as though it had been there since ould God's time.

"Ah, sure, it's shocking," Paddy would say, shaking his head sadly. "They'd take the eye out of your head nowadays and come back for the holes." Then, getting really carried away with the story, "Aye, sad though it is to say, they'd steal the cross off an ass's back and come back for the hooves!"

"You're desperate!" Eileen had been known to admonish him roundly, torn between disapproval and laughter. "The girls will be thinking it's all right to steal!"

"Yerrah, they will not!" Taking it as his cue, Paddy would wheel out and climb astride one of his favourite hobby-horses. "God made the woods for all of us the way we'd have a bit of shade if we needed it, or a bit of heat. Them Chadwicks are sitting up there in Beehive Hall roasting the arses off themselves in front of blazing fires, with not a thought for the rest of us shaking and shivering in our shifts. And who gave them the right to fence off Friar's Copse, that's what I'd like to know?" Here he would smash his fist down on the table or on his knee for emphasis, and answer his own question. "The bloody English! That's who! Coming over here and parcelling up our land like it was a pound of rashers with only the odd scrap thrown to the poor mongrel Irish. Just like the famine in the 1840s!" His voice would rise in direct proportion to his indignation. "Famine, me backside! There *was* no famine! Correct me if I'm wrong, but as far as I'm concerned a famine means a shortage of food and there was *no* shortage of food. There was a potato blight, that's all! A *potato* blight! Sure isn't Ireland a great agricultural country? Hadn't we got all sorts of other crops growing up and down the country? Wheat, barley, corn, the works! And what happened? The feckers shipped them off to England with never a thought for the poor Irish skeletons standing on the quayside with the dogs queuing up ready to gnaw on their bones!"

Eileen, fearing he might bring on a heart attack or stroke, would attempt to pour oil on troubled history. "All right, Paddy! A lot of water has flowed under the bridge since then."

"And a lot of blood flowed under it before. Don't forget that, girl!"

"I don't forget it! But neither will I carry it on me back like a dowager's hump. Time moves on. The English nowadays are a different breed and if the girls emigrate to England – and with the shortage of jobs round here, the *famine* of jobs round here, it looks like they'll have no option – you might even end up with a couple of Englishmen for sons-in-law. So my advice to you, Paddy McNab, is to leave the history in the past where it belongs, because what happened happened and what's gone is gone and no matter how much you rehash it and fret over it, it's something you can never change. Unlike your shirt, which could do with a good wash!"

"Ah, I suppose you're right." Gradually, the

twinkle would come back into his eyes and Eileen would breathe a sigh of relief as the hobby-horse was stabled for yet another night.

Mollie stayed close to the men on the way home, especially on the little boreen that skirted Friar's Copse and the back of Chadwicks' house. It wasn't the dark that made her nervous, though you couldn't see your hand in front of your face. Neither was it the thoughts that Sergeant O'Shea might happen upon them and their load of stolen timber. No! It was something much worse than that. Quite simply, Mollie was afraid that the ghost of Father O'Malley, tortured and murdered on this very boreen by the Black and Tans, would appear and frighten the life out of her. Mind you, Mollie wasn't alone in her terror. Many's the grown man would rather go a mile out of his way than set foot on the boreen at night. And after what happened to poor Miley Murphy, who could blame them? Sure wasn't the poor devil a gibbering wreck now and incarcerated in an asylum and likely to end his days there too by all accounts. Mollie remembered the night he had come banging on their door roaring and shouting like the banshee was after him.

"Open up! In the name of God, open up, would ye, and let me in!" *Bang! Bang! Bang!* "Oh, Sacred Heart! Would you let me in!"

The whole family roused from sleep, Mammy pale, clutching the neck of the nightdress she had expertly cobbled together out of odd scraps of material and which still bore the legend Odlum's down one side of it.

"Don't open it, Paddy!" Gathering Mollie and her sisters about her legs. "What if it's a madman come to murder us all?"

Daddy, dismissive. "Oh, don't be so ridiculous, Eileen!" And as the pounding continued, "Will ye hould yer whisht! I'm going as fast as I can!" Drawing back the bolt and staggering a little as the hysterical form of Miley almost toppled him.

"Aw Paddy, thanks be to God!" Miley, slamming the door behind him and shaking like a leaf. "Thanks be to the Blessed Virgin and the Sacred Heart!" Daddy led him to a chair as gratitude and relief caused him to thank a litany of saints, and confusion to bless one who was the furthest thing from a saint Ireland had ever known. "Thanks be to St Francis, St Martin, St Jude, St Peter, St Paul and Blessed Oliver Cromwell and all the saints!"

Daddy nodding to Mammy. Mammy correctly interpreting the gesture, going to the cupboard where Daddy kept a sizeable bottle of poteen and pouring a large mugful, which she handed to Miley, wrapping his shaking fingers around it.

"I seen him, Paddy! Eileen! Honest to God, I did!"

He took a large slurp of the poteen, choking a little as the fiery liquid caught at the back of his throat. "As plain as the nose on me face, I did."

"Calm down, Miley." Eileen patted his shoulder. "Now who did you say you saw?"

"Father . . . Father O'Malley!" And as they looked sceptical. "I did. I swear! Jumped out of the ditch round the back of Chadwicks', he did, all covered in blood and not a stitch on him."

Suddenly pale, Mammy had almost collapsed into a chair, miming the sign of the cross as she did so. "Did he say anything, Miley?" she asked, as Miley choked once more on a mouthful of poteen, drained the mug and held it out for a refill, his hands still palsied with fear.

"Aye, he did right enough, but I wasn't going to stick around conversing, like. Took to me heels and skedaddled so I did, and never stopped going till I hit your door."

"Are ye sure you weren't three sheets to the wind, Miley?" Paddy had asked suspiciously, knowing Miley's reputation with the bottle. "Maybe ye got a bad pint."

"Me arse in parsley, I did!" Miley was emphatic in denial. "Not a drop of the hard passed me lips this night, as God's my witness – not but what I hadn't the longing," he finished honestly. "But I didn't have the wherewithal and that's a fact!"

"The poor craythur!" Tears in her eyes, Mammy had shaken her head sadly. "Maybe it's prayers he's after. Maybe he can't rest in peace."

"Sure how could he rest in peace after the death those bastards gave him?" Paddy thumped the table. "And delivered into their hands by one of our own too. The feckin Judas! May he spend eternity roasting in hell with the devil shoving red hot pokers up his backside!"

Resisting an overwhelming urge to giggle, Mollie and her sisters had stayed very quiet. The grown-ups seemed to have forgotten they were there and they were loath to remind them, knowing they would be packed off to bed with a flea in their ear and so miss all the excitement. In full flow now Paddy continued, his voice bitter as he reflected once more on the injustices meted out to the Irish by the English, and this time Eileen did nothing to stop him for no one who had heard the story of the Black and Tans could fail to be horrified.

History being her favourite subject at school, Mollie knew all about the Black and Tans. "*They*," Sister Imelda said, the light of a zealot in her eyes, her mouth twisted with disgust, "were the flotsam and jetsam of the British Army, nothing but scum, through and through. Oh, they triumphed in the war, all right. But their triumph was shortlived, because whilst their compatriots were quick to welcome them home as conquering heroes and fierce quick to put out the bunting and dance in the streets, they weren't quite so quick to give up their jobs for them or to put their hands in their pockets to hand out aid. Small wonder then," she told them, clutching at the thick black rosary that hung from her waist, catching up the crucifix at the end and waving it at her audience, "that when the brass bands had finished playing and the bunting had been stuffed away, the crime rate suddenly soared and the prisons filled up with the same young soldiers who had so recently fought for liberty." Waving the cross with ardour, Sister Imelda had treated the children to a calculating eye. "It's an expensive business, you know, keeping a man in prison! And if you do your sums right, you'll see that it's even more expensive to keep hundreds and thousands of men in prison and it wasn't too long before the English government felt the bite. But as usual, the feckers didn't take too long to come up with a plan, which, surprise, surprise, involved riding roughshod over – who else but ourselves? As if we hadn't already suffered enough!" Chewing meditatively at the inside of her cheek, she expounded on the plan, calling it a way of killing two birds with one stone. "Offer the prisoners the choice of either completing their jail sentences or of going over to Ireland and belting ten bells out of the Paddies. Sure, who could resist that? That wasn't a choice at all. It was a gift! Nobody could lose – apart from the Irish. From the English Government's point of view, it would not only alleviate the strain on its purse but it would also take care of the Irish question. Where the prisoners were concerned, not only would freedom be restored, but they were also being given a free hand to take out all their rage and frustration on the poor Irish. All this and a handsome wage to boot! Naturally enough, it wasn't too long before the first lot of Black and Tans arrived, kitted out in the odd assortment of clothing, half khaki army uniform, half black police uniform, from which they gained their name. And with their arrival began one of the foulest and most painful periods in Irish history."

And poor Father O'Malley had been just one of their many victims.

Mollie knew all about Father O'Malley too. The nuns had seen to that. Indeed it was doubtful if there was a child left in all of Ireland who was unfamiliar with the details of his gory death right here in Friar's Copse.

"And 'twas one of our own that set him up! Can you credit that?" Sister Imelda had enquired of her pupils, her own open face patently displaying the fact that she herself could not. "Betrayed him the same way Judas Iscariot betrayed Jesus – and why? For what?" She answered the question herself, knowing by the blank look on her listeners' faces that she was unlikely to find enlightenment from that quarter. "For glory! That's what! Not even for thirty stinking pieces of silver, the dirty scutter!" Coming round to the front of her desk, she adopted a position of comfort, leaning her bottom against it so that she was half sitting, half-standing. Familiar with the signs, the children relaxed back in their seats, knowing that she was now in full flow and they could forget about fractions and geometry, for a while anyway.

"Ah, he was a grand man, a jewel in the crown of Catholicism!" Sister Imelda spoke as though she knew him personally. "And the Tans had it in their noses that he always seemed to get wind of when they were going to do a raid on someone's house and take their boys away. And what would he do only tip the family off, the way they could hide their children before the blackguards came." Looking reflective for a moment the nun wagged her head. "Indeed my own granny used to hide her lads down the cabbage patch thanks to the good priest giving her the nod and the wink. What is it, Bridie?" Annoyed at the interruption, Sister Imelda sent a quelling look to where Bridie McNamara had begun furiously waving her hand in the air in an effort to attract attention.

"Sure that's nothing, Sister!" Mission accomplished,

Bridie rose to her feet, sending a glance of triumph around the classroom. It wasn't often she had a chance to shine and by God she was going to milk this opportunity for all it was worth. "Sure that's nothing!" she said again. "Sure wasn't I *born* under a head of cabbage! And me brothers and sisters too." Wide-eyed, she let them in on a secret. "All except Marty! Mammy found him on the floor of the lavvy when she went out for a pee!"

Seeking the heavens, Sister Imelda's voice cracked like a whip on the chalky air. "Bridie McNamara! Sit down, shut your mouth and don't open it again till you've something sensible to say for yourself."

Staggered, Bridie did as she was told only to find herself on the end of poisonous looks from the rest of the class who resented anyone who had to gall to try and make themselves special. There wasn't a one of them, for God's sake, who *hadn't* been found under a head of cabbage, or a rhubarb leaf, or crawling up a hawthorn tree singing tiddly-oomp-boomp, come to that!

With a muttered imprecation for God to give her strength, Sister Imelda hauled desperately at the dangling thread of her narrative. "Now, where was I before that fool of a girl interrupted me? Oh yes, as I was saying before I was so rudely interrupted, the Tans weren't too impressed with Father O'Malley's activities, so weren't they the delighted boyos when a crawler by the name of Cassidy offered to serve them up his head on a plate. The plate bit's just a figure of speech," she added hastily, seeing Bridie's hand begin to ascend once more. Shifting a little, Imelda settled herself more comfortably. "Anyway, the plan was for Cassidy, who poor Father O'Malley himself had christened, and trusted as much as he trusted anybody, to lure him out on a bogus mission in the dead of night, and for the Tans to lie in wait for him. Did the plan work? Indeed, it did! Out he lured him on the pretext that somebody was lying hurt in Friar's Copse and, being the saint he was, Father O'Malley set off immediately to help, only to be ambushed by the Tans as he reached the little boreen at the back of the woods. And I hope they died roaring, every one of them," Sister Imelda finished, uncaring that the sentiment was strangely at variance with her Christian values.

Now, on that very same boreen, Mollie slipped her small hand into her father's pocket and willed herself to think about the apple-tart and the big mug of sweet tea that would be waiting for them when they got home. Still it was hard to suppress a sigh of relief when she finally spotted the oil-lamp Mammy always left burning in the cottage window.

"*Ah, sure the world is big and I am small . . .*" began her father, seemingly apropos of nothing.

"*. . . home is the best place after all!*" finished Mollie, and meant it.

"You'll come in for a while, eh, John-Joe? And you too, Cathal? I know Eileen would love to see you. She was only saying the other day that it was a while since you'd been round." Deftly manoeuvring the handcart round the back of the cottage, Paddy tipped the contents into a neat pile on the ground.

"Just try and stop me," John-Joe answered first, his nose twitching like a bloodhound at the lovely rich smell of apples and cloves emanating from inside the cottage, then springing back suddenly with a yelp of pain as, catapulting through the cottage door, Rose kicked him hard on the shin.

"Jaysus, Rosie! What did you do that for?" Genuinely puzzled, John-Joe rubbed tenderly at his leg, then reeled again as Rose turned her attentions to his midriff, pummelling him with small, though hard, clenched fists. "God almighty, you're killing me!" Desperately, he attempted to hold her away, at the same time appealing to his uncle and friend for help. "For the love of God, stop her, somebody, before she ruptures me bread-basket!"

Teasingly, Paddy cupped his ear. "What was that you were saying back in the woods about a *real* man? Ah, now John-Joe, what sort of a *real* man is it that can't handle an eight-year-old girl?"

"That's right." Cathal got in on the act. "And there's you thinking you can handle Oscar McBride, when he finds out about you and Bernie. Some chance! I'll tell you, I wouldn't like to be in your shoes."

"You're a big pig, John-Joe, so y'are!" Rose grunted, lack of breath finally forcing her to slow down. "You were supposed to marry me and now our Daisy saw you with that McBride one. Kissing!" Her voice rose accusingly. "On the mouth!"

"Ah now listen, Rose," John-Joe entreated, trying to duck past, before she got her second wind, "I was only practising."

"What d'ye mean, practising?" The small girl eyed him suspiciously, well used to being fobbed off by bigger and older people.

Sighing dramatically, John-Joe gave up his plan of escape and opted for diplomacy instead. "Who's my best girl?" he asked.

"Me?"

John-Joe nodded. "Exactly! But you're still just a little sprat, aren't you?" Again Rose nodded. "So I have to wait till you're grown up to marry you, don't I?"

"I suppose so," Rose agreed, more than willing to be charmed back into the good humour that came naturally to her.

Bending forward, John-Joe placed his hands on her shoulders. "So in the meantime I'm getting in a bit of practice, like. Learning how to kiss and that, the way you won't be disappointed when I whisk you off on me black charger."

"Oh!" Although prepared to go along with this line in plausibility, Rose wanted to get things quite clear in her mind. "But you don't love her?"

"Yerrah, divil the love!" John-Joe said scornfully, but with much mental crossing of the fingers.

"Well, that's all right, then." Appeased, Rose took him by one hand and Cathal by the other, leading them both into the house. "Besides, our Daisy said that one thinks her pee is lemonade. And it's not John-Joe, is it? It's just pee!"

Inside, Eileen bustled about with the teapot, while Daisy made herself important cutting the apple tart into uneven slices, reserving the biggest for Cathal. She watched the way his fair hair flopped forward onto his forehead and admired his nice eyes, grey with little green flecks in them. It didn't matter a bit that one of his front teeth was chipped. Yes, definitely, she told herself, one day I'm going to marry him.

"So, Cathal," Eileen took a seat opposite and poured him a large mug of tea, "you haven't been round for a bit. How's the family? All well, I hope?"

"Oh, grand, thank God, Mrs McNab." Gratefully, Cathal pulled the mug closer. "Did I tell you Lorcan's gone off to Dublin to train as a doctor? Imagine that, a doctor in the family!"

"Your mother must be dead proud."

"Oh, she is." Cathal nodded, smiling at Daisy as

she passed him yet another slice of apple tart, then unhygienically licked her fingers. "It's a right feather in her cap all right. And she's got all the bases covered now as well – a doctor to treat her if she becomes sick and a priest to pull a few strings with the Man Upstairs if by any chance she doesn't get better. What more could you want?" There was a slight bitterness in his voice that didn't go unnoticed by either Paddy or Eileen, who were both well aware of Miriam Power's raging ambitions for her family.

"I'm sure she's equally proud of you." Leaning across, Eileen squeezed his hand, finding herself somewhat dismayed when this small gesture of comfort led to his eyes filling up.

"No. No, she's not, Mrs McNab. I'm a disappointment to her." Furious at himself, he blinked the tears away. "And a trial. She's told me often enough. She wants me to be a barrister, you know." He gave a self-mocking shrug. "Me! A barrister! When I barely managed to scrape through my Inter Cert. Lord knows, I can hardly spell the word. Finn and Lorcan were always the brains of the family. Learning came easy to them, and good luck to the pair of them. I wish them every success." Then his face lit up with a passion Eileen and Paddy had never seen there before. "But as for me, I just want to be a farmer, that's all. I want to plant things and watch them grow. That's what makes me happy. I want to stand in a golden field of wheat and know that every sheaf, every blade was planted by me. I want to rise with the dawn, go outside and smell the earth. I want to milk cows and shear sheep. I want to raise chickens and goats and if ever I have a spare moment, I want to go down to the river, wade out into the middle and fish for trout." He brushed the back of his hand across his eyes. It came back wet and glistened in the light from the oil-lamp. Privy to his dream, everyone had fallen silent – even Rosie had come to stand at his knee and gaze up into his face with big solemn eyes. "Do you think I'm mad?" The question was directed to no one in particular, but both Paddy and Eileen rushed to answer it.

"Not at all." Moved, Paddy cleared his throat. "It sounds like a good sort of life to me. Doctors, priests and barristers are all well and good and all have their place, but it's the man who tills the land that puts food in the world's belly."

"True for you," Eileen agreed, feeling like her heart wanted to break for this young man and the simplicity of his dreams. "Sure where would we be without the farmer?"

"Have some more tart," Daisy said.

CHAPTER FIVE

"Good God Almighty, what on earth have you got there?" Startled, Eileen whipped round as her husband came in the door, the most decrepit-looking greyhound she had ever seen trailing at his heels.

"That! Or rather he," Paddy announced proudly, "is our fortune or will be, as soon as I've trained him up a bit."

"Fortune? Are you stone mad, man?" Eileen's eyebrows almost hit the roof and the greyhound, slightly wall-eyed, cringed back against his new master's legs recognising the tone of disapproval in Eileen's voice, and pleasantly confused when the kick in its bony ribs that usually followed failed to materialise. "Father Clarke's ould terrier has more go in it than that fleabag and that poor thing's only got three legs!"

Paddy bridled. "For your information, Mrs Know-It-All, Larkin here is out of Lord Kilbannon and a better racer never lived. Isn't that right, fella?" Leaning down, he patted the narrow head lightly and the wall-eyes gazed up in mute adoration. "Oh aye! We'll show them all a clean pair of heels, so we will, Larkin lad, won't we? We'll put them all to rout!"

"Huh!" Unimpressed, Eileen surveyed the sorry pair before her. "Larkin may or may not be out of Lord Whatever-you-call-him, but one thing's definite, Paddy McNab, and that's that you're straight out of the loony-bin!"

Unabashed, Paddy made a great fuss of the dog. "Oh, scoff all you want, woman, but it won't be long before you'll be scoffing your words and I hope they stick in your craw and choke you!" Both broke off their bantering as a sudden, unmelodious commotion from outside announced the arrival of the girls home from school.

"*Óró mo bháidín . . .*" Daisy's off-key soprano could be heard plainly approaching the cottage, as could the protesting voices of her sisters, "*ag snamh ar an gcuan . . .*"

"Would you shut your gob, Daisy!" Mollie roared, administering a sizable thump to her sister's back and causing her to break off in mid-phrase. "You'll frighten the life out of Mammy."

"Yeah!" Rose showed solidarity with her older sister. "She'll think you're being murdered."

"Ye're just jealous," Daisy snapped. "Just because I'm singing in the *Feis* and you lot aren't!"

Rolling her eyes dramatically, Mollie brought the Almighty in on the conversation. "Well, God help us all so! They must be scraping the bottom of the barrel when they're letting the likes of you croak." With a nudge, she encouraged her younger sister to put in her own ha'penny worth and Rose, more used to being the one on the wrong end of the stick, was only too happy to oblige.

"You're not the only one who can sing, Daisy McNab!" she said, puffing out her narrow chest importantly. "I learned a new song at school today too. Patsy Duggins was singing it. Do you want me to teach you?"

In the cottage her parents' heads jerked up as the strident tones of their youngest daughter suddenly ripped through the air.

"Hitler has only got one ball! Goering has no balls at all –"

Exchanging appalled glances, Paddy and Eileen left the wall-eyed Larkin to his own devices and, rushing outside, startled their youngest daughter into silence, at the same time frightening the wits out of the other pair.

Grabbing Rose by her shoulders, Eileen shook her

until her teeth rattled. "Sacred Heart of Jesus, you filthy little article!" Her voice came out in a sharp series of staccato bursts. "Where in God's name did you hear that dirt? Well?" she demanded, as Rose's head jerked backwards and forwards as if there was no bone in her neck. "Well, come on! Spit it out!"

"That's enough, Eileen." Prising his little daughter away from her irate mother, Paddy dropped to one knee, pulling Rose onto the other. "There now, love!" Delving into his trouser pocket he produced a hanky, wiping away the startled tears which, by now, were coursing down the little girl's face. "Sure you weren't to know there was any harm in it, were you?" His eyes rose to his wife who, a little calmer now, was regarding him with a mixture of equal parts guilt and annoyance.

Viciously she smoothed a strand of hair back from her eyes. "Oh, that's right, Paddy McNab! Let her off the hook! Let them all off the hook, why don't you? Just don't blame me when they grow up to be tinkers, that's all!"

Her sobs dying to just the odd sniff, Rose knuckled her eyes. "But, Mammy, everyone at school is singing it." Her voice was small and shaky. "Besides, what's wrong with it?"

"Yeah, what's wrong with it?" Daisy demanded, all animosity towards her younger sister temporarily forgotten in the necessity of siding against Mammy.

"It's only about them ould Germans not having any balls during the war." Helplessly her parents looked at each other as Daisy, determined to have her say, continued. "I love balls. Look!" Suddenly she rummaged in her schoolbag and produced a small rubber ball of indeterminate colour. Later she would bat it with her hand against the cottage wall, performing complicated manoeuvres in which the ball bounced over and through her legs.

Her father couldn't help but chuckle and even Eileen's lips twitched. "Well, it's not a very nice song, that's all!" Knowing she sounded lame, Eileen tried hard to inject some forcefulness into her assertion. "And I don't want to hear any of you singing it again. Is that clear?" Her glance raked her daughters, who nodding obediently, shuffled their feet into the ground, scuffing the polish off their boots. But there was a glint in Daisy's eyes that looked nothing like repentance. "All right, we'll say no more so!" Glad, at least, to have had the last word, though there was something about the victory that rang decidedly hollow, she turned to go back into the cottage, then shrieked as the bony form of Larkin shot past her, a bacon-joint clamped firmly in his jaws. Taking off in hot pursuit, Eileen gave vent to a number of colourful oaths that would have made the tinkers she so disdained blush from their ankles to the tops of their heads. "The hoors melt ye anyway, ye skinny

101

bugger!" she bellowed. "Just let me catch up with ye and I swear I'll have your hide for a rug!" Shaking her fist as his bony rump retreated further into the distance, she subsided onto the grass, her breath coming in sharp, painful gasps. "Enjoy the bacon, ye fecker, because it's humble pie you'll be eating from now on! Aye, and be thankful for it!"

Behind her Paddy dissolved with laughter, while the girls, tears and balls forgotten, galloped after her, screaming with merriment. For his part, Larkin ran on, and on, showing a clean pair of heels and stopping only when Eileen's threats had faded away into the distance. Then dropping his trophy, he admired it briefly, before devouring every scrap. Never having sampled bacon before, he found he liked the taste, and notwithstanding Eileen's curses decided he might venture back for more.

"Is he really ours, Daddy?" Mollie asked later as a replete but guilty-looking greyhound slunk in the door and prostrated himself on the floor.

Her father nodded. "Indeed he is, alannah. So what do you think, eh? Is he a winner or not?"

"He's gorgeous." Dropping to her knees beside the dog, Mollie reached out a hand to stroke the narrow head that felt surprisingly soft and silky. "There, boy," she crooned. "You're gorgeous, so you are. You're the most beautiful dog in the whole wide world." Unused to such demonstrations of affection, as well as such obvious lies, Larkin turned the full charm of his wall-eyes on her, his tongue darting out to cover her fingers in grateful licks.

"Where did you get him from, Daddy?" Daisy asked, squatting beside her sister, much to the greyhound's delight, for whom an audience, and an admiring one at that, was truly a novelty. Only Rose hung back, a little nervous of dogs ever since Father Clarke's little terrier had nipped her leg last summer.

"Daddy went to see a man about a dog," Mollie answered her sister's question, "only this time he brought him home with him. Didn't you, Daddy?"

Paddy chuckled heartily. "Something like that all right," he said, the truth being that he had won him in a game of poker that, according to Eileen, everyone else had the sense to deliberately lose.

"Will we be racing him? I mean racing him properly on a greyhound track and that?"

Their father nodded. "Aye, we will, and judging by the performance he gave earlier with the bacon, I'd say we're in with more than a chance." Suddenly his tone became mock-serious. "Still I'll expect you girls to give a hand with his training. I'll expect you to be up at dawn every day, putting him through his paces. And after school. And on weekends too. And especially during the school holidays."

"Oh, we will, Daddy," Mollie promised earnestly. "We'll run him ragged, won't we, fella?" Game for a laugh, Larkin panted happily, lips curling back to reveal long, yellow teeth, upon which Rose's trepidation vanished as if by magic.

"Look!" she said excitedly. "He's smiling!"

"As well he might, the bugger!" snapped her mother who, until now, had shown remarkable restraint. "With his belly full of prime bacon, while the rest of us will have to make do with a couple of eggs."

Nobody minded, least of all Larkin who, emitting a huge yawn of satisfaction, closed his eyes and went promptly to sleep.

CHAPTER SIX

Devlin lost no time in throwing up the foundations of his house. Paddy watched bitterly, standing at the door of the cottage, as day after day lorries loaded with building materials trundled past and workmen roughened the air with their coarse voices.

"Come away, love," Eileen would say, tugging at his elbow. "There's no point in upsetting yourself."

Sometimes her husband would give in, docilely allowing himself to be led away but more often than not he stood his ground, shrugging her off like a gnat from a horse.

"I *am* upset!" he'd say, gritting out the words. "And the way I see it I've a perfect right to be upset. And I'm angry too. I want to go out there and kill the lot of them."

"I know. I know." Eileen would pat his arm soothingly, afraid to show her own sorrow, for fear it would tip him over the edge and that, despite his promise to Father Clarke, he would snap and do Devlin an injury. And as the good priest had pointed out, it wouldn't bring their Liam back! Nothing would ever bring Liam back.

To give Devlin his due, he maintained a low profile, visiting the site only occasionally to check on the work in progress, and then staying no more than a short while and never ever catching his neighbours' eyes. But there was small consolation in that because there was no getting away from the fact that soon he would be there day in, day out, happily ensconced with the new wife they'd heard tell he'd married in England, a constant reminder of their tragic loss.

Stressed out, Paddy took to walking again, his footsteps inevitably leading him to the small cemetery where Liam was buried. Sitting down on the grave, his eyes would scan, without registering, the inscription painted on the little wrought-iron cross he himself had fashioned. Words from Eileen's heart, forever engraved on his own.

> *Liam McNab – only on loan*
> *A little angel – to God*
> *Gone safely home!*

One day, Paddy vowed, he would raise a marble

stone there, a Celtic cross with the inscription etched deeply in gold, the way no amount of wind or rain could ever erode the memory of his son. Liam had had his place in the world, and the world *would* remember!

In late April, when once more Paddy's feet led him to his child's grave it was to find, with a sudden uplifting lurch of the heart, that the rosebush he had planted the previous year had burst into generous early bud, giving the pale pink promise of roses. Masses of roses! Enough to stock the wee straw baskets of all three of Liam's sisters, as they marched at the head of the May procession and scattered the scented petals in his name.

Eileen would be thrilled when he told her. He wished she could come and see for herself but, since the day of the funeral, when they had lowered the tiny cheap coffin into the earth, and Eileen had collapsed, she had been unable to bring herself to visit the grave. And Paddy had no wish to force her. She would come in her own time, he reasoned, but until then she had her own way of dealing with the grief. Oh, he knew all about the gumboot on top of the dresser and the way she sat and cried her heart out with her poor arms empty and aching for the feel of a small warm body, long since grown cold. He'd seen her sometimes through the cottage window, when unaware of his presence she wept and lamented and cried out to God at the injustice of it all. And, as he turned quietly away, what was left of his own heart broke for her, over and over and over again.

With a quick mental apology to Liam for the shortness of that day's visit, Paddy turned and headed off across the cemetery, automatically noting as he passed old Harriet Miller's grave that her coffin was again peeking up through the earth. Old Harriet, he'd heard tell, had been a walking shrew of a woman when alive, and now that she was dead even the devil didn't appear to want her. Consequently her coffin, despite being buried time and time again, kept rising up out of the earth like a phoenix from the ashes, causing poor Batty the gravedigger no end of trouble.

"Jaysus!" he'd whine whenever Harriet put in another appearance. "No amount of concentrated ground will ever keep that one down." Sniffing aggrievedly he'd shamble off, spade at the ready. "For two pins I'd burn the hoor, so I would. Aye! And warm me backside at the flames!"

"Me head's bursting," Mollie complained bitterly upon awakening on the morning of the May Procession.

"So's mine!" Daisy joined in the whine.

And struggling up in bed, Rose, not to be outdone, patted her own head and added to the dirge.

"And mine!"

Gingerly Mollie raised a hand to her hair, wincing as she came in contact with the rags Mammy had twisted round her locks to form the long, dancing ringlets so beloved of Irish mothers. "Janey-mac! I think she's scalped me."

"For goodness' sake, I have not, Mollie McNab!" her mother scoffed, coming round the curtain. "Besides you have to suffer for style!"

"Why?" Rose demanded, but Eileen was not going to get drawn into that one.

"Because you do, that's all!" she said. "Now would you ever rise and shine or the Procession will be over before you've even gone out the door. Come on, now," she chivvied them, pulling back the bedclothes and smacking each of them smartly on the legs, to a mounting chorus of protest. "Shift yourselves!" Satisfied that they were well and truly awake she bustled off to lay out the clothes Aunty Kay had sent from America. Today, she thought, with satisfaction, they'd be as good as anyone else. Today, they could walk tall and hold their heads up high and if Mother Benignus had anything to say about the black patent shoes, well she'd better not say it in her hearing. That was all!

Since the episode of the patent shoes and sitting on a seat after a man got up, Mollie had been taken aside by Eileen and filled in on the true nature of the birds and the bees, and the real reason Breda Corcorcan got her baby. "Twas nothing to do either with buses or with her sitting on a seat after a man got up," Mammy said, and then went on to talk about a secret pocket in the woman's belly and how the man planted a tiny seed there, which then took nine months to grow into a baby. To tell the truth, Mollie still wasn't too clear on the whole logistics of the operation and whether or not shovels were involved, but as Mammy appeared to be quite sick during the telling, growing sweaty and very red in the face, before suddenly jumping up to "take a turn about the yard", Mollie hadn't felt able to quiz her any further. Still she had often pondered the matter since and had searched without success for the secret pocket in her own belly.

"Well, I'll be damned!" Paddy McNab gave a low, admiring whistle as twenty minutes later, washed, dressed and with their hair arranged into glossy bouncing ringlets, his daughters modelled their new finery, prancing up and down the small room, hands on hips like miniature women. "Talk about the belle of the ball! I'll have me work cut out for me today all right. I'll be beating off the fellas with a big stick and no mistake. Are you sure you're not changlings? I think me own mucky little daughters have been spirited away by the fairies and you three beauties left in their place."

Giggling behind their hands, the girls blushed. "You're terrible, Daddy," Daisy said, tossing her head and desperately hoping it was true and that he would be beating the boys off, especially Kevin Keithley, better known as Kiss-curl on account of the little coil of hair that lay blackly on his forehead like an inverted question-mark, and for whom she had recently developed a huge crush. Mind you, she'd die if her sisters found out, especially Mollie, who considered Kiss-curl to be an awful eejit and a fool. At the moment, however, her sister's mind was otherwise engaged as the worried grooves traversing her brow showed.

"Are you sure it'll be all right, Daddy," she asked. "After all, Mother Benignus –"

"Now look here!" Paddy raised a forestalling hand. "Didn't I tell you not to be minding Mother Benignus? Sister Imelda promised you could lead the procession, and in my book and in the Good Book, a promise is a promise and that's all there is to it. And if Mother Benignus doesn't like it, she'll just have to go and take a bleddy good run and jump at herself!"

"All ready then?" Eileen queried a moment later, giving one last maternal tug to Rose's sash. "Good! Off you go so, but remember, behave yourselves, keep your chin up and look the world straight in the eye. You're as good as anyone else and have as much right to walk through this world as they have. Just remember that, and also remember I love you with all my heart. I'm dead proud of you and I'll see you soon."

"All right, Mammy." Answering for all of them, Mollie set off with her sisters and father, the three little girls carefully and importantly clutching the baskets in which the rose petals from Liam's grave nestled.

Standing on the doorstep, Eileen admired her family as they disappeared off down the boreen, the girls fresh and innocent in pastels, their father, tall and handsome, his best and only suit sponged and pressed to within an inch of its life. Shading her eyes, she fancied she saw a small shadow tagging behind, but it was nothing more than the dimness thrown down by a passing cloud. Sighing, she went back indoors. There was just time for a quick tidy-up around the cottage, a lick and a promise as she called it, and then she would put on her best costume and watch proudly as her daughters led the May Procession through the streets of Galway and on to the cathedral for Mass.

"Right! Wait here!" 'Here' was a short distance from the convent gates. Paddy cupped his ear. "Listen! They'll be out in a minute."

Tugging at his hand Daisy attempted to pull him forward. "But Daddy, we're supposed to go inside."

Her father shook his head. "Trust me on this one," he told them. "You see *inside* is *their* property, and you play by their rules. But outside – " he made a funny face, "well, let's just say that's a whole different kettle of fish. Hold fire a moment now, girls. It won't be long."

Sure enough, a short time later the convent gates creaked open and a long crocodile of schoolgirls appeared in the entrance and started walking up the street towards where Paddy and the girls were standing. *"Mother of Christ, Star of the Sea . . . "* they sang in high discordant voices. *"Pray for the sinner! Pray for me!"*

"Right!" Paddy hissed urgently as they drew level. "In you go!" And almost before they knew what had happened, Mollie, Daisy and Rose found themselves pushed in at the front and leading the cavalcade, just as Daddy had promised.

Mother Benignus was gutted. Busy as she was bullying stragglers at the rear, it took a while before she discovered the subterfuge, and then, short of making a scene, there was little or nothing she could do about it. Looking at the thunderous faces of Nancy Doyle, Helen Maher and Majella McBride, so rudely pushed out of the limelight by the McNab brats, she could see the new roof for St. Joseph's flying away on wings. Well, let them have their moment of glory, she reflected grimly, as she watched Mollie and her sisters unconcernedly scatter pink rose-petals before them. If she couldn't have the pounds she'd so coveted, she'd settle for flesh instead – pounds of it! *"May is the month of Mary –"* she sang in a voice like a whipped cur, inclining her head graciously towards familiar bystanders, but with her mind wholly on the McNab girls and how she would make them suffer!

Eileen caught up with her husband outside the cathedral, where he, John-Joe and young Cathal Power had taken up a prime position at the top of the steps. Slipping her hand into his, she squeezed excitedly as the Procession hove into view.

"Ah, sure God love them," she remarked, as her daughters, faces glowing, drew near. "It's little enough pleasure they have."

"True for you," Paddy nodded his agreement, then burst out laughing as he caught sight of Mother Benignus, marching like a great black crow at the side of the queue. "Holy God! Would you look at the face on that?" He slapped his thigh in delight. "I swear I've seen a pleasanter look on a well-slapped backside." Around him, there was an outbreak of guffawing. Mother Benignus was not a popular nun, except, of course, amongst the 'lickers', and sure didn't you find a smattering of them in every walk of life?

In bed that night, worn out but very happy, Mollie,

Daisy and Rose, who fortunately, had no inkling of what Mother Benignus had in store for them, agreed it had been a very special day and one they would always remember. Daisy, in particular, had reason to feel gratified, having spotted Kiss-curl amongst the bystanders and received a lop-sided grin from him. One day, she thought, I'm going to marry him. That would be two husbands, so far, though Cathal , with his floppy fair hair, still had the edge!

Later, Paddy went down to O'Dwyer's in order to celebrate what had, all in all, been a good day, and to boast of how he had got one over on Mother Benignus. "Did you see the face on her?" he asked all and sundry. "I mean, did you ever see a puss like it in all your born days? Let that be a lesson to her. I might not have been born with a silver spoon in my mouth, but when it comes to wits, God must have given me her share."

Having made sure the girls were sound asleep, Eileen reached up and took down Liam's little gumboot, cradling it close, whilst Larkin, who had long since charmed his way into her heart, sat and watched with sad, liquid eyes. Liam would have loved him. Eileen could just picture the two of them, boy and dog, running and lepping like mad things in the fields around the house, or playing tag with the waves that broke in a froth of Carrickmacross lace down on the strand. Slowly she rose and went to stand by the window, gazing out to where the skeleton of Devlin's house crouched in the darkness like a prehistoric monster biding its time.

"You'll have no luck for it, Devlin," she said aloud. "For though the wheels of God grind slowly, they grind exceedingly small." Unconsciously her fingers stroked the soft contours of the boot she still clutched in her hand. "Isn't that right, boy?" Behind her Larkin whined his agreement, tail keeping time, thump, thump, thump, like a metronome. Her mind returned to its earlier train of thought. "Liam would have loved you, you know. Scrawny bag of bones that you are!" Delighted with the attention he was getting, the dog gave a quick bark and began to pull himself along, combat style, towards her. "Ah, sure we can't all be beauties, can we?" Tenderly, she leant down to pat his gaunt head. "Just look at Mother Benignus! Now there's a phizog that would frighten the Ould Boy himself." Chuckling, she hurried off to replace Liam's boot on top of the dresser, as the sudden strains of 'Kevin Barry' rent the air. Only later, when she was lying in bed, did she realise that for the first time ever she hadn't cried over the boot. And what was probably most surprising of all, she didn't feel guilty – felt instead a kind of peace creeping into her sore heart, an easing of sorrow, as if baby hands were soothing, stroking, telling her it was all right. For Eileen McNab, the healing had begun.

For Mother Benignus, revenge came sooner than anticipated, and all thanks to a migraine brought on by the failure of her more well-to-do pupils' parents to cough up for the new roof for the convent. Cullen's Powders having failed to work their magic, the only cure, she decided, was to walk it out and where better to do that than down by the sea where the ozone-scented air from the Atlantic was reputed to work miracles. Crunching slowly along, absent-mindedly fingering the thick black rosary that hung from her waist, she found herself startled to a halt by a sudden bout of excited cackles and shrieks coming from behind a large rock. Migraine temporarily forgotten, she found herself creeping up to the large seaweed-covered boulder, where peering over the edge she discovered the McNab girls rushing about in mad pursuit of a greyhound, so mangy it would have been better off dead.

"Aha!" she muttered softly, like a pantomime villain of old moving in for the kill. *"The Lord works in mysterious ways, his wonders to perform."*

"C'mon, Larkin!" Daisy yelled, cheerfully oblivious to all but getting the dog in shape for his first race. "You couldn't catch a three-legged stool at that rate! You couldn't catch chicken pox!"

"Yeah! C'mon, Larkin!" In order to tempt him, Mollie, flailing wildly, flung a small hand-ball purloined from Daisy's schoolbag the week before, as far away as she could. "Quick! Get the ball! Pretend it's Mother Big Knickers," she giggled, then choked as, like a vampire into full sunlight, a large, black form emerged from behind a nearby boulder. "Oh, Holy God!" Shrinking back, her hand rose to her mouth in disbelief.

"Janey-mac!" First Daisy, and then Rose echoed her horror. Only Larkin seemed delighted with the new addition to their party, barking a loud welcome and making playful forays in the nun's direction.

"Well, well, well! And what do we have here?" Placing her hands on her ample hips, Mother Benignus, pleasantly threatening, surveyed her captives. "Could it be the McNab brats, I wonder? Eh? Absenting themselves from school?" Transferring a rheumatic finger to her chin, she tapped meditatively. Guiltily the girls scrabbled bare toes in the sand and Larkin, suspecting this was a brand new game joined in with gusto, spraying sand in every direction till Mollie, under the Head Nun's gimlet glare, managed to subdue him, by dint of rugby-tackling him to the ground. "Now," said Mother Benignus icily, picking up a piece of driftwood, spinning the two eldest girls round and poking them in the back. "if you're quite ready, I suggest we continue this conversation back at St Joseph's. Or maybe it's a written invitation you're after. Would that be it? An RSVP?"

"Now, run that by me again – you, Mollie!" Paddy McNab held up his hand as all three girls almost fell over themselves in an effort to speak at once. "Start right from the very beginning."

As a prelude, Mollie wiped her nose on her sleeve, took a deep breath and shot a quick look at her sisters. "Well, she was walking along behind us, prodding us in the backs with a big stick she'd picked up off the strand." She screwed up her forehead in an effort to exactly describe the scene. "You know! The way you'd prod cattle." Her father nodded grimly, only too well able to imagine the spectacle. "And then when we reached the school, assembly had already started. Do you know what assembly is, Daddy?"

"I do!"

Satisfied, Mollie continued. "Anyways, she prodded the three of us onto the stage in front of everybody." Mollie could feel the cold sweat of humiliation creep over her once more as she recalled how the collective eyes of the hundred children and staff gathered in the hall had pinned themselves on herself and her sisters, their mouths opening in united disapproval or glee, according to their age and rank, as Mother

Benignus began the sonorous listing of their misdemeanours.

Scarcely able to contain his anger, Paddy listened grimly as the tale of his daughters' vilification unfolded.

"And," Mollie eventually finished on an aggrieved sniff, "she told everyone to take a good look at us the way they'd know in future what jail-bait looked like, so they could steer well clear. She said if you lie down with dogs, you get up with mange." Genuinely puzzled, she wrinkled her brow. "Although I don't know if she was talking about us or Larkin."

"Oh, she did, did she?" By the time Mollie finished up, there was smoke coming out of Paddy's ears. "Jail-bait, is it? Mange, is it?" he asked, fuming. " I'll give her bleddy jail-bait, so I will! I'll give her bleddy mange!" Thumping his fist down on the table, he dislodged the book he'd been reading, so that it fell down and hit Larkin on the head, sending him skulking off into a corner. "The cheek of that one! None of my daughters will end up in jail! The McNabs are a respectable family. There's no jailbirds among our lot, but I doubt if she can say the same, considering she's old Brick Brennan's niece and wasn't he one of the biggest blackguards in Ireland!" He grinned sourly. "Used to crack on that he was a builder but, for God's sake, the only building the old sod ever did was to build a tissue of lies. After a while it got so that nobody could recognise the truth – not even himself!" Bending down, Paddy retrieved the book, set it down on the table with a bang. "I'll tell you what, Eily, I've a damn good mind to go round there and knock the living daylights out of her, nun or no nun!"

Eileen, who had listened to the story unravel with as much disgust as her husband, was nevertheless quick to intervene when it looked like the hot-headed Paddy might go and compound matters. "Now listen here, Paddy McNab!" She shook her finger at him, doing, did she but know it, an almost perfect imitation of Mother Benignus telling off a recalcitrant pupil. "The last thing we need right now is you going round there and putting your big hoof in your mouth."

"But we can't just do nothing!" Paddy dragged distracted fingers through his hair, causing it to stand out in little peaks.

Impatient, Eileen shook her head. "I didn't say we were going to do nothing, now did I, but there's more ways of choking a cat than stuffing him with butter, as the old saying goes and more ways of getting even than by simply adding two and two."

A slow smile spread across Paddy's face as he caught her drift. When it came to a battle of sheer wits, he had to hand it to her. Eily came up trumps every time. "Well, I should have known better than to underestimate you. So what exactly have you got in mind?"

"Yeah, Mam, what have you got in mind?" Mollie asked, more than a little sorry that she wouldn't have the opportunity to watch her father go round and beat the living daylights out of the Head Nun.

"You'll find out soon enough, madam," her mother replied with a glance that included the other girls. "And by the way, just because I'm mad with Mother Benignus doesn't mean I'm not mad with you lot as well. So if you're thinking of mitching school again, don't! Because next time, it won't be Mother Benignus you have to worry about." She poked herself in the chest, fixed them with a gimlet glare. "It'll be me!"

"We won't, Mam. Promise!" Mollie, as usual the mouthpiece, answered both for herself and her sisters, but she'd crossed her fingers behind her back the way it wasn't really a lie.

In any case there was no time for further discussion, as moments later John-Joe arrived at the door with the news that Father Clarke's housekeeper had died.

"Heaven be good to her!" Upon hearing the news, Eileen blessed herself. "She was one in a million, poor Maisie!" Smiling in fond remembrance, her gaze encompassed all the occupants of the room. "Maisie was my godmother. Did I ever tell you that?

Mind you, it was never a role she took very seriously. She bought me knitting needles and a couple of balls of navy wool for a christening present. Can you credit that?" Eileen's face broke out into a broad grin. "What did she think I was going to do? Sit up in the cradle and knit a pair of socks? Heaven help her, the poor woman hadn't the sense she was born with. Still, that's one funeral we'll have to go to, right enough!"

Neither Mollie nor her sisters had ever seen a dead body before and if they'd gone purposely looking they couldn't have found an uglier cadaver than Maisie Barry's, or one more guaranteed to frighten the life out of them.

As it was, Eileen had thought long and hard before finally deciding to allow the children to attend the wake. Poor old Maisie had been good to them, God rest her soul, and many's the thruppenny bit she'd slipped them when Eileen's back was turned.

Paddy had agreed, though with reservations. "Aye, I suppose it'll do them no harm to pay their respects, though I hope they won't be frightened."

"Frightened? Why on earth should they be?" Eileen had demanded. "Sure poor ould Maisie never hurt a hair on their heads when she was alive and she's even less likely to now that the breath's left her body."

"Don't I know all that?" Paddy was scathing. "Still, kids are funny animals. You never know what's going on between their ears!"

Playfully Eileen clipped his own ear. "Not half as funny as you! Now will you hould yer whisht and come to bed."

Laughing, Paddy climbed between the much-mended sheets. "You're a wicked woman, Eileen McNab, so you are."

"So I am," Eileen had replied cheekily, then shrieked as Paddy's cold hand found its way onto her knee.

"Did I ever tell you I love you," Paddy murmured, burying his nose in her lavender-scented hair. He loved the way she loosened it at night, letting it ripple down over her shoulders and back, to her waist, in an undulating wave of gleaming red. Despite giving birth to four children, Eileen's figure had held up well, but now it was the figure of a woman as opposed to that of a girl, a little more full in the bosom, a little curvier round the hips. All to the good, as far as Paddy was concerned. The more there was of her, the more there was to love.

"Tell me again," she demanded, snuggling into him and smiling up at him from a face almost as young-looking and unlined as her own daughters'.

"I love you," he said obediently, dropping a kiss on her willing lips. "I love you more today than I did yesterday. And tomorrow, I'll love you more than today. And from now until eternity, I'll love you a little bit more every single day. How does that sound?"

Eileen's answer was to kiss him again.

The following day, the girls stood surveying the terrible vision which for some reason was laid out on the kitchen table.

"Why has she got pennies on her eyes?" Daisy asked in a sibilant whisper that caused some adults to frown, others to smile.

"Them's to hold her eyes down," Mollie answered knowledgeably.

"What?" Daisy was horrified. "In case they pop out, do you mean?"

"Like on springs?" Rose was scarcely able to tear her eyes away from the corpse with its waxy, marble face and clasped hands, through which somebody had woven a string of rosary beads.

Feeling infinitely superior, Mollie shook her head. "No, ye stupid eejits! They're to keep her eyelids closed the way she won't be looking at people."

"But she's dead, Mollie," Daisy pointed out with a logic that could not be faulted. "How could she be looking at anybody when she's dead?"

Unable to answer that one Mollie rapidly lost all

patience. "Ah, would *you* shut your gob, Daisy McNab, and don't be annoying me!"

"Shut your own gob," Daisy shot back, then was suddenly shocked into silence herself as a piercing shriek rent the air.

"Jaysus! Tis the banshee!" John Knowles, a sprightly septuagenarian, crossed himself then reached for the bottle of poteen some thoughtful person had laid at the corpse's feet to help her on her journey. "Maisie always said it followed her family. And didn't she meet it herself the night her father died and she out in the stable calving a cow? All dressed in white, she said it was, waving a comb in her face like it was a sword and roarin' like a mad thing."

"Banshee me arse! Would you go way outta that!" Paddy interjected scornfully, having imbibed, by this time what his wife termed a quare ould skinful. "Tis only Donal having a good keen for himself." No sooner had the words left his mouth than another almighty shriek assailed his ears and the ears of everybody in the room, except those of the one for whom it was intended.

"Ah, Maisie! Why did you die, Maisie?" Donal, Maisie Barry's nephew who had never had a good word to say about her when she was alive and who, in times of drink, had often been known to refer to her as 'that fat ould hoor' prostrated himself across her inert body. "Why did you, die, Maisie? Why did ye lave me? Why did you dieeeeeee?"

"Hey, Mister!" A little voice piped up as the last syllables faded away and before Donal had a chance to renew his interrogation of the corpse. "Sure she can't answer you. She's dead."

It was a long time before Rose McNab was to understand what she had said that was so funny that it had some of the more irreverent grown-ups snorting from behind their hands. Still she knew she must have done something right when somebody slipped a couple of bright, shiny coppers into her hand with the admonishment that she hide them quick before anyone caught on. Rose herself didn't catch on till she caught sight of Maisie Barry staring horribly at her from out of dead-fish, blue eyes from which someone had robbed the pennies – bright shiny pennies exactly like the ones clutched in her sweaty little hand. It was a vision Rose was to carry with her well into adulthood and the cause of many a broken night's sleep and countless rows between her parents, each of whom blamed the other for allowing her to attend the wake.

CHAPTER SEVEN

Paddy wasn't sure about Eileen's plan. Oh, it was clever, he'd give her that, but flying the Proddy colours? Now that rankled, as well it might to a Catholic born and bred.

"Tis just a temporary measure, you big gombeen!" Impatient, Eileen brushed away his reservations. "You just wait and see. They'll break their necks to get our girls back into St Joseph's. We'll have Mother Benignus beating a path to our door in an effort to get them back, so we will." She nodded in far-seeing satisfaction. "In fact, it wouldn't surprise me if the Bishop himself wasn't called in. Heads could roll over this, you know."

Paddy remained sceptical, but gave in to her as usual. "Aye, well maybe," is all he said.

And so it was that Eileen enrolled her daughters

at Cherry Bank Elementary, a school so desperate to justify its existence to the Board of Education, such was the scarcity of pupils, that it was only too happy to welcome the Catholic McNab children across what had been up till then solely Protestant portals.

Those portals never having encountered anybody so lively or so completely uninhibited, the girls proved to be a big hit at Cherry Bank. Even when Mollie loftily informed her classmates that they were all destined for hell seeing as how they dug with the wrong foot, nobody took offence. Instead, with her cloud of fiery hair and quicksilver, irreverent tongue, she was the focus of intense interest and the source of much competition between the boys who vied with each other in ever-increasing displays of stupidity for her attention. Sadly for them, Mollie and her sisters' stay at Cherry Bank was of fleeting duration as Eileen's prediction came true and a succession of outraged pious feet, starting with Father Clarke's, beat a path to her door.

"It won't do, Eileen." Taking a sip from the cup of tea Eileen had set before him, he shook his head emphatically. "You're endangering their immortal souls. And for what? To get one up on Mother Benignus. I thought better of you than that."

Cut to the quick, Eileen decided against offering him a fresh-baked scone, though she knew well the tongue was hanging out of his head at the lovely smell wafting on the air. "Well, do you know what, Father?" Deliberately, she busied herself lining the scones up one by one on the wire tray. "At the moment I'm more concerned about their mortal souls and the effect the treatment they've been having up at the convent is having on them, than anything else. As for the Protestants –" Determinedly she overrode Father Clarke as the word 'Protestant' almost sent him into an apoplexy that had him bobbing up and down in his chair, "my daughters have met with nothing but kindness up at Cherry Bank and that's a fact!" She nodded emphatically. "It strikes me that the whole kit and caboodle up at St Joseph's could do with taking a leaf out of the Cherry Bank book and that Mother Benignus should be the first one to take note."

Much to Father Clarke's surprise, because he had always found her very biddable, Eileen McNab on this particular issue was proving as immoveable as the Rock of Cashel and it was with a growing sense of panic that he realised that if he couldn't get her to see sense then, as true as eggs were eggs, he'd have the Bishop breathing down his neck. And Bishop Fahy, with his reputation as a Tartar, was not a man anyone wanted breathing down their neck. For two pins, it was said, he'd feck you off to some little hole-in-the-wall parish where you'd spend your life officiating at funerals and living hand-to-mouth in a mouldy run-down presbytery. The mere thought was enough to have him back-pedalling furiously. "Now, Eileen," he reached a placatory hand across the table. It was the sort of hand, Eileen couldn't help but notice, that had never done a day's hard work in its life. Fat and white and dimpled, with perfectly manicured nails, it was a far cry from Paddy's work-roughened and calloused hands. "I'm not saying that things up at St Joseph's couldn't have been handled differently. Sure isn't there room for improvement in all walks of life and maybe Mother Benignus got a bit carried away with the story?" He shrugged an appeal, tried his best to sound bluff. "And sure, God love her, isn't she a martyr to the migraine? And people suffering the torments aren't always best placed for making sound judgments. But doesn't that only go to show that she's human too and that there's none of us, not a one, neither you, me, nor the Pope himself, who can claim to be perfect. Let she who is without sin cast the first stone!"

"That sounds more like an excuse than an apology to me, Father." Turning away for a moment, Eileen checked on another batch of scones in the oven, decided they needed another five minutes browning and closed the door on an aromatic waft of steam. "And I'm not in the mood to listen to excuses. What I do want to hear is an apology and I want to hear it issue from Mother Benignus' own lips, for I've no intention of ever entrusting my daughters again to somebody who makes fish of the poor and flesh of those that have a few bob in their pockets."

Dismayed by her recalcitrance and clearly not relishing the thoughts of bearding Mother Benignus in her lair, Father Clarke sighed and rose from his chair. "Well, if that's your final word, I'll see what I can do. But you're not making this easy for me, Eileen. In fact, you're putting me in a terribly embarrassing situation. Diplomacy is what's called for here and I wouldn't like St Joseph's to think I'm interfering."

"Well, I'm sorry about that, Father." Coldly, Eileen led the way to the door, opening it wide to let him pass. "But sometimes people have to interfere. Look at the Good Samaritan – some people might have said he was interfering. And maybe he was, but it was all for the good, wasn't it?"

"Aye, I suppose so." The words were dragged out of the priest, who couldn't help but feel a bit put out that Eileen was encroaching on his own territory. Sermons were his department, not hers! Standing for a moment outside the cottage, he pulled his scarf up around his neck in an effort to ward off the biting, unseasonable wind that had characterised the day, and when he set off it was with head down, shoulders rounded and the demeanour of a man on his way to the firing squad.

And so it was that Eileen McNab's prediction
came to pass and the McNabs were honoured with a
visit from Mother Benignus. With a face that would
trip a tinker, she took the chair Eileen pulled out but
not before surreptitiously checking it with her
fingertip for dirt. The gesture was not lost upon
Eileen, who compressed her lips and decided against
offering the nun anything to eat or drink. "I'll come
straight to the point, Mrs McNab." Mother Benignus
managed to look down her long nose at Eileen which
was quite a feat considering she was sitting down
and Eileen was standing up. "This situation cannot
be allowed to continue."

Taking up a battle stance, Eileen folded her arms
across her chest. "Oh? And just what situation might
that be, Mother?"

Mother Benignus tutted. "Come now, Mrs McNab,
I'm a very busy woman, so let's not play games. I'm
sure we can get any – er – little misunderstandings
ironed out and things back to normal without further
ado."

Pulling out a chair, Eileen sat down opposite the
nun. She was rapidly beginning to lose the awe and
respect she had always accorded to members of the
religious. There was nothing like seeing your loved
ones hurt and humiliated for putting things in
perspective.

"Well now, Mother, I'm not all that sure that your

idea of normality and mine are the same thing at all."
She scraped her chair a little closer to the table,
setting Mother Benignus' teeth on edge. "You see, I
don't see that it's normal to humiliate a child and set
them up for ridicule in front of the other children in
the school. I don't call that normal at all." Warming
to her theme, Eileen found herself unstabling and
leading out a hobby-horse Paddy would have been
proud of. She wagged her finger across the table.
"Hitler did that, you know! He debased the Jews and
victimised them. He made a mock of them before
everyone else and encouraged everyone to bash hell
out of them. He set them up for ridicule, made them
wear yellow stars and tattooed numbers on their
arms, the way the local farmers here brand sheep
and cattle. That's right, branded them, like animals,
took away their humanity and heaped humiliation
after humiliation on their heads!" Mother Benignus
recoiled as Eileen's finger, whipping up and down
through the air, increased in its fury. "And we all saw
what that led to, didn't we? A whole nation practically
wiped out. Men, women and children! All because
some dirty little article didn't like the cut of their jib!"
Pausing for breath, she couldn't help but notice that
the nun was beginning to look visibly shell-shocked,
her normally high colour giving way to a kind of
sickly green pallor of the kind more often seen on the
faces of newly-drowned corpses. Nevertheless, Eileen

was on a roll and in the mood to stick the knife in, all the way up to the hilt. "And that's what you are, Mother, a Hitler! A dictator! A bully!"

Shocked to the core, Mother Benignus rose shakily to her feet, finding it necessary to cling onto the table edge for support. "I hardly think that's fair, Mrs McNab. More than that, I find it extremely insulting and a waste of both our valuable time." Extracting a large white handkerchief from her pocket, she blew volubly into it. "I came here today in the vain hope that, like civilised people, we might try and rationally discuss the little matter of your daughters' education. Effect, if you will, an *entente cordiale*. I see now I was wrong. Good day to you." Let the Bishop do his worst, she thought bitterly as, considerably less erect than when she'd first arrived, she headed for the door. Bishop, Cardinal or Pope, there was no way she was going to stay and trade insults with an ignoramus like Eileen McNab. Hitler indeed! The cheek!

"Oh, hold your horses!" Alarmed, Eileen backtracked a bit, trying to block the nun's exit. True, she'd meant to give the woman a good tongue-lashing, but she hadn't meant to alienate her so much that the girls were stuck in Cherry Bank forever. Nice and all as the Protestants had proved to be, the girls were still Catholics and as such needed to be educated in their own faith. And St Joseph's, Mother

Benignus notwithstanding, was a damn good school with a good reputation. "Look!" Placatingly, she reached out a hand, thought better of it and snatched it back again. "If I send the girls back to St. Joseph's, I'll expect them to be treated the same as everyone else – neither better nor worse, mind."

Sensing that the showdown with the bishop might not after all come to fruition, Mother Benignus turned hopefully on the no-man's-land of the doorstep, though she was careful to keep her face composed and her expression bland. "I think I can safely promise you, Mrs McNab, that your daughters will be treated fairly."

"All right!" Eileen hoisted the white flag. "They'll be back at school on Monday. By the way –" she called after the nun, anxious to cement newly re-established relations, "would you like to take a scone or two home for your tea?"

The white flag might have been raised, the peace treaty signed, but Mother Benignus didn't hesitate to fire the one remaining shot left in her blunderbuss. "I don't think so, Mrs McNab. I have a delicate stomach."

"Suit yourself!" Eileen muttered, closing the door with a bang. "Hitler!"

Paddy was suitably impressed by his wife's victory, the girls less so.

"Why do we have to go back to that dump?" Mollie asked heatedly. "I like Cherry Bank."

"So do I!" Daisy agreed but didn't add that principally she liked it because it was a mixed school and, even at the tender age of nine, Daisy was popular with the boys. She had already spotted someone else she intended to marry.

"Yeah, why do we have to go back to that dump?" Rose asked, a smaller echo of her elder sister.

"Because you just do, that's why," their mother told them aggravatingly.

"And what if Mother Benignus does the same thing to us all over again?" Anxiety wrote itself across Mollie's brow.

"She won't!" Paddy was quick to reassure the young girl. "Your mother gave her such a flea in her ear that it'll be a miracle if she's not down on her knees kissing the feet off you all on Monday morning."

"Did you, Mammy?" Daisy asked, while Rose merely looked puzzled at the logistics of such an operation.

Eileen adjusted her bosom proudly. "Well, I suppose I did give her something to think about."

Paddy laughed. "That's the understatement of the year. I only wish I'd been a fly on the wall."

In bed later that night, Daisy nudged Mollie awake. "Listen!" she commanded her sleepy sister.

"What?" Mollie asked crankily, and then giggled

as she too heard it. Out in the kitchen Mammy was singing, softly but recognisably none the less.

"*Hitler has only got one ball, Mother Benignus has no balls at all!*"

As it happened the girls had only to endure a few more weeks at St Joseph's before the school broke up for the long summer holidays.

"Yippee!" shouted Mollie erupting through the convent gates and breaking into an old rhyme she had cleverly reworked to suit her own circumstances.

> *No more Geography, no more French,*
> *No more sitting on a hard old bench!*
> *Kick up tables, kick up chairs,*
> *Kick Mother Big Knickers down the stairs!*"

Giggling, her sisters caught up with her, and arm in arm like the three musketeers they set off for the beach where a less mangy but still wall-eyed Larkin awaited them. Kicking off their shoes, they charged up the beach with the dog racing excitedly around them.

"Larkin's getting really fast now!" Daisy panted as eventually the three of them collapsed in a breathless heap onto the sand, while Larkin took himself off to bark futilely at the incoming tide, jumping back exaggeratedly whenever a ripple broke over his front paws.

"Yeah. Daddy said we can enter him in a race next week," Mollie said casually, her sparkling eyes betraying her excitement.

"What?" Daisy and Rose yelled in tandem. "Really, Mollie? You mean a proper race?"

Mollie nodded importantly. "Really and truly. We have to take him down to the dog-track on Saturday and enter him in –" her brow furrowed in concentration, "the Gold Challenger race."

"Janey!" Her sister's were suitably awed.

"What's the prize?" Daisy, who had a mercenary streak, demanded.

"Five pounds and a gold cup."

"Wow!" Wide-eyed, Daisy thought of all the things she could do with five pounds.

"But you have to give the gold cup back the next year if someone else wins the race," Mollie explained.

"What? That's stupid! What about the money?" Daisy asked. "Do you have to give that back too?"

Mollie shook her head. "No, you get to keep that."

"Well, that's all right then." Relieved, Daisy set about training Larkin with a vengeance till, worn out, the dog decided enough was enough and took himself home.

"You can't enter that thing!" The official down at the

dog-track was horrified at the sight of a wall-eyed Larkin and his determined, young owners. "Sure I'd be a laughing-stock if I allowed you to put him up for the race. I'd be laughed out of Galway, so I would. The only place that fella's fit for is the knacker's yard."

"We can *so* enter him!" Mollie stamped her foot. "He's a greyhound, isn't he?" Dubious, the man ran his eyes over Larkin's less than appealing frame. He might have started life as a greyhound, his look seemed to imply, but something terrible had happened somewhere along the way. "And this is a greyhounds' race," Mollie continued unabashed and happily completely unaware of the official's thoughts. "*And* here's the one shilling entry fee!"

In the face of such determination, the man knew when he was beaten. "All right so!" he said, backing down, and with a quick look around to make sure no one was witness to his shame. "But I must be stone mad. I must want me bleddy head examined!"

"C'mon, Larkin!" Victoriously Mollie led Larkin out to the track where with some difficulty she managed to manoeuvre him into one of the traps.

"Is he going to win, Mollie?" Rose asked, her face alight with excitement.

"Course he is!" Mollie said staunchly, then all three children held their breath as the traps were sprung and the hare came coursing up the field with only Larkin apparently showing any interest in catching him. The other contenders, it appeared, were far more interested in Larkin and the tasty coating of cod-liver oil Mollie had applied to his coat in an effort to make it shiny. Alarmed at all this attention Larkin took to his skinny heels and ran as he had never run before, passing out even the hare, such was his hurry.

Holy God! The greyhound track official couldn't believe his eyes. It won! The scurrilous cur actually won! Never in all his born days had he seen the likes. Were it not for the fact that the McNab girls were so young and so innocent-looking, he would undoubtedly think there were nefarious goings-on afoot! Still shaking his head in disbelief he went off to present the prizes. Unsurprisingly, perhaps, Mollie and her sisters were first in line.

"Thanks very much!" Daisy, shoving Mollie out of the way, quickly pocketed the fiver as Rose proudly raised the cup above her head.

"Yeah, thanks very much," Mollie said bending to pat Larkin, then extending her hand in what she hoped was a grown-up fashion.

Half-heartedly the steward shook it, still shaking his head at what appeared to be the eighth wonder of the world. "Well, I don't know how you did it at all, so I don't. No, damn me if I can figure it out." A moment later, when he released Mollie's hand and found his own covered in a slick of cod-liver oil, he was given the answer. "Jaysus!" Horrified, he made as if to grab the cup back out of Rose's hands but she held firm. "You cheating little buggers, ye! Give me back that cup! And the money, come on now!" In a panic he dived at Daisy, having as little chance did he but know it of relieving her of the fiver, as of beating the hare himself. Frantically he racked his brains for a solution. Maybe he should reconvene the race, this time without the skinny brute who was looking at him so accusingly and, how could he have missed it, reeking to the heavens of cod-liver oil. Maybe he could bluff it out. Say it was due to a technicality or something. He knew one thing though, and that was that there'd be hell to pay if this got out. He'd be run out of Ireland, so he would, unable to set foot on a dog-track for the rest of his natural, and all on account of three bleddy kids who had managed to pull the wool over his eyes. Red-faced, indignant but ultimately helpless he finally stalked off, deciding that the best thing was to keep his mouth well shut and pray that nobody ever found out.

"Stop laughing, Daddy!" Aggrieved, Rose glared at her father.

"I can't help meself." Guiltily, but with shoulders still heaving, Paddy looked at the three indignant faces of his daughters. "Cod-liver oil, eh? God, that's a good one, eh, Eileen?"

Eileen nodded happily, delighted with the five-pound note and having mentally already spent it over and over again.

"Larkin won fair and square, didn't you, boy?" Mollie patted the ungainly head from which a fishy aroma still wafted. "Still, I don't think we'll enter him for any more stupid ould races, not if they're going to try and cheat us out of the prizes!"

Making a huge effort to control his mirth in the face of their distress, Paddy agreed. "Aye, retire him while he's on top," he advised. "That way you can say no one ever beat him and he'll always be a champion."

Agreeing wholeheartedly with this suggestion, the girls bore the champion off for a run on the beach.

Later that evening, Paddy was amazed to receive a visit from Tom Bailey, a local farmer so mean that people said he'd bargain with you over the steam from his pee.

"What can I do for you, Mr Bailey?" Paddy asked, keeping him standing on the doorstep.

"Tis about the hound." Showing his impatient nature in the shuffling of his feet, the other man came straight to the point.

Paddy raised his eyebrows. "What hound?" Then, as light dawned. "Oh, Larkin you mean."

"Aye, if that's what you're after calling him."

Paddy nodded. "After James Larkin, the great Trade Unionist, you know."

The farmer shuffled some more. "With all due respect, McNab, if it was a history lesson I wanted, I'd go to the library."

Paddy frowned at his visitor's rudeness. "And with all due respect to you, Mr Bailey, what exactly is it you want?" A worried frown gathered between his eyes. "He hasn't been worrying your sheep, has he?" It seemed unlikely. Larkin was frightened of his own shadow, but it wouldn't be the first time a seemingly meek and mild dog had turned vicious predator when confronted by a field of sheep.

Bailey shook his head and Paddy found himself releasing the breath he wasn't aware he had been holding.

"I'll give you five guineas for him, and no arguments!" Rummaging in his breast pocket, the farmer produced a wad of grubby notes, which he proceeded to thumb through as though the bargain had already been struck.

Whatever he'd been expecting, Paddy hadn't been expecting that and his eyebrows climbed so high they almost disappeared beneath his hairline.

Mistaking the other man's surprise for reluctance, Bailey, with a jerky movement, as though it hurt him to make it, thrust the notes beneath Paddy's nose. "Go on, take it! Before I change me mind."

Stepping back a pace, Paddy shook his head. "I can't, Mr Bailey." His voice was rueful. There were a lot of things he and Eileen could do with five guineas, but it would break the girls' hearts to part with the dog and no amount of money could compensate for a child's broken heart.

Knowing nothing of his thoughts, the farmer glared and, not for the first time, Paddy noticed his eyes were the pink you'd find on a pig. "'Tis a fair offer, McNab! Take it or leave it!"

"I'll leave it so and bid you goodnight." Making to close the door, Paddy was prevented from doing so by the other man thrusting his foot through the aperture.

"Ten bob more and we'll spit on it!" Nonplussed, Bailey peeled another note off the roll. He'd thought McNab would have jumped at the offer, seeing as how he hadn't tuppence to bless himself with. Sure, hadn't he, himself, run him off his property not so long ago, when he'd come to the farm looking for work.

"The dog's not for sale!" Paddy made his voice firm, though it near choked him to turn down such an offer. Wasn't that typical all the same? This morning they hadn't the price of a pound of rashers but now, thanks to Larkin and the girls' ingenuity, they already had one fiver and here he was turning down even more.

Bailey's pink-rimmed eyes shot fire. "Is that your final word?"

Paddy nodded. "It is, Mr Bailey, but with the kind of money you're offering, couldn't you buy yourself a litter of greyhounds?"

Angrily, the farmer scuffled on the doorstep. "Aye, I dare say I could, McNab, but not one with the makings of a Master McGrath."

This time Paddy's eyebrows did disappear beneath his hairline and his voice rose incredulously. "The makings of a Master McGrath?"

The other man narrowed his piggy eyes. "Aye, after today's performance down at the track, I reckon with the right training – and that takes both money and experience - that hound could be a champion to outrank all champions."

"Is that a fact?" Paddy, for whom the penny had only just dropped, found it hard to restrain the hilarity he could feel building in his chest. "A champion to outrank all champions, you say?"

"I do!"

Paddy gave a low whistle of amazement. "Fancy that! And there was I thinking it was all down to the cod-liver oil the kids slapped on him to make his coat shiny."

Paddy wasn't to be the only one for whom a penny dropped that night. "Cod-liver oil?" Bailey's pink eyes took on the red glow of madness. "Cod-liver oil?"

Paddy grinned. "Aye, that's the boyo! Cod-liver

oil. Sure wouldn't you run like the bejaysus too if you thought half a dozen hungry hounds were after your hide?"

"Oh feck!" Incredulous, the farmer backed off away from the door as if he'd suddenly discovered the inhabitants to be possessed of the black plague. "A pig in a poke!" Disbelieving, he shook his head. "Imagine it! Me, Tom Bailey, of all people, nearly bought a pig in an poke. Just wait until I get me hands on that bastard steward. He'll never work again! So help me, God. I'll kneecap the fecker, so I will. I'll string him up in Friar's Copse and let the crows pluck out his eyeballs!"

An imp of mischief taking hold of him, Paddy spat on his palm in the time-honoured fashion of countrymen sealing a bargain. "Ah, go on then, Mr Bailey, you've twisted me arm. Ten bob more and the hound's yours! You've got yourself a deal."

"Deal? Deal!" Bailey swore, turning a face grotesque in its disbelief towards the other man. "Go eff yourself, McNab, and your mangy cur while you're at it!" Shaking his fist at Paddy, he retreated back the way he'd come, only twice as quickly. "And mind, if ever I find the bugger within a mile of me farm, I'll fill him that full of shot he'll come home as a watering-can!"

"Did ye ever in all your life hear the likes of that?" Paddy chuckled as he went back into the cottage.

"Did you see the look on his face when I told him about the cod-liver oil? I thought he'd have a heart attack."

"Oh he got his comeuppance tonight, all right." Eileen agreed with satisfaction. "Still I wouldn't like to be that poor man down at the dog-track when Bailey gets hold of him."

Paddy sniffed. "Ah, that fella's all mouth and trousers! There's no way he's going to let on to anybody what happened here tonight. Wouldn't he be a right laughing-stock? And there's plenty around here would take pleasure rubbing salt into his wounds."

"Well, nobody likes a bad egg." Eileen rose from where she'd been darning socks by the fire, stretching her hands high above her head to relieve the stiffness that had set in around her shoulders. "And Bailey is bad through and through. And I'll tell you something else," she turned down the oil-lamp, immediately plunging the room into deep shadow, "if he'd offered us a hundred pounds I still wouldn't have parted with Larkin."

Over by the fire, stretched out to his full length and still reeking like the inside of a fishing trawler, the subject of their discourse turned over, farted, opened a surprised eye and went promptly back to sleep.

"On second thoughts –" Eileen began.

CHAPTER EIGHT

As the roof went up on Devlin's house, Paddy took to walking again, all hours of the day and night. Eileen worried but said nothing. There was nothing she *could* say, no magic pill or potion she could give him to ease his suffering. All she could do was be there when he wanted her, listen if he wanted to talk and hold him when he wanted to be held. Too busy fighting her own demons, she could not fight his. Sometimes, though, when she woke to find only space where Paddy should have been, she would rise and go to the window, willing her eyes to penetrate the thick curtain of night beyond, endeavouring in vain to pinpoint her husband and accompany him, if only in spirit, on his lonely walks. At other times, she would simply lie restlessly awake, waiting for dawn to paint her ceiling with the beginnings of yet another day, so she too could find a way of submerging her sorrow beneath the unrelenting demands of her growing young family.

And lately, she'd been plagued by one of those awful feelings of premonition that seemed to crop up at key moments in her life. A nebulous kind of uneasiness, unseen and untouchable, it hovered like an evil spirit on the periphery of her consciousness, leaving her in no doubt that something awful, something inevitable was going to happen, and happen soon. Rising from the bed, after yet another night spent tossing and turning and praying for Paddy, Eileen wandered stiffly over to the window, wiping the condensation from the glass with her hand. The last time the feeling had been this strong, it had presaged the death of little Liam. On another occasion, it has been that of her mother. What now, she wondered peering out into the early morning gloom, and finding herself startled by the unexpected sight of a lorry slowly making its way up along the promontory, its headlights slicing through the early morning mist like eyes that could see right through into her soul. What now?

With a mounting sense of doom and kind of terrible hypnotic fascination she watched the truck draw nearer, rumbling inevitably onward till, finally, it rolled to a clattering halt outside Devlin's brand new house.

"*Ryan's Removals,*" Eileen read on the side of the van. "*We really know how to move you!*" Suddenly she felt sick. Feverish. They really knew how to move her all right. Enraged, she watched as a moment later a car pulled in behind the van and Devlin and his clearly pregnant wife got out. Pregnant! Eileen wanted to scream at the injustice of it all. Devlin's wife, pregnant! And it would be a boy! She just knew it, could feel it in her water! Warm hay and dandelions! Little boy smells, and achingly mischievous laughter. 'What's heaven like, Mammy?'

"No!" Eileen whimpered, watching as Devlin swept his bride up into his arms and made to carry her over the threshold. "No!" Eileen's voice, the dying protest of a wounded animal, rose in a shriek that brought her daughters panicking bolt upright from their dreams.

Back from his wanderings, Paddy was just in time to catch her as she hurtled out the door, a carving knife she had grabbed from the drawer caught in her hand.

"No, Eily!" With difficulty he wrested the knife from her, struggled to restrain her. "That's not the way!"

But, like a lion defending her cubs, Eileen fought him vigorously, teeth bared. "Let me go, Paddy! For the love of God, let me go! He killed my child! He killed Liam!"

"I know, love. I know!" Wrapping his arms around her so that her arms were pinioned to her sides, he held her gently but firmly till all the fight went out of her and she leaned limply, weeping against his chest. Above her head his eyes sought those of Devlin and his plainly bewildered and frightened wife, set once more upon her feet, her hand protectively cupping the bulge beneath her dress. There was hate in one man's eyes. Something unreadable in the other's. For a moment, as Devlin stared him out, Paddy thought it looked like guilt or even shame, but masked by the blackness of hell, it was difficult to be sure. Then, dropping his eyes, Devlin ushered the young woman into her new home before firmly closing the door against Eileen's sobs.

"I thought I'd be all right, Paddy. Really I did." Eileen, her face swollen and suffused with misery, pushed away the hot cup of sweet tea Mollie had placed before her, before going to join her sisters who were cuddled up to each other, grave eyes fixed anxiously on their mother. "I thought I could cope. I mean I've been building up to it for a long time and I thought I could handle it." Impatiently, she swiped away a tear. "But when I saw *her*, it was like – it was like something just went bang in my head. I just couldn't stop myself. I'm telling you, Paddy. I wanted to kill him. And I wanted to kill her too, although I've never clapped eyes on the girl before in my life."

Paddy nodded grimly. "'Twas a shock all right!" Strangely enough, he had never thought further than how he'd feel about having Devlin living opposite him. It had never occurred to him that one day Devlin's own son might be running around the same meadows, climbing on the same trees and fishing in the same ponds as their Liam had done, catching butterflies and grasshoppers in a net and proudly bringing them home for his parents' inspection. And Devlin's heir was already baking!

"It's a strange thing, but I'd have thought it would be me restraining you instead of the other way around." Eileen stared at her fingers, interlaced so tightly the knuckles were white.

"And it could well have been, if it wasn't for something that happened last night."

Detecting a peculiar note in his voice, Eileen looked up. The cold claw of fear was back all of a sudden. That nameless bird of prey, hovering around her head in ever-diminishing circles, making it difficult for her to catch a breath. "Last night?" The words were barely above a whisper. "Why? What happened?"

Clearing his throat Paddy glanced meaningfully over at the girls. What he had to say was plainly not for their ears. Interpreting the look, Eileen immediately dispatched them outside, despite a trio of mutinous faces.

When the door had closed behind them, Paddy seated himself at the table, leaned forward, gently unlocked his wife's fingers and cradled them between his own. "There's no easy way to say this, Eileen. I only wish there was." He dipped his head and when he spoke again, there was a broken quality to his voice. "It's young Cathal Power. I found him in Friar's Copse, last night. He'd only gone and hung himself, poor lad."

The bird of prey beat at her with his wings, covered her with a great dark suffocating shadow and for the second time in only a short period, Eileen's voice rose in a shriek of pain. "Oh, no! Not Cathal! Oh, Sacred Heart, no!" Pulling her hands free, they flew to her heart, which had started pounding so hard it felt like it was struggling to burst through her chest. "Oh, don't tell me he's dead, Paddy! Please don't tell me he's dead! Oh, he can't be dead! He can't be!" Frantically, she searched around for anything, anything at all that might prove Paddy wrong, show him he had made a terrible mistake. It wasn't Cathal. It was some other poor boy. "He was here just the other night. Remember? Wednesday night, it was. He was here and I had to tell Daisy off for teasing him. She never knows when to stop, that child. The smallest bit of encouragement and the reins are off." She was gabbling and they both knew it, but somehow she felt as long as she didn't hear him actually say the words, everything would somehow be all right. It would all be a mistake. Just a mistake.

"His body was still warm when I cut him down." Elbows on the table, Paddy cradled his head between his palms. "I couldn't help thinking that if I'd happened along a moment or two before –" He broke off, as the latch lifted and John-Joe, his face bleached to an unearthly pallor, stumbled in.

"That's foolish thinking, Uncle Paddy!" Catching the tail-end of the conversation, John-Joe deliberately made his voice harsh. Even so, it was obvious that his own tears were not too far away. "Even if you had managed to save him, there would have been another time. Poor Cathal – it was on the cards for ages. If it's anyone's fault it's mine. I should have known. I should have read the signs. I should have been there for him."

Paddy was bitter. "No, lad, you've nothing to blame yourself for. If you want to lay the blame with anyone, lay it at the right door. It's that ould bitch of a mother of his that drove him to it. Her and her hoity-toity notions, wanting him to be a barrister. A barrister, if you don't mind!"

"She didn't know how good she'd got it with those lads of hers," Eileen bit hard upon her lip. "But then some people are never satisfied. Why couldn't she leave the child alone? Sure all most of us want is for our children to be healthy and happy. When Judgment Day comes, does it matter if they've letters after their names or not? Does it matter if people tip the cap and kow-tow to them. Surely to God, isn't the most important thing that they turn out to be normal decent human beings?" Her voice caught. "Do you recall that day you went round to her, Paddy?"

Paddy nodded, remembering well how egged on by both Eileen and John-Joe, who were becoming increasingly worried about Cathal, he had made it his business to try and talk some sense into the woman, though, as a rule, he was not one to interfere in other people's affairs. "Water will always find its own level, Mrs Power," he'd told her. "Give the lad a chance, and he might surprise you one day!" He'd tried placating her too. "Sure isn't it the lucky woman you are to have a doctor and a priest in the family. Isn't that enough for you? And barristers are nothing but crooks in fancy wigs, anyway. Everyone knows that. And, at least farming is an honest occupation."

Shaking back the head of black hair that hadn't got a grey strand in it, although she was well into her forties – the way a mare would toss its mane, proud like, as Paddy was to relate to his wife later – Miriam had bent the look of Lucifer upon him.

"Be about your business, Mr McNab," she'd told him, never one to mince her words. "What I do with my family is my affair. And as for your saying about water – let me tell you another one." Again she had tossed the glossy mane. "Lie down with dogs and you get up with fleas. Good day to you!" And she had stormed back into her big house without a backward glance, closing her big door against him, proud as a queen before a fall.

"Some people don't deserve to have children," Eileen mused tearfully, thinking of the gentle Cathal and how they would all miss his welcome visits and the way he would always put his head round the back door and sniff the air appreciatively.

"Ma's on the warpath again!" he'd say. Then, with a wink, "Is that scones I'm smelling or is it just wishful thinking?"

And Eileen would laugh and never begrudge him the bit of food she could spare, because despite all the Powers' money, their son, beneath his large adolescent frame, was nothing but skin and bone. "Go on then, you big lug, sit yourself down."

"I suppose it was the Leaving Cert that did for him," Paddy reflected thoughtfully, as John-Joe nodded. "The results are due out any day now, aren't they?"

"And, no doubt, poor Cathal was terrified he'd failed and couldn't face the music." It was a mystery to Eileen how parents could put pressure on their children like that. Oh, education was important, a passport to the world as it were, but at the end of the day you could only do your best, and no examination was worth killing yourself over. "Who broke the news?" she asked.

"Sergeant O'Shea. I couldn't have trusted meself to go with him. God knows what I might have said to the woman. I don't mind telling you I'd have found it hard to keep me hands from her throat."

Eileen could well understand that. Sure, how could a man who had lost his son in such tragic circumstances condole with a woman who had driven hers to his death?

"Do you know something, Paddy?" she said, tears standing like diamonds on her cheeks. "I think Father Clarke might well be right. Look what Miriam Power sent out on the tide all these years. And just look what it brought back. Maybe I'll leave Devlin to the tide after all."

Outside the shouts of the three young children playing tig reminded them that life, with all its vagaries, could at times also be warm and joyful. But, right now, sorrow had the upper hand.

A few short miles away, high above the Regional Hospital in Galway, seagulls wheeled and shrieked, their raucous cries masking the heartbroken wails of a mother below. And as the tears of guilt and sorrow slipped down her face, sanity too slipped quietly away. Before the earth was flat on Cathal's grave, Miriam Power had gone to join him.

"Love," Father Clarke said, officiating at the funeral, "comes in many guises. It's not necessarily hearts and flowers and wearing it all on your sleeve. Love," he said, as the first spadeful of dirt rattled on the wooden lid of the coffin and echoed dully, "is a funny thing. Sometimes, there's no accounting for it at all."

CHAPTER NINE

As the summer wore on, an uneasy truce sprang up between the McNabs and their new neighbours, achieved principally by dint of studiously ignoring each other's existence. The girls, naturally enough, were eaten up with curiosity about Devlin's wife, who was not only much younger than her husband but beautiful as well, with a cloud of soft blonde hair that reminded the girls of the lovely big Crolly dolls on sale in the big stores in Galway. Added to that she was English! *"English!"* the girls told each other in hushed awestruck whispers, unsure whether this was something to be lauded or deplored, but delighted by the novelty either way.

Eileen wasn't the least bit curious and if she appeared to be glancing out the window more often than usual, it was merely because she thought it might rain and she needed to bring the washing in, or she was looking out for the postman, or to see was that Paddy or the girls coming up the boreen. The fact that she always knew when Mrs Devlin was coming or going, or emerging to plant flowers outside her front door was also down to coincidence, pure and simple, and God help anyone who had the temerity to suggest anything else.

The planting flowers bit made Paddy laugh his head off. "I wish her joy," he'd said, wishing her anything but. "If she can coax so much as a leaf to grow up here with the wind and the salt blowing in from the sea, she's a better man than I am!"

Eileen had laughed too, but in truth her green fingers itched in sympathy. As a new bride, she too had had a go at planting flowers, but apart from a woody-looking fuchsia bush, which produced an occasional sad and short-lived display of blossoms, her efforts had all come to zero.

Watching Mrs Devlin down on her knees one day, with a small trug of colourful plants beside her, Eileen couldn't help musing that for someone who was married to a murderer, she looked incredibly happy. Would it all change, she wondered after the baby was born? There was nothing like having a child of your own to put things into perspective, and judging from the size of the young woman's bump, that time was not too far off. It was strange to think that under other circumstances they might even have been friends. As if something of Eileen's thought's had transmitted themselves to the other woman, she glanced up suddenly, causing Eileen to jump guiltily back from the window. Ridiculous! As if she'd been caught doing something that she shouldn't. Eileen cooled her suddenly hot cheeks between the palms of her hands. Where was the law that said she couldn't look out her own window? Still, she felt uncomfortable, tainted almost, as if she had intruded upon something private. Placing a calming hand over her heart which, unaccountably, had started pounding, she moved away to put the kettle on, only to be startled a moment later by a soft tap on the door.

"Now who the devil could that be?" she muttered to Larkin, who left off chewing one of Daisy's balls and gazed adoringly up at her. "Just a moment," she called, giving her clothes a hurried smooth down, before opening the door. "Oh," she said a moment later, taking an involuntary step backwards and feeling her face stiffen into a kind of rigor mortis. "It's – it's you."

"Yes, I'm sorry to disturb you, Mrs McNab. I'm Coral Devlin." Up close, Mrs Devlin proved to be even prettier, with lightly tanned skin, dark soulful eyes and a soft, almost childish mouth that seemed to tremble either on the verge of laughter or tears. By contrast, Eileen suddenly felt old and tired, though in truth there probably wasn't more than ten years between them, and her own, normally generous, mouth drew itself into a tight narrow line.

"I know fine well who you are, Mrs Devlin." The words came out almost on a gasp. "What I don't know is how you've got the brass nerve to go landing yourself up on my doorstep."

"I – I'm sorry." Timidly, the young woman attempted a smile. "It's just that what with us being neighbours and –" breaking off, she held out a terracotta pot in which a bright red geranium nestled, eagerly, almost like a child. "Look, I-I brought you this. I thought it might look nice outside your door. It's such a lovely shade, don't you think?"

Scathing, Eileen ignored it. It would take a damn sight more than a flower in a pot to assuage the bad blood running like the Red Sea between the two households. Deliberately, she made her voice sharp. "Us being neighbours is not of my choosing, Mrs Devlin."

"Coral . . . please," the young woman interjected.

"Mrs Devlin," Eileen held firm, "'twas your murdering husband that chose to build his house next to us, the way we could be reminded of our grief every time we looked out the window or stepped outside our own front door." Almost absent-mindedly she noticed the other's arms, still clutching the flowerpot, move slowly down till they appeared to be cradling the unborn child beneath her dress.

"No – no, it wasn't like that – it wasn't like that at all," the girl started to protest. "None of that was down to Mick, honestly it wasn't. I saw your house from a boat one day and it – it looked so pretty, like something out of a picture book and I insisted – and I didn't know – oh, look, I'm sorry." Breaking off as she saw the patent disbelief on her neighbour's face, she dipped her head. "I shouldn't have come here. It was stupid of me. Of course, I heard about the accident and I really sympathise over the loss of your little boy." For a moment her bottom lip wobbled and she looked as though she were about to cry. "B-but there's nobody else around for miles and I did so hope we might be friends."

Like a shot, Eileen understood. The girl was lonely! And miles away from her own kith and kin that wasn't so surprising. It couldn't be easy being a stranger in another land, especially a land that didn't have much time for the English. Still, she hardened her heart till it felt like stone in her breast. For Coral Devlin the loneliness would be appeased at the end of the day when her husband came back from his work and when her child was born. For Eileen McNab, the loneliness would fester forever more, for little Liam was never coming home.

The pain of the thought knifed at her heart and

made her cruel. "We can never be friends, Mrs Devlin," she said baldly. "Sure how in the name of God could you expect me to be friends with the wife of the man who killed my son? What would we find to talk about? Eh? Tell me that. Not your husband, that's for sure! Not your child, when it's born. Are you callous enough to think I could stand round cooing over the cradle, watching you and that murderer you married cuddle, kiss it and make plans for its future, knowing all the while that my own son lies cold and silent in the grave, because your damn husband sent him there?" She stepped forward as the other woman took an involuntary step back. "Has it ever crossed your mind to think of how it feels to me, knowing I'll never hear him call my name again, or feel the soft caress of his warm breath as he drifts off to sleep in my arms sucking his thumb? How do you think it feels to know the hopes and dreams you cherished are lying six feet under the earth in a wooden box? To know the plans *we* made for his future will never now be realised." Her voice stumbled. "And at night, sometimes, when there's a storm say, when the rain is coming down in torrents, the lightning is ripping the sky apart and the wind is screaming either in rage or agony, how do you think it feels to know that your child is out there on his own in the dark, that he might be frightened and lonely and calling for you?" The tears started up in her eyes. Angrily she dashed them away. "Oh, I know there's no logic in it. I know Liam is dead. I know he can't feel or hear or see anything. But my heart doesn't know that!" Impassioned, she banged against her chest with a clenched fist. "My heart doesn't know that, Mrs Devlin, because that's the mother in me. And soon, Mrs Devlin, when your own baby is born you'll know what that feeling is like and maybe you'll come to understand better the way I am today and why it is I can't extend the *céad míle fáilte* to you."

"I'm sorry." Shakily and with tears glittering on her lashes, Mrs Devlin half-turned away. "It was stupid of me to come here," she said again. "Stupid and insensitive. I don't know what I could have been thinking."

Eileen's eyes gave off angry sparks. "Aye, it was that! And just so you know, Mrs Devlin, not everybody's so sure Liam's death *was* an accident!"

"You were right to run her, Eily!" Paddy nodded reassuringly as, over dinner, his wife recounted the events of earlier.

"Then why do I feel so bad about it?" Eileen's brow folded itself into deep creases. "Why do I feel ashamed?"

"Because you're soft-hearted, that's why!" Spearing

a potato, Paddy peeled back the skin to reveal the lush white floury flesh inside. "Just remember you don't owe that one anything. Who the hell is she anyway, only a bleddy Brit Devlin had to go abroad to find, since no decent, respectable Irish girl would have him!" He pointed his knife at her. "So don't you go worrying your head, d'ye hear me? She's probably over there laughing up her sleeve at us right now."

Eileen shook her head. "No, I don't think so, Paddy. She seemed genuine enough to me. She's no more than a child herself, really. Rising twenty, if that, I'd say." Automatically she brought a forkful of food up to her own lips, put it down without tasting it. "And do you know what, she said something about it all being her idea to build here. Do you think that's true?"

"No! I don't believe a word of it." Unmoved, Paddy helped himself to the salt, sprinkled it lavishly between first finger and thumb over his food. "That's all rubbish. Misguided loyalty, and I suppose you can't blame the girl for trying to put the best slant on things. Still she made her own bed. So she'd better get used to lying on it!"

Echoes of Eileen's father came back to her. *"When you make your bed, you'd better learn to settle on it, lumps, bumps, fleas and all."*

"Well, I think you were dead mean, Mammy,"

Daisy interrupted, having pondered over the story with furrowed brow. "It's not Mrs Devlin's fault if her husband killed our Liam."

Surprisingly both Mollie and Rose backed her up. "Yeah, I think Mrs Devlin is nice!" Mollie added. "She always smiles at us whenever we see her, so she does."

"And I think she looks like a fairy princess," Rose, said, still at an age to believe passionately in fairytales.

"Now listen to me, you lot." Paddy bent his gaze so that it encompassed all three of his daughters. His voice was low, serious, the kind he used when he meant business. "You better stay well away from that woman, do you hear me? If I so much as see one of you even breathing in her direction, I'll take me belt to you. Is that clear?" Receiving no response, he repeated himself, spacing out the words so there could be no doubt of their meaning. "I said, is that clear?"

"Yes, Daddy!" Mollie replied, whilst her sisters nodded, the mere threat of the broad leather belt enough to bring them to heel.

"Good!" Satisfied, he pushed his plate away, rose and unhooked his jacket from the back of the door. "I'm off down to O'Dwyer's. I won't be late." Pocketing Dicken's *Great Expectations*, which he was reading for the regulars down at the pub, he dropped a quick kiss on Eileen's lips and, with a wink for his daughters, disappeared out the door. A moment later, following an almighty clatter, he was back, a smashed terracotta flower-pot in his hands. "Who the hell left this on the doorstep? I could have broken my bleddy neck."

To give Mollie her due she hadn't meant to fraternise with the enemy but when she caught sight of Mrs Devlin frantically beckoning her round the side of her house one day, she didn't know what else to do. Her parents had, after all, instilled in her a healthy respect for adults, and whatever else Mrs Devlin was, she was certainly that.

"Quick!" Mrs Devlin hissed as Mollie, with a frantic glance round about, made her decision and ran like the wind till she was safely out of view if Mammy should happen to look out the window. Close to, Mrs Devlin with her gilded blonde hair and velvet-brown eyes really was like a princess. Mollie could scarcely take her eyes off her.

"Look, I have something for you, Mollie." Taken aback at this use of her name, Mollie started and looked wary. "Oh, I heard your sisters calling you," Coral Devlin explained dismissively. "I know their names too. Daisy and Rose, isn't it?" Mollie nodded. "I watch you playing all the time." The young woman smiled. "And that great hound of yours."

"That's Larkin!" Mollie volunteered shyly. "He's a big softy really. Da says it's just as well we've nothing worth robbing because Larkin would take the thieves by the hand and show them where the loot was hidden."

Mrs Devlin looked doubtful. "Hmm, I'll take your word for it. Now look at this."

"What is it?" Mollie asked, as, like a magician pulling a rabbit out of a hat, Mrs Devlin produced a big oval box from behind her back. Covered in a kind of red, flock paper, the likes of which Mollie had never seen before, it was wrapped around with the widest of gold ribbons and finished off in a big bow.

"Why, it's a box of chocolates, of course," the woman explained, as Mollie's eyes opened to the extent where they were in danger of falling out of her head.

"Really?" Mollie had seen boxes of chocolates before in some of the shops in Galway, but never anything like this work of art.

"Really, and it's for you!" Coral offered, holding it out.

"I can't, Mrs Devlin!" Jumping back as if she was scalded, Mollie folded her arms protectively across her chest. Lord knows, she would have loved the chocolates, could almost feel them melting on her tongue, but Daddy would kill her if he got wind of it.

Bewildered, because this wasn't at all the reaction she'd expected, the woman smiled a little uncertainly.

"Of course, you can. And call me Coral, will you? Mrs Devlin makes me sound so old and, really, I'm not all that much older than you, you know."

"I can't! Honest!" Deeply rueful, Mollie shook her head. "Daddy would have my guts for garters, so he would."

"Does he have to know?" Mrs Devlin placed a lightly tanned hand upon Mollie's shoulder. "Listen, Mollie, if you and your sisters don't eat these chocolates they'll be going in the rubbish. They will!" she stressed, as Mollie looked dubious. "You see, I can't really eat them since I got – well . . ." She patted her expanding tummy. "They just make me feel sick. As for Mr Devlin, *he* never eats sweets, though he keeps buying them for me no matter how often I tell him I don't want them."

At this revelation, Mollie's eyes widened still further. How could anybody possibly not want sweets, especially chocolates like the ones Mrs Devlin was going to throw in the rubbish? "Are you sure they're going in the rubbish?" she asked, wavering a little but wanting matters clear in her own mind.

"Definite! And if I were to throw them out that would be a terrible sin, wouldn't it?" Although not in Ireland all that long, Coral Devlin had already learned a little of what made the Catholic Irish tick. "And you could save me, Mollie McNab, from committing that terrible sin, couldn't you?"

"I could!" Mollie was sure about that and magnanimous in her relief at having her dilemma not only solved, but in such a way that made it not only right, but imperative to take the chocolates, if poor Mrs Devlin wasn't to spend eternity roasting in the fires of hell alongside of her husband. Because he was going to hell, that was definite. There was no way he was going to be allowed into heaven with Liam.

Trying hard not to smile, Coral watched, as, conscience salved, Mollie's hands eagerly reached out for the box, her fingers stroking the ornate covering as though it were live and about to purr. "Now, you'll be sure to share them with your sisters, Mollie, won't you?" she cautioned.

"Yes, of course, Mrs Dev – I mean, Coral." Mollie nodded earnestly. It was a lie she would live to regret, as racked by tummy-ache later that night, she vomited up a mush of what, if her mother had been more worldly-wise, she would have recognised as strawberry creams, lime barrels and hazelnut whirls all over the bedroom floor. Instead, long after her daughter lay sleeping, Eileen lay awake vowing to haul her off to Dr McBride the following morning, although where the money for that was going to come from, God alone knew.

Beside her, shifting uneasily in his sleep, Paddy, coughed softly, immediately setting her off on another tangent of worry. Although a blacksmith by trade, Paddy only ever seemed to get odd jobs these days, usually labouring jobs, hard graft that didn't do his chest any good. Though wrong about most things where Paddy was concerned, her father had been right about one thing, anyway. There was precious little work around for blacksmiths these days which was a real shame, not only because it was what Paddy was trained for, but also because it had given him the chance to exercise his more creative side and sometimes, after the run-of-the-mill jobs were finished, he used to play about designing things: ornate plant holders and door-knockers, fire irons and ornaments like the little figurine of the donkey and cart that stood on their own mantelpiece. Eileen sighed as she remembered how he had also designed and made the simple iron cross that guarded Liam's grave, honing and re-honing, polishing and re-polishing, working himself to the point of exhaustion till the dull base metal took on the gleam of gold and flashed like a halo in the sun.

Not that Paddy was the sort to complain. Many's the day found him rising before dawn, tramping ten miles or more, all on the promise of a couple of days' work. And whatever he earned he brought straight home, unlike a lot of the men hereabouts who, with never a thought for their wives and children, went straight down to O'Dwyer's and pissed it all up against the wall. Never mind that their children's bellies were tripping them up with the hunger! Oh, her Paddy was a good one right enough, and well respected. His formal education might have come to an early conclusion, but his thirst for knowledge and the sharing of that knowledge knew no bounds. On fine summer evenings he was often to be found sitting on the low stone wall outside the cottage reading the paper aloud to a group of men who would come from miles around, just to listen to the latest news or to hang on his every word as he recounted the story of *America's Most Wanted Man*, that was being re-serialised in the *Independent*.

"Yerrah, he'd never have gotten away with that carry-on over here!" she'd overheard one member of his audience comment once, scornfully dismissive of the exploits of the infamous John Dillinger. "Sure, Sergeant O'Shea would have had him by the short and curlies before ever he'd a chance to pull the trigger." Others had remained unconvinced. He sounded like a right bucko to them. One even had it on good authority that Dillinger wasn't killed at all but was alive and kicking and living just over the border in County Clare.

Which remark hugely incensed the first speaker, who, himself, had had his collar felt by the guard on one account or another more times that he cared to recall. "Ah, not at all. That's ould codology. Sure he'd have had no chance with Sergeant O'Shea."

At this juncture, someone else, much less in awe of the good sergeant's capabilities felt it incumbent upon himself to shove his oar in. "Sergeant O'Shea, me arse! Would you go way with yourself! That fella couldn't find his flies in the dark, much less John Dillinger!"

Every Saturday night in winter, when the rains lashed and the winds battered, they would congregate down at O'Dwyer's, some bearing letters they could not read from relatives long since gone abroad to London, America or even Australia, but eager to keep faith with their roots.

One by one, Paddy would work his way through them. "It's from Mary in New York. She's just had another baby. A boy, this time. Six pounds, three ounces. She's called him Seamus, after your father, and she says he's the spit of you, Benjy, right down to the big nose." Holding out his hand for the next envelope, he'd quickly scan the postmark. "From Australia! D'ye see the stamp? From your Uncle John. He says, don't bother coming over. The place is full of bloody criminals. Criminals and sheep and feck all else!" And so it would go until, invariably, he'd get to Jim Gallagher, whose son, Padraig, had moved to Bristol, and sent the exact same letter month after month. "Right, Jim. Padraig says he hopes this finds you well, as this leaves him. He's got a job on a building site. The work's hard, but the pay is mighty.

He says, can you give his regards to his mammy and that he's enclosing a pound, but not this week."

"Aye, and not next week nor the week after, come to that." Hawking and spitting into the spittoon the disgruntled father would bang his pint glass down on the counter. "You'd be waiting till Tibb's Eve before that fecker would put his hand in his pocket. To tell, the truth, I'm surprised he didn't send the letter by carrier pigeon to save himself the stamp!"

The times Eileen loved most though, the times that made her glow with happiness were late in the evening when, with the children fast asleep in bed, Paddy, his head in a book, would share with her as she sewed or ironed whatever pearls of wisdom he came across.

"Did you know, Eileen, that penicillin is a mould?"

"A mould? Go way outta that!"

"I'm telling you, it's a mould!" Then, with a wink, "Tis no wonder our lot were never a day sick in their lives with the amount of the stuff we've got up in the rafters."

Now, Eileen smiled to herself in the darkness. If only she could lighten his load a bit, get a little job, maybe sewing or cleaning a few hours a week or something of the sort. But first she'd have to see what Dr McBride had to say about Mollie.

CHAPTER TEN

As it happened Dr McBride had nothing to say about Mollie for when morning came Mollie, it seemed, had staged a miraculous recovery and when at breakfast she fought Daisy for the heel off the loaf, Eileen knew she had nothing to worry about on that score. Still, as she watched Paddy march off on his quest for another day's work, with only a couple of dripping-sandwiches in his pocket to tide him over till dinner, she remembered her vow of the night before and decided to start looking for work herself that very day. And so, an hour later, dressed in her Sunday coat and hat, and having placed Mollie in charge of her sisters, she set off on the long walk into Galway.

"Bring us home something nice, Mammy," Rose called before she disappeared around a bend in the road.

"I will in me hat!" Eileen called back. But maybe, just maybe, if she *did* find what she was looking for, she might just run to a quarter of bull's-eyes.

An hour later, Eileen shuddered as she passed the Spanish Arch where the infamous Judge Lynch had taken out his own son and hanged him in public for killing his rival in love, a young Spanish boy. It was beyond her how anyone could take a life, let alone the life of their own child, no matter what they were supposed to have done. Now the deeds of both father and son had passed into history and lynching had become an everyday word, though Eileen doubted if many people outside of Ireland knew about its grisly origin. Hurrying past she walked the short distance to Eyre Square, stopping every now and then to admire the merchandise displayed in the windows of the big stores. Not for the first time, she wondered what it would be like to be able to simply walk in and choose a whole new rig-out; shoes, hat, handbag, the works, and not feel intimidated by the salesgirls with their hard assessing stares – all of *them* done up to dig in a matchbox with their navy skirts and white blouses with the Peter Pan collars.

Since the girls were born, Eileen had never had anything which was not either a hand-me-down, or run up by herself on the old Singer sewing machine left to her by Paddy's mother, who must have guessed something of what it had cost her to give up the golden opportunity of working at McVeigh's. And, truth to tell, sometimes, she couldn't help but wonder how her life might have turned out had she chosen to go down that particular path, but then she thought of Paddy and the children and any inkling of regret vanished as if by magic. She kept her hand in at the sewing though, running up skirts and frocks for the girls and herself, whenever she could get her hands on a half-decent piece of material and, when she put her mind to it, she had even been known to turn out a grand shirt for Paddy. When John-Joe's sisters, Nuala and Mary, had got wed, Eileen had designed and made both their wedding dresses for them: Nuala's out of oyster-coloured slipper satin she had gone all the way to O'Connell Street in Dublin for and Mary's out of a lovely raw silk, with a smattering of pearl beads around the sweetheart neckline. It had been a pleasure working with such materials, though she went through agonies worrying that Mollie and her sisters might maul the fabric with their sticky fingers. So, just to be on the safe side she did most of the work when the children were in bed and Paddy was either down in O'Dwyer's or engrossed in some book by the fireside. The dresses had been an unqualified success and soon Eileen found her dressmaking abilities in huge demand, with requests coming in left, right and centre, though she found herself being paid in kind, more often than not, rather than hard cash. In the end Paddy had called a halt to it.

"You'll wear yourself out, Eileen," he'd warned. "You can be kind to a fault, you know. There's more than one round here quick to take advantage. Look at that Mrs Middleton. All those sheets and pillowcases you patched for her and what does she give you? A dozen eggs and six of them rotten!"

Eileen protested. "I know Paddy but –"

"But me no buts, woman! You're going around like death warmed up from tiredness and if you're not careful you'll go into a decline."

Eileen had laughed at that. "Divil the chance! I'm as tough as ould boots." Nonetheless it was only after she'd stopped taking on any more sewing that she realised just how drained she had become.

Still, she reflected now, as she dawdled in front of Kiely's window, wouldn't it be great if she could get a proper sewing job in a shop or a factory maybe, with a proper wage packet at the end of every week? Well, she might not have any fancy qualifications or letters after her name, but she could sew a straight seam, couldn't she, which was more than whoever sewed that navy shift frock in the window could do. Talk about a botched job! One of the seams was all rucked and the hem was up one side and down the other. And Kiely's were asking five guineas for it. Astounded at the gall, Eileen shook her head, then wheeled round as a hand clamped itself onto her shoulder.

"Window-shopping, are you, Mrs McNab?" The voice, much to Eileen's annoyance, seemed to imply that that was all Eileen could afford to do and belonged to Mrs Bailey, every bit as unpleasant as her husband, the farmer who'd been after Larkin.

"As a matter of fact, Mrs Bailey, I was just looking at that navy frock and if it wasn't for the fact that the seams must have been sewn by the One-Eyed Reilly, I might even have bought it." Forcing herself to sound, casual, dismissive even, Eileen told the lie with aplomb but Mrs Bailey, who was known for having the nose of a bloodhound, wasn't to be put off that easily.

"Ah, sure they've plenty more inside." Grabbing Eileen by the arm she practically frog-marched her into the shop. "C'mon, I'll go in with you."

Short of making a scene there was little else Eileen could do but accompany her. Still she almost died with embarrassment when the ould bitch clicked her fingers and called for the manager. "My friend has a complaint to make." She poked Eileen in the back. "Haven't you, Mrs McNab?"

"I have not!" Panicking, Eileen blushed to the roots of her hair, but it was too late. The other woman's stentorian tones brought the eyes of customers and staff alike swivelling curiously in their direction.

"Indeed?" Unfurling herself from some dark corner of the shop, a human icicle, with a perm that extended all the way onto her forehead like the fringe on a Charolais bull, raked Eileen with cold blue eyes.

"'Well, go on then!" Mrs. Bailey prompted, ablaze with mischief and in no way fazed by the superior attitude of the manageress. "Tell her about the frock."

"The . . . gown?" One of icicle's eyebrows arched itself into a scornful question mark.

"That navy frock in the window –" The cynosure of all eyes, Eileen, despite wishing that the ground would open up and swallow her whole, felt she had no option now but to brave things out.

"The *La Belle* model, you mean?" The manageress made a sort of salaam motion towards the dress, giving the impression that in another moment she would be flat on the ground and prostrating herself. "Exclusively from Bond Street."

"If that's the one with the botched seams and crooked hem, then I suppose I do." In for a penny, in for a pound, thought Eileen, neither knowing nor caring where Bond Street might be.

"B-botched seams? C-crooked hem?" Shocked, the manageress gave a faint stagger and grappled at the high collar of her blouse, pulling it away from her bony throat as though it were choking her. In bygone days, she would have called for the McKenzie's smelling salts or burnt feathers. "Clarisse!" Faintly she beckoned towards a young salesgirl who, judging from her fresh Irish buttermilk complexion, was more likely to be called Bridget or Mary.

"Yes, Madame Bovary?" Anxious-eyed, anxious-voiced, anxiety dripping from every pore, the young woman scuttled over.

"Fetch the *La Belle* from the window." Faint or not, a quick glance round had demonstrated the importance of putting this upstart scarecrow in her place before the clients, fickle at the best of times, really started to believe there was something amiss with Kiely's merchandise and took their custom elsewhere. And, as a hefty part of the manageress's wages were made up of sales commission, this wouldn't do at all. Almost reverently she took the garment from the young assistant, draping it across her forearms and holding it out, like an offering to the gods. "From Bond Street, London, ladies!" Sharp-eyed, her glance scanned the onlookers, who craned forward for a better view. "Selected by Kiely's with an eye to the discerning woman."

"Selected and sewn by Saul of the Cataracts, if you ask me." Sure of her turf for once, Eileen gave a great hoot of derision. "Would you just look at that seam?" Obligingly the audience crowded closer and one even rooted in her handbag and took out her spectacles for a better look. "I've seen a straighter seam up a bandy leg." She rolled her eyes. "As for the hem!"

Barging her way to the front, a large bucolic woman dressed from head to toe in Galway tweed wrenched the dress away, stretching it this way and that in a way that threatened to send the manageress into an early grave. "She's right, you know. That hem's more up and down than my ould lad and he's a right moody bastard. Just ask anyone," she instructed. "Con O'Rouke of Spittal. Anyone will tell you!"

Around her, heads nodded shrewdly – some because they agreed the hem was a holy hames, more because they had first-hand evidence that her husband was a right moody bastard.

"It can be saved though." Taking it from her, Eileen examined it judiciously. "It just needs unpicking and someone who knows what they're doing to sew it up again. The material's good and the design, though nothing special, works well."

"I might even be tempted to buy it meself then." The woman in tweed with the bastard for a husband announced, cheerfully oblivious to the fact that it wouldn't go past even one of her knees.

Less impressed, Madame Bovary's eyebrows once more pinned themselves high on her forehead, as sneering around she attempted to elicit a cheap snigger at the expense of the bag-of-rags who was continuing to examine the dress between her work-roughened hands.

"I bow to your superior knowledge, I'm sure." The taunt was laced with arsenic. "You that's so obviously dressed in the height of fashion, yourself. Ladies, would you look at that hat! Is that a work of art, or what? And the coat?" Elongating her already long neck to reptilian proportions, she stuck her head out at right angles and bared her fangs. "Isn't that the kind of thing the tinkers wear?"

"Enough!" His voice cracking on the air, a well-dressed, grey-haired little dumpling of a man appeared suddenly out of nowhere, startling the manageress into an embarrassed silence, which she tried to cover by pretending something urgent required her immediate attention at the far side of the room and loping off there in long strides.

"Brendan Kiely." Almost dancing on his little feet, the man introduced himself to a surprised and somewhat bewildered Eileen. "Proprietor, for my sins, of Kiely's Emporium, Galway, Cork and soon, God willing, Dublin." Shorter than her, he twinkled up at her, encasing her hands between his own in an avuncular way that made her warm to him at once. "Now, I think you and I may have a bit of business to discuss. Something to our mutual advantage." He quirked an eyebrow. "So, Mrs . . .?"

"McNab." Stunned at the turn events were taking, Eileen could barely find her voice.

"Mrs McNab." He inclined his head. "Perhaps

you would be so good as to accompany me into the back room. And Clarisse, please be so kind as to bring both the dress and a cup of tea for Mrs McNab and myself. There's a good girl."

Outside, the excitement over, the small crowd of shoppers began to disperse, and within minutes there was nobody left apart from the manageress who had frozen into a remarkable impression of Lot's wife and Mrs Bailey, who still cherished the fond hope that she would yet have something to crow over.

Almost before she knew it, Eileen found herself seated at a large work-table on which a sewing-machine vied for space alongside bolts of material, industrial-sized spools of thread and a pile of labels suspiciously bearing the legend *La Belle of Bond Street*. In half an hour she had unpicked, and resewn the navy frock so that its seams were perfectly symmetrical and the hem as straight as a die. In another five minutes she had accepted a job as seamstress at Kiely's, five days a week, nine to five, to be paid at a rate which if it wouldn't exactly buy her a mansion, would at least keep the wolves from the door and lighten the load on Paddy's shoulders.

"Welcome aboard, Mrs McNab!" Cherubic face alight with good will, Mr Kiely pumped her hand heartily before disappearing into his office and leaving Clarisse to show her out.

"I'm glad you're starting here," the young girl said frankly. "We could do with someone to stick up to old sour-puss." Her head jerked towards the manageress outside.

Eileen grinned. "Thanks, Clarisse, I'll do my best."

"Ah, I'm only Clarisse to the customers," the girl confided, adding, much to Eileen's amusement, "Me real name's Bridget. As for that one," again her head jerked towards the manageress, "that's Assumpta Hickey. She got Madame Bovary out of some book or other." She looked considering for a moment. "I suppose you'll have to have a French name too. How about Marie-Antoinette?"

Eileen laughed. "Right so, Marie Antoinette it is!" Then, as she spotted Mrs Bailey, "Oh, Mrs Bailey, are you still here?"

Attempting to hoist a concerned look on her face, Mrs Bailey succeeded only in looking sly. "Well, I thought I'd better wait and see what happened to you as in a manner of speaking it was me that got you into it."

"You did me a great turn, so you did." Delighted with the way things had turned out, Eileen waved a magnanimous hand. "All credit to you, Mrs Bailey. It's down to yourself that I start work here on Monday. As a seamstress, if you don't mind."

Mrs Bailey very much minded, minded so much that she was completely gutted. Desperately she cast around for an excuse to leave, unable to bear another moment of the McNab one's gloating. "That's great, Mrs McNab," she said lamely, the words sticking in her craw, "but I'd better go now. My Tom's been a bit off-colour recently. I thought I'd nip into the chemist and get something for him."

It was Eileen's turn to pretend concern. "Oh, dear, is that a fact? Well, you know what you'll get him, Mrs Bailey?" She wagged her head authoritatively. "Cod-liver oil!"

"Cod-liver oil?"

"Aye, that's right!" Struggling not to laugh, Eileen nodded with conviction. "The biggest bottle you can find and before you know it he'll be racing around like Master McGrath."

"Hadn't I an awful nerve though, going into a shop without the price of a pair of socks in my pocket, and complaining about a dress I couldn't afford to buy in a month of Sundays?"

Still amazed at her own daring, Eileen was regaling her husband with the morning's events. Paddy smiled but the smile, she noticed, did not quite reach his eyes.

Sensitive to all his moods, Eileen knew at once what was wrong. Suppressing her jubilation, she put down her cup of tea, reached across the table and took hold of his hand. "Now you're not going to give me all that ould codology about a woman's place being in the home, are you?" Earnestly she sought his eyes. "Because we can't afford false pride, Paddy, and me doing a bit of sewing up at Kiely's won't make you any less of a man. Besides, now that the girls are older and I've more time on me hands, I'd enjoy getting out of the house, meeting people and such like." Sensing a softening in him she pressed home her advantage. "You and me are a team, Paddy McNab. Haven't you supported me and the girls for years, and now that jobs are scarcer, isn't it only right that I should pull my weight?"

His thumb stroked circles on the back of her hand. "You've always pulled your weight, Eileen love, and I'm delighted about the job. Really I am! It's just that I wish I could do more. It seems wrong that you should have to go out to work. All wrong."

"And what more can you do, eh? Look at you! Up at all hours, tramping the highways and byways of Galway, demeaning yourself in front of people who aren't fit to lick the dirt from your boots. And all so the girls and I don't go hungry." Eileen bristled, her voice catching a little. "Let me tell you, Paddy, you won't be doing us any favours if you kill yourself, you know."

Bending his head, Paddy stared hard at their intertwined fingers. He couldn't deny the truth of her words. There were days recently when his chest had felt like a pair of bellows and he was always conscious that the bronchitis that had carried away both his parents and one brother was only one cough away. Picking up her hand, he kissed her fingers. "Ah, don't be worrying your head about me! Sure everyone knows it's hard to kill a bad thing."

Eileen sighed. "Bad thing? The truth is, you're the best thing that ever happened to me."

"And you to me, Eileen." Paddy was fervent.

"Well, that goes without saying," Eileen joked to lighten a mood which had become somewhat sombre, a state of affairs that did not last long as Larkin, followed by the children, careered through the door having spent the best part of the day romping down on the strand.

"Does that mean we'll be rich, Mammy?" Daisy, always with an eye to the family coffers, asked when Eileen had finished sharing her news with them.

Eileen laughed. "Not exactly, but you know what they say – look after the pennies today and the pounds will build palaces tomorrow. And Mr Kiely says I can take home any remnants I like, so I'll be able to keep you well supplied with style."

"Will you make me a dress like Cinderella?" Rose asked hopefully, coming to stand at her mother's knee.

"You're wearing one already!" Daisy scoffed,

pointing at the well-worn, much-patched dress her sister was wearing.

Furious, Rose rounded on her. "Shut up, Daisy. I mean a frilly one!"

Reaching out, Eileen gently pushed Rose's thick black hair away from her eyes, where it had a habit of falling. "Ah, you never know your luck!" she said. "Anyway, there's something else I have to tell you. Your mother's got a new name. What do you think of that?"

"What do you mean, Mammy?" Mollie asked. "Which bit have you changed and will we have to change ours too?"

"Ah no, Mollie, I'm only to be called a different name at work. A French name! We all have to be called by a French name." She made her voice lah-di-dah. "To impress the customers – and I'm Marie Antoinette."

"That's stupid!" Prosaic as always, Daisy didn't follow the logic.

"Marie Antoinette was stupid!" Mollie gave an unladylike snort. "We learned about her in history. When she was told that all the poor French people were starving and had no bread, she said they should eat cake."

"Huh! There's nothing stupid about that." Scornful of her sister's knowledge, Daisy gave her a sharp push. "I'd prefer to eat cake any time, so I would, especially currant cake like Mammy makes."

"Yeah, so would I!" Rose agreed and, reminded of her stomach, which in Eileen's opinion resembled nothing so much as a bottomless pit, launched into her favourite complaint. "I'm starving, Mammy. What's for dinner?"

Ruefully, Marie-Antoinette rose and began to peel a stack of potatoes. There was nothing like children to bring you down to earth with a bump, she reflected. Nothing at all!

CHAPTER ELEVEN

After the episode with the box of chocolates Mollie felt that it would be downright rude to continue to ignore Mrs Devlin and so a secret friendship had sprung up between the two of them and Mollie had come to love visiting her house. Apart from Coral herself, for whom she couldn't help but develop a deep, if guilty, affection, Devlin's house fascinated her. Whereas her own home was nothing more than a simple thatched cottage, theirs was a big grey two-storey affair, with a neatly slated herringbone roof, which Daddy had sourly remarked was built with the wages of sin and which he hoped would be blown to Kingdom Come with the next good storm. Upstairs there were four bedrooms, two of which remained empty and which Coral told her were reserved for the guests she hoped might come to stay after the baby was born, the most important being her mother and brother who would be travelling over from England. Of the remaining two, the smallest had been kitted out as a nursery with pale primrose wallpaper on which doe-eyed baby farm animals gambolled and where a white-painted wooden cot, complete with a lace canopy, was already set up and awaiting its new occupant. In the meantime, Coral had placed her own old teddy bear, Winston, inside. Sporting only one eye, and a battered nose, his golden plush was frayed, even bald in places; it was a sign, Coral said, that he had been well loved, and to demonstrate that love she still took him out occasionally, kissed him, cuddled him and nursed him on her knee. Mollie was thrilled to pieces. Never in her whole life had she seen anything like it, never even imagined that a newborn baby might actually have a whole room to itself or that a grown-up woman might still play with a teddy bear. It was a wonder she didn't burst under the strain of having to keep all these wonders to herself and, indeed, there were times when she found herself sailing a bit close to the wind, especially if Daisy or Rose were boasting about something which paled into insignificance compared to what she knew.

"Listen, ye big eejits," she itched to say in her most superior voice, "wait till I tell you about . . . " But, miraculously, she didn't. Miraculously she managed to keep her mouth closed, because, more than anything, she wanted to keep on visiting Coral. She wanted to keep on trying on Coral's clothes and high-heel shoes, while Coral sat on the side of the bed and chuckled hysterically at the state of her staggering up and down the room like a miniature drunk. She wanted to go on sitting in front of Coral's big oak dressing-table with the triple mirrors, a big square one in the centre, flanked by two smaller oval ones on either side, trying on her lipstick, smearing it inexpertly all over her mouth so that it looked like she'd been licking the lid off a strawberry-jam pot. She wanted to keep on adorning herself with the contents of Coral's jewellery box, the one that played 'Clementine' whenever the lid was lifted, layering on the blue crystal necklace on top of the pearl one and the multi-coloured beaded one on top of that with various gold and silver chains topping the lot, so that Coral took to calling her the Lord Mayor and doffing an imaginary hat to her.

To Mollie, used to sharing a tin bath in front of the fire with her two sisters, Coral's bathroom with its huge white, claw-footed enamel bath, crouching in the centre of the room like some sort of prehistoric monster, was a further and continuing source of amazement, and a great part of her very first visit was spent in turning the taps on and off again just for the sheer novelty of seeing actual running water.

When it came to the flushing toilet, she was a bit more wary because of the whooshing and gargling noise it made and the way the water frothed and bubbled up in the pan. "Aren't you afraid it might suck you in?" she'd asked, fearfully backing away. But, reassured by a laughing Coral that there was no chance of that happening whatsoever, she soon lost her fear and admitted that it was lot better than the one in the outhouse at home, where a rusty old rain-barrel with a plank of wood across the top, out of which a circle had been cut, had to suffice. The fact that there were no spiders waiting to pounce on her was a further bonus, as was the flowery disinfectant, a far cry from the stench of Jeyes' Fluid with which her mother regularly attacked the germs. Or Germans, as Rosie called them, prompting her father to wonder why on earth Churchill never thought to issue it to the British troops.

When Mollie had had enough of playing upstairs she went downstairs via the polished banisters, sliding expertly all the way, though not before she'd almost broken her neck a couple of times.

Downstairs was the kitchen, where a huge Aga cooker, on which there was always something savoury bubbling, gave off a fierce heat. Leading off that was a smaller room known as the scullery. To Mollie's eyes this last was an Aladdin's cave where Coral stored all sorts of interesting knick-knacks:

sacks of potatoes, vegetables and Odlums flour, dirty laundry in a big wicker basket, galvanised buckets, a washboard and a huge big iron mangle that would almost wrench the arm out of your socket.

Lastly, and best of all, there was the parlour, where Mollie liked to sit, sipping home-made lemonade from a crystal glass and pretending she was like the 'quality' of London Coral told her about. In contrast to the whitewashed walls of the McNabs' cottage, the walls of this room were covered with a soft bluey-green paper reminiscent of the sea on a warm summer's day. A collection of gilt-framed, sepia photographs marched grimly up along one wall, whilst an assortment of coloured prints were dotted randomly round the others. Mollie didn't like the photographs, the subjects of which seemed to peer down their long Victorian noses, their long-dead eyes and expressions forbidding, following her around the room as though she might break or steal something. The chocolate-box prints with their gaudy flowers, horses and ships on the sea were much more to her taste, along with the many porcelain figurines, shepherds, shepherdesses and crinoline ladies, scattered about on occasional tables, which her own mother would no doubt have summarily dismissed as nothing but dust collectors and a criminal waste of money.

But to the uncritical Mollie, all this was nothing

short of heaven, and at every opportunity, whenever she could shake off her sisters and often on the pretext of visiting her friend, Delia Mackey, she went straight across to Devlin's house, where, delighted with her company, Coral would regale her with tales of her life in London.

"I lived in Tooting. That's in South West London," Coral told her, "on a little street called Totterdown."

Tooting! Totterdown! Mollie lapped up the names as though they were some new and exotic fruit. There was magic in those names. St Martin-in-the-Fields! That was another one. And Coral had gone to a school called Burntwood, which sounded a whole lot better than St Joseph's, more the kind of place where there would be midnight feasts and girls called Gladys and Daphne who said 'jolly' a lot and 'how splendid' like the characters in the *Famous Five* books. They would drink ginger beer, eat something called macaroons and play some peculiar game called lacrosse.

She learned about Green Park too. That was a park in the centre of London, so called, Coral said, because no flowers would grow there on account of it being the site where hundreds of plague victims were buried. Mollie wasn't sure what a plague was. She only knew *she* was one.

"God, you're a right plague!" her mother or teachers would often say. "Go away and stop plaguing me."

"Who did you live with?" she asked once, biting

into a piece of cake Coral told her was called Angel cake, and which really did taste heavenly.

"Oh, my mother and my brother, Jason." A little sad, Coral cleared her throat. "My dad died when I was only ten. He was a fire warden during the Blitz and one night he was caught out during a bombing raid and didn't reach the tube station on time. That's where people used to shelter, you know, Mollie, in the Underground train stations, way down in the tunnels, all up and down the platforms. Some people used to bring sandwiches and flasks of tea and make a bit of a picnic out of it and once, someone even managed to get a piano down there – don't ask me how – and we all sat round singing 'Knees Up Mother Brown' and 'Roll Out The Barrel'. But mostly we were miserable and scared. The noise of the bombs kept us awake and sometimes we'd try to guess where they were falling. 'Oh, there goes Balham,' somebody would say, or 'God help the poor souls up town; they're taking a battering tonight.' And sometimes there'd be a terrible kind of screeching noise and then a huge bang nearby, and you'd know the Jerries had scored a direct hit and wonder whether it was your house that was in smithereens or your neighbour's, and how many had been killed." Her eyes misted over. "You'd hear people praying out loud then, even if they weren't the sort to pray usually, and babies crying and mothers shushing them and others cursing and swearing and roaring about what they'd like to do if ever they got their hands on that Hitler fella. Then later, the all-clear would sound, and we'd all come blinking like moles up into the light and sometimes, Mollie, when you reached the top it was like stepping out into another world. Sometimes it would feel like you'd been spirited away and set down in a completely different place. Because whole streets of houses would be razed to the ground and nothing would look familiar. And the dust! The dust was everywhere, clouds of it that painted itself onto your clothes and lodged itself in your hair and eyes and clogged your lungs, and thick black palls of smoke that sent the sky into mourning, so sometimes day was as black as night and the birds got confused and didn't sing at all. Imagine that, Mollie, a world without birdsong. Now that's a sad world indeed!"

Wide-eyed, Mollie hung on Coral's every word, never tiring of hearing the same thing over and over again, often prompting her when it looked as though Coral might deviate or become distracted.

"Tell me about the food, Coral."

"If you could call it that." As always, Coral wrinkled her nose at the memory. "Awful! Truly awful! Powdered eggs and Spam and, if you were lucky, a few mouldy vegetables that you had to queue round the block for – and no chocolate. Not so much as the sniff of a bar till the Yanks came and I must say they were very generous. I fell in love with one, you know, though I was only a child. Guy Berensen, he was called, and he came from somewhere in the Deep South. Orlando, I think." Affecting a Southern drawl, Coral would chuck Mollie under the chin. "'Say, lil girl, ya want some bubblegum?' Of course, it was really my mother he was after and I suppose he saw me as a good way of getting round her, though she never took the bait. After my father died, she never so much as looked at another man. Still, I got the benefit and Guy fed me chocolate and bubblegum till it was coming out my ears and, best of all, taught me to jive to 'Chattanooga Choo Choo'."

"Will you teach me?" Mollie begged. "Will you teach me to jive?"

And despite her ever-increasing girth, Coral did, and many a happy hour was spent in the company of Coral's small record player, Glenn Miller and "The Boogie-Woogie Bugle Boy from Company B".

Eventually when they ran out of puff, Coral would tell her about the evacuation, when she and hundreds more children from London had been sent off down the country to stay with relatives and friends and even complete strangers.

"For our own safety," Coral said. "Although we didn't see it like that. I think most of us would have preferred staying with our own families, even if it did mean blackouts and nights spent down the Underground. Still, I was luckier than most, because I had an aunt who lived on a farm way down in Devon. At first though, I was lonely, frightened and terribly homesick. I'd never been away from my family before, not even for a night, and I missed my mother and Jason like you wouldn't believe." She grinned. "Added to that, I'd never seen farm animals up close before and they scared me to death. They were so big. Now, don't laugh, Mollie, but the first time a cow mooed at me, I cried for an hour and locked myself in my bedroom in case it came after me."

Of course, Mollie did laugh. Scornfully! "Imagine being frightened of a stupid old cow," she said. "I'm not frightened of anything, except spiders. And Mother Benignus."

"Well, you must remember, I'd never seen a real-live cow before," Coral reminded her. "It looked awful big and scary and when it stuck its huge long tongue out, I thought it was going to eat me. Still, after a while, I became a bit of an expert. I used to help drive the cattle home at night for the milking, mix up the swill for the pigs and feed the chickens. I knew all their names too, and it was my job to collect the eggs. Before long, I could even tell which one of them was being sneaky and laying out somewhere."

Her face darkened. "Not every one was so lucky, mind. I remember being in town with my aunt one day when a new group of evacuees arrived. There were tons of them, Mollie, some only about three or four, little more than babies really, with big frightened teary eyes and snotty noses, clutching gas-mask boxes in their little hands and with labels pinned to their coats with their names on. A huge bully of a woman, dressed head to toe in tweed, and with a voice like the crack of a whip, forced them all to line up against a wall and then people came and picked a child to take home, sometimes prodding and poking them as if they were animals. The bigger boys and girls were the first to go, being quickly claimed by farmers or people with businesses in search of cheap labour, and the prettiest children by women who had none of their own and who were desperate to lavish their love on someone. They were the luckiest evacuees, although often the women's hearts were broken when the war ended and the children they had become so attached to went back home to their own mothers. People weren't so quick to take the more unattractive children, though, the ones who were pale and sickly, with scabs on their hands and knees, the ones with bad eyesight or who were afflicted by rickets or polio and often they'd be left standing for hours, faint with tiredness, hunger and loneliness, desperately waiting for someone to come and give them a home." A frown gathered between Coral's eyes, and her lips formed themselves into a bitter twist. "And some of them were beaten, Mollie, thrashed and made to work like slaves by the very people who were supposed to be protecting them, while others were sent abroad to places like Australia, without their parents even knowing and with no way of tracing them when the war ended and so many never came back again."

"That must have been terrible." Mollie had heard of Australia. There was nothing there but deserts and kangaroos and funny-looking wild men with bones through their noses, who spent their lives throwing boomerangs. "You were lucky you had your aunt, weren't you?"

Coral nodded. "Very. She was lovely, my Aunty Sarah, and my uncle and cousins. I couldn't have asked for better." Getting to her feet, Coral went into the kitchen, replenished the lemonade jug, came back and continued reminiscing. "I remember one day when my aunt had finished shopping, we passed the spot where the evacuees had been and there was one little boy still standing there, all on his own. I'll bring that picture to the grave with me. It was one of the saddest sights I've ever seen. His face was dirty, with tear-stains all down his cheeks, showing up the clean pink skin underneath. He must have had lice or ringworm or something, because his head had been shaved and his clothes were no more than rags, the sleeves of his jumper ending several inches above his skinny wrists and his trousers flapping round his ankles like those on a scarecrow. Nobody wanted him, Mollie. Nobody wanted this poor little child that stood there, shivering and shaking, his head bent in a shame he never should have been feeling. And then my aunt, God bless her, did something that raised her head and shoulders above anyone I have ever met, before or since. Handing her shopping basket to me, she went over, bent down and took him in her arms and she cradled him there till he stopped shaking, letting the warmth of her own body and all the love in her heart seep into him. Then, she took him by the hand and brought him home."

"And what happened to him, Coral?" Mollie asked in a croaky voice, moved to tears by the story.

Leaning over, Coral tweaked her nose. "Ah, wipe your eyes, Mollie, and don't fret. There's a happy ending. He stayed with the family, even after the war ended and, believe it or not, ended up marrying one of my cousins. He's six foot tall now, with a thick black head of curly hair on him and everybody who knows Neil Alton worships the ground he walks on. But you know, it just goes to show, what one simple act of kindness can lead to, and the way the choices we make affect our lives and the lives of all those around us."

"And what about you, Coral? Did you stay there till the war ended?" Eagerly, Mollie held out her glass for a top-up.

Coral shook her head. "No, after a few months my mother came and took me home again. She said that if we were going to die, then she'd sooner we all died together. But we didn't die and here I am! So, all told, I've nothing to complain about, really. I've been blessed with a pretty good life and a wonderful family which is more than a lot of people can say."

"And is your husband wonderful?" Mollie asked, genuinely interested.

"Yes, Mollie, I think he's wonderful."

"Well, we don't." Mollie was blunt. "He killed our Liam, you know."

Two bright spots of colour crept up Coral's cheeks, giving her the look of a Dutch porcelain doll. "I know, Mollie. I also know that if he could turn back the hands of time and bring your Liam back to life, he would. I know he can't sleep at night for thinking of it, but gets up and paces the floor till he's fit to wear out the carpet." Misting over, her eyes gazed far-seeingly over her young guest's head as though she'd forgotten her presence, and was simply speaking her thoughts aloud. "And I've heard him crying: crying like a baby when he thinks there's no one around." She gave a little shiver, brought her focus back to Mollie. "But I don't let on, never let him know what I've seen and heard because that would diminish him. And he's a proud man. And a good man! I just pray that one day he'll find peace and stop beating himself up over the terrible tragedy, the terrible accident that cost your Liam his life and my husband his peace of mind."

"He was drunk the day of the funeral," Mollie accused. "Daddy saw him, outside O'Dwyer's, staggering about without a care in the world and drunk as a lord!"

Coral Devlin sighed again as she looked at Mollie's set little face, the indignation that lit up her eyes from within, so that they flashed like twin sapphires in sunlight. "What your father saw, Mollie, was bravado. Do you know what that is?"

The child shook her head. It sounded like some sort of a Cowboy and Indian film but she wasn't going to say that in case Coral thought she was stupid.

"Bravado is when somebody is putting a brave face on things. It's pretending you don't care, when all the while your heart is breaking."

"Oh!" Mollie was glad she hadn't said anything about Cowboys and Indians. "I felt like that when my best friend, Delia Mackey, went off with someone else and wouldn't talk to me any more."

Coral Devlin smiled at her candour. "It hurts, doesn't it? And believe it or not, Mollie, my husband was also hurting that day. If he was drunk, then, believe me, he was because he was drowning his sorrows and not because he wished to cause your family any further grief. Can you understand that?"

"I – I think so," Mollie nodded, feeling as Coral had no doubt intended, a mite more sympathy toward her husband.

Nonetheless, as Mollie heard his key in the front door, she skedaddled like a bat out of hell straight out the back.

Coral sighed deeply, pondering the strange fate that had brought her here to the Atlantic coast to be neighbour to a family who hated her, her beloved husband and her unborn child . . .

CHAPTER TWELVE

Coral Devlin had just turned eighteen when first she'd set eyes on the big Irishman who was destined to become her husband. In fact, left to her own devices, she wouldn't have gone out at all that evening, except that Fate in the dumpy shape of her best friend, Noreen McDermott, beckoned. Worn out after a hard day's nursing, Coral's idea of a great evening was to relax in front of the fire with a good book, maybe listen to a play on the radio, then turn in for an early night. But, Noreen had different plans, ones that involved Coral, and so she set about nagging her with gusto.

"Oh, don't be such a wet blanket, Coral. Time enough to sit home doing your knitting and listening to the radio when you're old and grey. Get up those stairs and get your glad-rags on girl, because we're off to the Galtymore!"

"But I don't like Irish music, Nore," Coral remembered protesting timidly, not wishing to cause offence. "It's all didley-didley-doo and old men playing accordions and fiddles and jumping around like frogs."

Noreen waved a scornful hand. "Listen, there's nothing didley-doo about the Galtymore. This place is the real thing, a proper ballroom, with one of those big mirror-ball things spinning round in the middle of the ceiling and ne'er an accordion, fiddle or frog in sight. They have *proper* bands there, Coral, I'm telling you. Showbands! And gorgeous men all over the place!" Turning her back, she wrapped her arms about herself, one hand on her shoulder, the other cradling her waist, running it suggestively up and down. *"If you were the only girl in the world,"* she sang, then twisting round, fell dramatically to her knees, hands held out in supplication. "Ah, come on! Say you'll come. It'll be great, I promise, and, for all you know, your future husband might even be there."

"I doubt it," Coral laughed, catching something of Noreen's excitement despite herself. "Anyway, I don't intend getting married for ages yet. I'm far too young."

Knowing victory was near, a smile split Noreen's face. "Look, you can stay an old maid forever, for all

I care. It can be just you, a rocking chair and twenty cats for the rest of your life, so long as you come tonight. Just for the fun. The worst that can happen is that you enjoy yourself and, tell me, where's the harm in that?"

"None, I suppose," Coral admitted, throwing in the towel. "Just don't go lining me up with any old farmers, though, or you won't see me for dust."

"As if I would," Noreen scoffed. "I had enough of those back home, myself. Nothing will do me now but Stewart Grainger."

On Noreen's insistence, because she didn't want her friend 'making a show of her', Coral took extra care with her appearance that night, teasing out her long blonde hair so that it fell in soft bouncing waves about her shoulders and carefully matching her lipstick to the cerise colour of the full-skirted dress she'd bought with her first wages as a student nurse. For a whole week, every time she passed Ely's Department store, she'd stood gazing at it in the plate-glass window, her eyes greedily taking in the sweetheart neckline, the little puff sleeves and the mountain of buckram underskirts peeping snowily out just below the hemline, terrified that by the time pay day came round, it would no longer be there. But it had been and now it was hers and when she saw the raw envy reflected in her friend's face, she knew she'd made the right choice.

"God Almighty," Noreen complained, watching Coral primp and preen before the mirror, "I should have my head examined for asking you to come along." She flapped her fingers. "Just make sure you don't stand beside me, that's all, or I'll never get a dance."

"Oh, don't be so daft!" Coral tossed the compliment away, knowing how sensitive her friend was about her own looks, the mop of carroty hair that headed off in whatever direction it chose and that no one, God, man or army could subdue, and her figure that erred on the side of plump. "You look gorgeous, Nore. Stop putting yourself down, because . . ."

"I know. I know. There's plenty of people only too willing and ready to do that for me," Noreen finished. "Ah, I'll do, I suppose. I've seen worse – in Madame Tussaud's!" In no way fooled, she made a little moue, then her irrepressible high spirits re-asserting themselves, grabbed her clutch-bag and a cardigan that she slung carelessly over her shoulders and headed for the door. "Well, come on, Cinderella, your pumpkin awaits!"

As it happened, both girls barely left the dance floor all evening and it was only much later on a visit to the powder room that they got a chance to catch up and compare notes.

"Did you see that fella watching you, all night," Noreen demanded, peering into the washroom mirror and examining her teeth for signs of stray lipstick. "The tall chap with the curly black hair and spivvy suit?" She shot Coral a sideways look. "Come on, you must have seen him. He never took his eyes off you."

"Oh, him!" Nodding, Coral pretended nonchalance. Of course, she'd seen him, brooding darkly at the side of the floor, watching her every move, but making no move to ask her to dance himself. He wasn't the kind you could miss and other women had noticed him too, several of whom went and stood close to him, chattering like magpies and fiddling with their dresses and hair, anything in a vain bid to attract his attention. "Well, what about him?"

"Just steer clear of him," Noreen advised, and then, hurriedly, in case her friend got the wrong idea. "Oh, don't get me wrong. I'm not jealous or anything. It's just that I know him from back home and he's got a bit of a reputation, that's all."

Intrigued, Coral powdered her nose and fluffed her hair up at the back. "What kind of reputation? With the women, do you mean? Did he get some girl into trouble?"

Beside her, Noreen, touched up her own face. "No, nothing like that. He ran over and killed some young child in Galway a while back. Rumour has it he'd been drinking. Others aren't so sure it was an accident at all." She made a round 'o' of her mouth, swiped a tube of lipstick across her bottom lip, then rubbed her fingertip across it to spread the colour. "He's known for having a very bad temper and for being a hard taskmaster." Smacking her lips together, Noreen made a final check, then blew herself a satisfied kiss in the mirror. "Mind you, the girl that marries him won't want for anything. He's not short of a few bob, the same Mick Devlin. But then, whoever heard of a poor building contractor? My father always said that they're the ones with the money and it's on fools like himself that rich men build houses."

"So what do you think he's doing over here in London?" Flicking open a small box of mascara, Coral extracted the brush from within, spat on the bristles to wet it and brushed carefully at her lashes, her dark pansy eyes gaining in mystery and depth with every stroke.

Noreen shook her head. "How do I know? Probably visiting friends or family, if he's got any here, or doing a bit of business. Don't you know well the likes of him will have his finger in all sorts of pies? Most of them unsavoury."

"Maybe it's not him at all. Maybe you're confusing him with somebody else." Snapping the box of mascara shut, Coral slipped it back in her handbag, took out a bottle of Evening in Paris and spritzed lightly at her wrists and throat. "Don't they say everybody has a doppelgänger – isn't that what it's called? And maybe that man out there is his."

"Rubbish! It's him all right." Noreen frowned as a woman in the last stages of incontinence barged roughly past her and disappeared into a toilet stall. A moment later, there was a long sigh of relief. "I went to school with his sister. He was quite a bit older than her, as I recall, and all the girls were mad for him. Well, admittedly, he is very handsome – you don't get many with those looks to the pound. These days, mind, most of them would cross over to the other side of the street if they saw him coming." She bent a stern look on her friend. "And if you've a grain of sense, you'll do the same. So don't go having your head turned, just because he's been staring at you."

"All right, Mummy," Coral made her voice tiny. "If you say so, Mummy. After all, it's no skin off my nose. Now are you coming back out, or are you just going to stay there lecturing the thin air?" With a careless grin, she led the way back to the dance floor, where, giving the lie to her words, the first thing she did was to sneak a quick look at Mick Devlin, only to find he was no longer there and that his place had been taken by a total stranger with a set of less than perfect teeth, which he bared invitingly in her direction. Her gaze bouncing chillingly over him, Coral let her eyes stray around the room, but there was no sign of Mick Devlin anywhere amongst the dancers or bystanders, or even amongst the throng of men holding up the bar at the far end of the dance-hall. Strange, but after that, the magic seemed to evaporate from the evening, and the music, which up till then had been quite perfect, disintegrated into a mere cacophony of discordant notes that set her teeth on edge and gave her a thumping headache.

The following Saturday found the tables turned and Coral begging Noreen to go dancing. In truth, she hadn't been able to get Mick Devlin out of her head all week, and found him popping into her thoughts at the strangest of times, circling round and round like one of those annoyingly catchy tunes or an itch that needed scratching. By the time the weekend came round she felt as though she would go mad if she didn't see him one more time. And so, dressed up to the nines, this time in a fitted navy silk polka-dot dress that moulded itself to her curves, high white sling-back shoes and her hair loosely piled up in a mass of blonde curls, she made her way to the Galtymore, with Noreen quizzing her all the way.

"I don't know why you're so keen to go dancing again," she remarked with a sly sideways look as arm-in-arm they neared the Galtymore, "considering how I had to almost twist your arm the last time."

"Well, I enjoyed myself," Coral said in what she hoped were tones of complete innocence, then piling on the flattery to throw Noreen and her bloodhound's nose off the scent, "You were perfectly right, Nore. There's no harm in having a bit of fun. Heaven knows we work hard enough all week and, like you said, there'll be plenty of time to stop home when I'm old and past it." She squeezed her friend's arm. "Besides, I hear there's a really good band playing tonight."

"Oh, really? What are they called?" Coral didn't need to see Noreen's face to see Doubting Thomas written all over it. Noreen was shrewd and could, in her own words, take anyone to the crossroads and leave them there. Not that Coral was familiar with all of Noreen's Irish sayings, but she guessed that one meant that her friend wasn't one to be hoodwinked easily. And she certainly wasn't going to be fooled by Coral who, honest as the day was long, began to splutter and trip over her tongue.

"Oh, I forget, now. B-but I know they're supposed to be good. It-it said so in the paper. Rave reviews and all that."

"Oh, is that a fact? What paper was that then?" Unrelenting, Noreen pressed further. "Would that be *The Times*, *The Independent* or maybe it was the made-up one in your head?" Bending a stern look on her friend, she swung her round to face her, raising her voice crossly. "Now, listen here, Coral Browne, you'd want to get up a darn sight earlier in the morning if you want to pull the wool over my eyes. I'm not so green as I'm cabbage-looking, you know. Don't think I don't know what's really going on in that feeble mind of yours. It's him, isn't it? Mick-bloody-Devlin – the man with the devil in his name!"

"Noreen, stop it!!" Embarrassed because people had turned to stare, Coral pulled away. "I don't know what you're talking about. Are you completely mad?"

"Not so mad that I can't see inside your woolly head!" Noreen snapped back. "Do you think I'm a complete eejit? Do you think I haven't a working brain-cell in me head? All week, you've been hinting round the subject and going all dreamy, looking like one of them film stars down the picture house. Well, I'm telling you now you'd better wake up to yourself. You're not Jayne Mansfield. You're not Vivien Leigh. You're Coral Browne, a student nurse from plain old Tooting, and if you play with Mick Devlin, you're going to wind up with more than just your fingers burned." Her complexion thrown into ghostly relief by a streetlight overhead, she made one last-ditch appeal. "So, please, Coral, can you not just put him out of your mind? Let's just go and enjoy ourselves. Let's just get back to normal, because, honest to God, I'm going to go off my bloody head if you don't stop mooning."

"Everything is normal," Coral insisted, "and I'm

not mooning, Noreen. It's all in your imagination. Maybe you've been working too hard. You should tell Matron you need a break." Crossing her fingers behind her back, she then proceeded to tell one of the biggest lies of her entire life. "Whether you believe it or not, the truth is I'm not the least bit interested in Mick Devlin. I couldn't care less if I never set eyes on him again, or if he dropped off the edge of the earth. So there!"

"Oh good! So, you won't be disappointed that he's not here tonight then," Noreen observed with satisfaction, quickly scanning the room as they made their way into the dance-hall. "With any luck he'll have gone back to his father in hell!"

"Of course not," Coral scoffed. "Like I said, I couldn't care less if I never saw him again!" But like a glass of flat champagne, the fizz had gone out the evening before it even got started. At least for her!

As the evening wore on and a succession of men led her out onto the dance floor, she glanced hopefully about, but there was no sign of Mick Devlin that night at the Galtymore, or the following Saturday, nor the one after that and, finally, she just had to accept that most likely he had gone back home to Ireland. Yet, still, it proved impossible to get him out of her head. Like an unwanted lodger, he had taken up residence in her life. It was as though his very image – the thick, wavy black hair, the tormented dark eyes, the look of intensity – had all burned themselves onto her brain and were indelibly imprinted there forever more. And on her soul. And on her heart. Without his ever having spoken one word to her, without his ever having laid one finger on her, Coral realised with something of a shock that she'd completely and utterly lost her heart. To Mick Devlin, a tall dark Irish stranger! A man with a shady past. A man, as Noreen had pointed out, with the devil in his name.

CHAPTER THIRTEEN

Eileen enjoyed working at Kiely's despite Madame Bovary's long face and flaying tongue, which she used on every possible occasion and mostly against her. By contrast, young Bridget was like a breath of fresh air. If her own girls turned out as well, Eileen felt she wouldn't have a thing to complain about. A complete softy, there wasn't an ounce of malice in the whole of her body, just a heart of pure gold and a willingness both to please and be pleased.

To someone as creative with her needle as Eileen, the work was both rewarding and easy and she had a right giggle sewing on the *La Belle of Bond Street* labels. Still, she couldn't help thinking that the 'cleehontell', as Madame Bovary called them, would get an awful kick up the backside if they knew the way they were being hoodwinked. Bond Street, how are you! Mind you, there was a limit to her sympathy. The way she saw it, anyone who would willingly splash out five guineas or more on their own back, when the same kind of money would feed a family of four for a week or more, deserved nothing less than a good trouncing.

Occasionally, these days, if things got really busy on the shop floor, Mr Kiely called on her to help out with serving the customers, a task she really enjoyed. And in her smart navy skirt, white blouse and court shoes, all courtesy of her employer, Eileen felt as though she was really coming up in the world. Oh, she was able to put on the act as good as any of them! "Yes, modom. That suits you down to the ground, so it does, modom. Now maybe if you teamed it with a little black hat? There you go – just perfect! Just some gloves now to complete the outfit – to draw it all together? After all, you can't have one thing laughing at the other." Mr Kiely was delighted with her, remarking that she had a real way with people and was a true saleswoman if ever there was one. And, currying points with the boss, Madame Bovary agreed loudly, only she called it "the common touch" and Eileen wondered if she was the only one to notice the way her long nose wrinkled and her vowels lingered over the word 'common'.

Madame Bovary aside, Eileen's confidence grew with every day and it wasn't long before she thought about submitting some of her own designs to Mr Kiely, though Paddy cautioned her to wait a bit longer. "Creep before you walk," is how he put it, when she broached the subject in bed one night. "That Madame Bovary sounds like a right vicious article – better not to antagonise her too much, eh? A woman scorned, wouldn't you say?" And, taking his advice, Eileen agreed to bide her time. For far too long life had given her and hers nothing but backhanders. Now, it was slowly getting better and she'd no wish to rock the boat, purely for the sake of a bit of vanity. Yes, for once Eileen felt her cup close to running over. The girls had settled back into St Joseph's, where, true to her word, Mother Benignus had left them well alone, and Paddy had recently commenced work for a local farmer. It wasn't much, mind, just a bit of labouring, but it was a start and had done wonders for his ego. These days they were like a couple of honeymooners, giggling and stealing kisses whenever they were alone.

The thought brought a blush to Eileen's cheeks and, coming into the room with a bundle of invoices Mr Kiely found his eyes drawn to her where she sat, head bent in a halo of light, tongue protruding slightly as she concentrated on threading up the sewing machine. A few strands of hair had come loose from her topknot and waved gently around her fine-boned face. A man not immune to beauty,

Brendan Kiely sighed with pleasure at the sight. With her cloud of flame-red hair, eyes the exact colour of a field of bluebells and slender, though shapely figure, Eileen McNab was a picture to stir any man's blood. Were it not for the fact that she was happily married and the mother of three young girls, he might be tempted to . . . Smothering the thought in its infancy, he dragged his gaze away, though it only took a split second for Madame Bovary, who was hot on his heels, to see which way the wind blew – the McNab one, looking as though butter wouldn't melt, and Mr Kiely like an old dog with his tongue hanging out. A moment later found her storming back out to the shop floor, where poor Bridget bore the brunt of a tirade that had very little to do with ladies' fashions and everything to do with jealousy.

"Eileen!" Clarisse, stuck her head breathlessly round the workshop door. "There's someone here asking to see you."

"To see me?" Puzzled, Eileen looked up from the seams of the dress she'd been tacking together. There was an added sparkle in Bridget-Clarisse's eyes and a definite flush to her cheeks, all of which told Eileen clearer than any words that whoever it was, was definitely male. "Are you sure?" Nobody ever visited her at her place of work, or ever would unless . . .

unless . . . Feeling her maternal instincts swing suddenly onto red alert, Eileen half struggled up from the chair.

"Sez he's your nephew?" Bridget continued, blissfully unaware of the terrifying emotions she had unwittingly stirred up in the other woman's breast.

"Oh, John-Joe!" Exhaling her relief, Eileen sank back down again, her heart still racing nineteen to the dozen. "Yes, he's my nephew all right, though why he couldn't wait to see me at home is anyone's guess." Expectantly, she turned towards the door. "Well, go on then, Bridget – don't just stand around making the place untidy – send him in."

"Okay, but Frosty Drawers won't like it!" The young girl jerked her head to indicate that the manageress was nearby and lurking.

"Now when did I ever take notice of that one?" Eileen asked in a voice loud enough to be heard at the top of Mount Errigal and, a moment later, an uncomfortable looking John-Joe found himself being ushered through.

"How ya, Aunty Eileen." Leaning down, he bestowed a quick hug on her, then blushed to the roots of his hair, as swivelling round the room his gaze encountered a huddle of glassy-eyed, naked mannequins waiting to be dressed and put back in the window.

"And to what do I owe this honour?" A gleam in

her eye, Eileen unceremoniously pushed a hank of material off a stool beside her onto the floor, patting the seat invitingly. "Let me guess, it'll be one of two things – girls – or girls. Did you fall out with Bernie? Is that what it is? I'm right, amn't I? I'm right, and you couldn't wait for the benefit of your old aunty's advice." Gaily she twinkled up at him, sobering immediately as the blood drained suddenly away from his face, leaving him looking like death warmed up. "Aw no, John-Joe!" Alarmed, her hand flew to her mouth, as she guessed the exact nature of his visit. "Oh, please no, not that! Tell me you're not that stupid!"

Miserably he nodded, and in a voice choked with tears, translated her fears into the words she'd hoped never to hear. "It's Bernie. She's expecting!"

"Aw, Christ, John-Joe!" A shiver went through her as someone walked over her grave and the feeling, that awful, terrible familiar feeling of foreboding once more rose up out of nowhere and threatened to overpower her. "What the bleddy hell did you think you were doing? Didn't you know better? Have you no sense at all?" Distraught, she took in the hunch of his shoulders, the head bent penitently forward and felt her heart turn over for this boy who was more like her own son than a nephew. Life hadn't been easy for him either. His mother had walked out on the family when he was eight and his sisters only just turned ten. And now that both Nuala and Mary had married and left home, life must have been pretty lonely with just him and his father rattling around on the farm. And it wasn't even as if he had his best friend, poor Cathal, any more.

Unable to meet her eyes, he shuffled uncomfortably. "Twas just the once, Aunty Eileen. Just the once. I swear."

"Sure it only takes the once, lad, that's all." Sighing at his ignorance, Eileen jumped abruptly to her feet and began pacing the floor, looking for answers from the bare walls and the naked mannequins, but the walls stayed silent and the mannequins, if there was any wisdom at all behind their glassy eyes, chose not to share it. After a few moments' fruitless pacing, she straightened her back and stuck her chin out, as if gearing up for battle. "Well, there's no use wailing over spilt milk, I suppose. What's done is done and you won't be the only ones round here having to get wed with the print still wet on the banns." She narrowed her eyes. "You are getting married, I take it?"

John-Joe nodded.

"When?"

"Soon."

"And McBride?" Eileen frowned with worry. "I don't suppose he'll take it too well. No offence, John-Joe, but I think he had his sights set on greater things.

Since his wife died he's all but wrapped those girls of his in cotton wool. And now . . . this! He'll go off his head, no word of a lie."

It was John-Joe's turn to pace slowly back and forth. "Maybe, but he won't know until it's too late. We're catching the boat, Aunty Eileen."

"What?" Eileen's eyebrows shot up. "To England, you mean?"

John-Joe nodded. "Aye. Tomorrow. There's one leaving at eight o'clock tomorrow evening from Dún Laoghaire. That gives us the entire day to travel to Dublin and get out to the port. We'll have plenty of time."

"But your home, your family is here!" Her heart sinking, Eileen tried to reason with him because how would she bear it if she lost him too? "Listen, John-Joe, you don't know anyone in England. Not a sinner! What would you do? Where would you go?"

Holding up his hand, John-Joe stemmed the tide of her questions. "Look, Aunty Eileen – haven't I a strong back on me and hands like shovels. I'm bound to find work on a building-site or something. As for home . . ." Despite his best attempts at keeping a stiff upper lip, a wobble entered his voice, "*sure* I'll miss it. But no one will ever be able to say that I ran from my responsibilities, so they won't."

Eileen inclined her head. "No, they won't, but they will say that you ran from McBride."

"True enough," John-Joe nodded, "and if it was up to me, we'd stay and face the whole thing out, but Bernie's terrified of the ould bugger. From what she tells me, he didn't so much wrap them in cotton wool as smother them. She's counting the minutes till she can get away from him."

His aunt folded her lips into a grim line. "Terrified, is she? Not so terrified she thought to keep her legs closed!" Immediately ashamed, she strove to be fair. How did that old saying go? It takes two to tango. Well, it took two to make a baby too, which made them equally responsible. Not that there was any sense in apportioning blame, anyway. The baby was on its way and that was that. "Listen, John-Joe." She took him in her arms as if he were still the same small child she used to carry on her back and not the towering young giant he'd become. "Running away is not the way to play this. Far better to take the bull by the horns, than go skulking away like a thief in the night and losing all that's dear to you, as well as your self-respect. Oh, I know it seems right now that you've got the worries of the entire world on your shoulders, but one day it'll pass. I promise you that. It'll all blow over." Reaching up, she stroked a finger down along his cheekbone. "Stay here with your family, with the people who love you. Because, let me tell you, there's small comfort in strangers. Especially those across the water."

Regret filled his face. "Ah, I can't stay, Aunty Eileen, even if I wanted to. I promised Bernie we'd make a new life for ourselves. I can't let her down now."

"And what about letting your father down? And Nuala and Mary? What have they got to say about it?"

John-Joe's eyes slid away. "I haven't told them yet."

"But you will?" Eileen scanned his face. "You won't just go sneaking off, will you, John-Joe? You're better than that, aren't you? And heaven knows *they* deserve better." Especially poor Dick, whose wife had already deserted him, without so much as a goodbye or the courtesy of an explanation. How on earth would he cope if his only son did the same?

Something of her thoughts must have shown on her face because when John-Joe answered, his voice was strong again and his gaze direct. "No, I won't go sneaking off, Aunty Eileen. I will tell them. I just have to get things clear in my own mind first, okay?"

"Okay, but I won't pretend I'm happy about it. Still, if your mind is made up there's no more to be said, and I wish you and Bernie all the luck in the world and I'll light a candle it all works out for you."

As John-Joe gave a weak smile of thanks and headed for the door, Eileen called him back a moment, putting a restraining hand on his arm.

"And you'll be sure to come and say goodbye to Paddy and the girls too before you go?"

"Of course. That goes without saying." He covered her hand with his own. "I'll be round later tonight, and thanks, Aunty Eileen. You've been like a mother to me. Better than a mother. Better than mine, anyway." Gruff, he dropped a self-conscious kiss on her cheek then hurried for the door, his eyes suspiciously bright.

"And John-Joe," Eileen called urgently, possessed of a sudden fierce urge to pull him back and keep him by her side. "You will take care of yourself, won't you? You will be careful? Promise me."

"I promise," he said.

Behind him Eileen broke down and wept, while Bridget crept quietly in and placed a cup of tea before her – the first of countless cups administered that afternoon, each accompanied by vague comforting pats on the back.

"You're a good girl, Bridget," Eileen told her tearfully. "He'd have done a whole lot better if his eye had lighted on you, so he would."

If there was any consolation to be found at all in the day, it was that Madame Bovary – for reasons best known only to herself – left her well alone. No doubt, she had other fish to fry, other souls to torment, but for that small mercy at least Eileen was thankful.

CHAPTER FOURTEEN

Whipps Cross Hospital was a bundle of activity as Coral came on duty one evening. A passenger train had been derailed a few hours earlier and a fleet of ambulances were busy ferrying the victims to hospitals all over the city.

"You go over and work on A & E," Matron instructed her. "They have need of all hands on deck over there at the moment."

Her eyes ran approvingly over the young woman, crisply efficient in her navy and white striped probationer's uniform. Coral Browne was that rare thing, a born nurse, intelligent and willing, able to muck in where needed without making a song and dance. The patients loved her and even the notoriously difficult Mrs Goldstein over on Cavell Ward behaved herself for Coral. Matron only hoped she would stay the course and not throw it all up to go off and marry some fool of a man. She'd seen too many excellent nurses come to grief like that. Love! It was nothing but a big cod, designed to keep women firmly under the thumb. But not Gladys Thompson! Unconsciously adjusting her sizeable bosom, Matron disappeared back into her office, as, orders received, Coral hurried away down the corridor.

"God almighty, it's desperate in here." Noreen, who had also been despatched to casualty, greeted her at the door, her hands full of bloody bandages. "We've our work cut out for us tonight all right." She jerked her chin over her shoulder. "There's a load more just come in on stretchers. Why don't you start there, though it's already too late for some of the poor bastards." She shook her head in disgust. "Who'd be a nurse, I ask you!"

Wide-eyed with horror, Coral took in the carnage unfolding before her eyes, the throngs of wounded and walking wounded, all wailing and clamouring for attention and the doctors and nurses running around like headless chickens themselves.

"Here, nurse," a doctor beckoned imperiously, "come and give us a hand here." Pushing a drip bag into her hand, he motioned her to follow as his patient was wheeled urgently through to the operating theatre, blood splashing copiously from a wound in his side.

When she came back, Coral found herself running hither and yon, setting up drips, washing and bandaging wounds, administering advice and sympathy and where necessary covering up the dead. Occasionally she and a white-faced Noreen hurried past each other, with no time for more than an empathetic pat on the arm, or a shared look of mutual exhaustion.

It was past midnight before the last ambulance discharged its grisly load and things began to calm down. Hurrying over, Coral followed one of the stretchers into an empty bay on the ward, angling the light so that it shone full on the occupant's bruised and battered face.

"There now." Picking up a cloth, she leaned over and dabbed at the man's face, exerting pressure where a long cut just above his eye streamed blood. "You just hold on and the doctor will be with you in a minute. In the meantime, I'll make you as comfortable as I can."

Weakly, the man tried to push her hand away. "Look, don't bother with me. I'm all right." He struggled to sit up. "There's others far worse off – go and see to them first."

"Hush!" Gently she pushed him back. "Now you just lie down and don't you fret yourself. The others are all being seen to already, and that's a right nasty cut you've got on your head. You're going to need stitches in that. Tell me, do you hurt anywhere else?"

"All over," he told her, squinting with pain, "but it's nothing, just aches and pains. I don't think anything is broken. Experimentally, he moved both arms and legs, smiling wryly up at her through bloodied lips. "There's more than one will be sorry to learn that."

"Nonsense!" Stemming the blood, Coral, as a temporary measure, taped a clean bandage over his brow, then concentrated on wiping the rest of his face clean, dabbing the blood gently from around his mouth and eyes. "There now, that's much better" she said jokily. "You're beginning to look less like a pound of minced meat and more like a human being and – oh, good heavens!" Startled, she jumped back as his dark eyes swept over her. "It's you! You're that man from the Galtymore!" Despite herself, she started to shake.

"Aye. I'm surprised you recognise me. I recognised you at once!" A fine sheen of sweat started up on his brow as pain racketed suddenly through his entire body. "I didn't think you'd so much as glanced at me that night, though I couldn't take my eyes off you."

If only he knew! Flustered, Coral turned away to cover her confusion, her heart beating so hard she was convinced it would tear free of her body. "Let's not talk about it now – not while you're so ill. I – I'll just go and fetch the doctor."

"No. Don't go!" His hand came up, clamped her

wrist, put a bloody imprint on the skin. "Please, don't. Stay with me."

"She can't!" Noreen's voice dropped suddenly between them with all the force of an exploding bomb. "She's wanted somewhere else." There was steel in her voice, as she freed Coral's wrist from his grasp. "Go on, Coral. Matron is looking for you. I'll take over here."

"Coral . . ." The man looked longingly after her, as half-hesitating, she started to walk away. "What a beautiful name! And just right for her too. A delicate, fragile piece of coral!"

"Too delicate and fragile for the likes of you, Mick Devlin," Noreen snapped. "So you just keep your fancy poetic words and your mucky hands to yourself. Don't think because you've left Galway that you can walk away from your past, because your sins will always find you out. And, where Coral's concerned, rest assured, I've made damn sure of it." Seconds later found her running for the doctor, as with a groan the man fell back on the stretcher, blood spurting suddenly from his mouth.

"Before you start bawling, he's not dead!" Erupting into the locker room where Coral was changing out of her uniform, Noreen yawned cavernously, fanning her fingers in front of her mouth. "Mind you, it was touch and go for a while, but the devil looks after his own and so it looks like he'll make it after all."

Relief making her weak, Coral felt her knees suddenly give way and she groped for a nearby bench with nerveless fingers. "Oh, thank God," she said, sinking down and cradling her head between her hands. "Oh, thank God!"

"Well, there's no need to be so dramatic!" Noreen shrugged out of her own uniform and kicked it to one side. "It's not as if you even know him. Not *really*! I mean a couple of glances exchanged on a dance floor and a few words over a bloody face doesn't exactly add up to the romance of the decade. Besides it wasn't so long ago that you swore blind you'd no more interest in him than in the man in the moon." Reaching for her civvies, a mud-brown shirtwaister dress that did her absolutely no favours at all and flat brown lace-up brogues that only served to emphasise the thickness of her ankles, she raised a disdainful eyebrow. "Besides which, we're talking Mick Devlin here. Not Clark Gable. You know – Mick . . . Devlin . . ." she dragged out the name. "Who, lest you forget, was the one who killed that little child over in Galway and who, if it came down to a popularity vote between himself and Hitler, would undoubtedly end up coming in last."

"You don't think you might be guilty of judging him too harshly?" Coral felt her hackles rise.

Sometimes Noreen McDermott was far too opinionated for her own good. "After all there are always two sides to every story."

"Not in this case." Noreen stepped into her dress, yanked it up over her hips where it had a tendency to cling and began the lengthy process of fastening all the buttons. "One side is dead, remember? If I've told you once, I've told you a million times, forget Mick Devlin." Exasperated, she dragged the material across her ample bosom, forcing button and buttonhole into a gaping and tenuous alliance. "Even before all that business with the child, he had a terrible reputation. People don't accumulate the kind of wealth and power he has without stepping on a few bodies along the way. So do yourself a favour, go find yourself a nice doctor, why don't you? For God's sake, if I had half your looks, it wouldn't be Mick Devlin I'd be looking to, I can tell you. It would be to the highest in the land."

"Oh, I don't know why you're making such a big song and dance!" Getting to her feet, Coral, dressed only in her slip, angrily shook out her own uniform and hung it on a peg, pulling the front towards her the better to examine a stain on the collar. "Is it a crime now to enquire after a patient? Did they pass some by-law that makes it illegal? Is it forbidden to show a bit of concern for your fellow man?" Reaching for a pale blue jersey and a simple navy skirt, she tugged first one on and then the other, turning the skirt back to front in order to do up the zipper.

"And what about the other fifty or so poor souls all lying out there on stretchers or in the morgue?" Noreen pointed her chin towards the doorway. "Tell me, does your concern extend to them as well, or would that be going too far in the line of duty?" Squatting down awkwardly, she began to tie her shoelaces. "Oh, you can fool some of the people some of the time with your Florence Nightingale act, but you can't fool me! Don't forget, I saw your face earlier on when you thought that Mick Devlin was on his way to meet his Maker. Talk about wearing your heart on your sleeve!" Straightening up, she winced and held a hand to the small of her back, which, as always after a hard day's work, was stiff and aching. "If you've never listened to me before, Coral," she said, "listen to me now. Don't have any truck with that fella. Did you ever hear that old saying about never troubling trouble till trouble troubles you? Well, take it from me, that man is trouble with a capital T."

"Oh, that's just rubbish!" Coral spoke through a kirby-grip clenched between her teeth. "Anyone would think we were on our way up to the altar." Twisting up her hair at the back to form a loose chignon, she extracted the grip and stabbed it through the blonde roll. "Look, I admit he interests me and that I like him. But that's all, Noreen. It's not like I'm planning to run off to Gretna Green with him or anything."

"Oh, yeah?" Ever the cynic, Noreen raised her eyebrows. "Well, if it's interest you're after, go down and open a bank account. Long-term, it's a safer investment and will make you much happier." Picking up a hairbrush, she commenced dragging it through her own wiry hair, gave it up as a thankless task a moment later and stuffed it into an untidy bun. "Now, enough is enough and it's been a hell of a long day. What do you say we shake the dust of this place off our feet and go home?" With a roll of her shoulders, she gave herself a kind of all-over-loosening shiver. "Thank God, I'm off tomorrow and I can't wait to have a long lie-in. What about you? Are you off?"

Coral shook her head. "No. I'm on duty for the rest of the week. Although things have quietened down a bit now after the emergency, Matron felt it would be better to have as many people on call as possible. Especially as things have got a bit behind on Cavell. I'm surprised she's letting you off."

"She had no choice," Noreen scoffed. "Nothing comes between me and my day off." Sceptically, Noreen watched as, folding up her uniform, Coral prepared to take it home for washing. "Mind you, it's all very convenient for you, isn't it? I mean, you'll be right on hand to keep an eye on Devlin, once he's out of intensive and back on the ward."

"Oh, drop it, Noreen, can't you?" Flushing with annoyance, Coral busied herself tidying away her belongings. "Anyone would think you were jealous."

"Well, anyone would be wrong then, wouldn't they? But, fine! Fine! If that's what you think, I won't say another word, except on your own head be it!" Hurt, Noreen picked up her handbag and, rigid with indignation, stomped for the door.

"Oh, wait, Nore!" Coral picked up her own bag and hurried after her. "For heaven's sake! I didn't mean it like that."

"So, how are you feeling today? Better?" Having first ascertained that the coast was clear, Coral sat herself gingerly down on the side of Mick Devlin's bed. If Matron caught her, she'd have her up on the triple charges of sitting on a patient's bed, deserting her post, and what was almost worse, fraternising with a male patient.

"All the better for seeing you." Trying to smile, he ended up wincing instead as pain attacked him from all sides. "You're an angel, do you know that?"

"And you're a silver-tongued devil!" Coral, laughed off the compliment, but inside her heart had started singing. It was no good, she told herself. Noreen could warn her off as much as she liked, but the minute Coral looked into those eyes, stormy and black as midnight one minute, soft and clear as a rock pool the next, she was in over her head and drowning. "Are you comfortable," she asked, trying to cover her confusion with the brisk cloak of professionalism. "Is there anything I can get you?" Never mind that it wasn't her place to get him anything and that the other nurses were shooting her funny looks and whispering behind their hands.

"Just yourself," he said, his mellifluous Irish accent lapping over her and heating her blood like the sun on a warm summer's day. "You're all the tonic I need."

Coral dipped her head. "So, why didn't you ask me to dance?" There, the question was out! The question that had been nagging at her for months, ever since she'd first laid eyes on him, standing at the side of the dance floor, brooding darkly. "That night, at the Galtymore. Why didn't you ask me to dance?"

"*Would* you have danced with me?" He turned the question full circle.

"Maybe." A soft smile teased her lips and dimples came and went at the side of her cheeks. "Definitely."

"Even after your friend told you all about me?" A note of steel entered his voice. "Because I know she did. I know by the way you look at me that you know far more about me than I do about you."

"Well, I must say that's a bit of an assumption!" A flush covering her face, Coral plucked idly at the bed cover.

"Is it? Well, I'm sorry if I'm wrong, but it's just that I've got used to people talking about me and these days I tend to assume the worst. Besides, I recognised Noreen McDermott. I've had dealings with her family. More than that, I recognised the look of contempt on her face." He smiled, but without a trace of humour. "Then, when you went off together, it seemed pointless me staying around. It seems that where I'm concerned, the whole world thinks they can act as judge and jury." The words were without self-pity, more a statement of fact.

Gently, Coral took his hand. It was square and honest, used to hard work. "Isn't that what you did to me? Didn't you judge me, without trusting me to make up my own mind?"

"Would the verdict have been any different?" He issued her with a challenge, but left his hand in hers, squeezing her fingers gently. "People call me a murderer. Oh, not to my face. That would be biting the hand that feeds more than a few of them. But behind my back, or in little asides as I walk down the street. Often, they don't even have to say anything. It's there written all over their faces. There goes Devlin, the murderer! And I feel tainted, like I've got the mark of Cain on me." He struggled to sit up. "So, tell me, darling, would you have danced with a murderer? With everybody standing round and pointing the finger? Would you have danced with me all the same?"

"Shush!" Alarmed as he began to get agitated and worried about the attention they were attracting, Coral pushed him gently back down against the bed, smoothing her hand across his brow where thick black waves tumbled erratically onto the tanned skin, giving him an almost gypsy look. "Don't upset yourself or I won't be able to come and visit you any more. Not least because Matron will have given me the boot! Remember, you've only just come out of intensive."

"So, you will visit me again?" Exhausted, he lay back obediently, but there was urgency about his voice not lost on Coral. "Even after everything you know?"

Coral nodded. "I'll come and visit."

"Is that a promise? You won't let me down?"

"It's a promise!" she said, then surprising even herself, leaned over and kissed him lightly on the mouth, feeling a shock go through her entire system as their lips met.

"You're a fool, Coral Browne." Angrily, Noreen pushed her unfinished cup of tea away. "You're infatuated, that's what you are. You're infatuated with Mick Devlin because he's not like any other man you've ever met." She slapped the palm of her hand down flat on the table, startling other diners in the staff canteen and earning inquisitive looks. "But I've met his likes before, plenty of times. Big, rough, country Irishmen with film-star looks, who could charm the birds off the trees one minute and wring their necks the next. So you be careful he doesn't end up wringing your neck."

"He's not like that." Coral bit her lip. "He's good and he's kind and –"

"Don't tell me," Noreen cut her off. "He's in line for canonisation by the Pope." She furrowed her brow. "Tell me, are we talking about the same Mick Devlin here or a changeling the fairies have left in the night, because the one I know of is far from good and kind. The one I know would walk roughshod over anyone who got in his way. I'm telling you, Coral, that fella's wealth was built on other men's sweat."

"I never said he was a saint." Coral glared at her friend over the rim of her cup. "But then again, I don't know anybody who is. And, fair enough, so he drives a hard bargain. That's only good business, Noreen, not a crime. Nobody ever got to the top of the ladder by hanging on the bottom rung. Sometimes you have to stick your neck above the parapet, even if that makes you unpopular with other people."

"And sometimes people who stick their necks above the parapet get shot," Noreen sneered. "And sometimes people like Mick Devlin deserve to get shot!"

Sighing, Coral put down her cup and covered her eyes with her hands for a second. "Okay, let's take a slightly broader view here. *You* say Mick is hard and selfish and that his success is built on other men's labour. Another way of looking at it might be to say that Mick's drive and ambition has enabled those men to hang on to the coat-tails of his success. It's thanks to him that they have jobs to go to, that they can pay their rent and put food on their families' tables. But," grabbing her teaspoon, she rapped on the table as Noreen opened her mouth to interrupt, "as is often the case, some people don't like to be seen to be under a compliment and so they turn around and badmouth the good Samaritan."

"Good Samaritan!" Noreen began to cough and splutter in an exaggerated fashion. "Good Samaritan, my foot! My God, Coral you've really gone beyond the pale when you can mention Mick Devlin's name and the Good Samaritan in the same breath. Oh, it's true what they say! There's none so blind as those who will not see." Suddenly all humour left her face, leaving in its place a cold and cynical mask with two icy shards of glass for eyes. "And what about the child, Coral? Can you take a broader view there too?

Will you preach Good Samaritans to the parents as they kneel devastated beside their child's grave?"

Coral dropped her eyes. "We haven't talked about that yet. Well, not in any detail, anyway. I don't see it as my place."

"But you will? Please tell me you're not just going to skim over it?"

Coral nodded. "I will. When the time is right. When I'm ready and when he's ready. But I'm telling you now, Noreen, that whatever Mick and I discuss will be kept between the two of us and nobody else. And whatever I decide – whether I decide to go out with him or not – will be a decision made by me and me alone. And you're going to have to live with that."

Ostentatiously pushing her empty mug away, Noreen leant down and picked her handbag from the side of her chair. "Fair enough. I won't go wasting any more good breath on you. I've done my duty and there's no more I can do. I only hope that, at the end of the day, when you look at yourself in the mirror, you can say without shadow of a doubt that the decision you've made is the right one. Because *you're* going to have to live with that!"

CHAPTER FIFTEEN

It was dark down by Friar's Copse. John-Joe thought longingly of the many times he, his Uncle Paddy and his friend Cathal Power had traipsed this road with a pile of fresh timber hidden beneath an old tarpaulin in a wheelbarrow. If only he could turn back time this would be just such another night, instead of the night he had come to take his leave of the McNab family. He felt embarrassed about seeing Paddy, couldn't help but feel that he had let him down. It wasn't all that long ago that his uncle had codded him something rotten over Bernie. John-Joe could still see him in his mind's eye, clutching at his chest like a maniac and begging for a doctor. Even now, he couldn't suppress a smile at the sly dig. And little Rose would be heartbroken too. Just as his own father had been. John-Joe flinched at the memory of the shock on his face.

"But what about the farm, son?" Dick Brady had shaken his head at the enormity of John-Joe's news. "Every blessed furrow I ploughed, every blessed seed I planted, 'twas all for you. You can't just up and leave for England. Bring the lassie home, can't you? We're not so bad. We'll make her welcome – and the baby." But John-Joe *had* left, hardening his heart against the pleadings of the figure that, silhouetted in the light from the open doorway seemed suddenly so much smaller, so much frailer than the giant of a man who had towered over him as a boy. In those days, John-Joe truly believed that his father could put the whole world to rights. One hug, one wave from his large capable hands and what only moments before had seemed like a disaster, seemed suddenly as nothing, a mere blip blown out of all proportion. But not any more! There were some things even his father couldn't fix. And this was one of them!

Sharp needles of rain began to fall as he skirted round the back of Beehive Hall causing him to turn up his collar and bend his head down against it, so that when the man suddenly appeared from nowhere, gun cocked and at the ready, he was taken completely by surprise.

"Stop where you are, you bastard!"

Rooted to the spot, John-Joe gasped as a watery finger of moonlight parted the canopy of branches above and his aggressor's face, white as the negative of a photograph, became recognisable. "Dr – Dr McBride?" Catching in his throat, his voice barely made it past his lips. "Is – is that you?"

"Aye, it's me all right." McBride's voice was as loaded as the gun he pointed at John-Joe's head. "Bernie's father! You remember Bernie, don't you, the one you raped like she was some tuppeny-ha'penny little tinker off the side of the road, instead of a fine young woman with breeding and background? And a father that cares about her!"

"R-raped?" Horrified, John-Joe stuttered over the word. "Before God, Dr McBride, I never raped Bernie! I love her!" Instinctively backing away, he felt his shoulder come into sharp contact with a tree, dislodging a heavy splatter of raindrops that trailed icily down his face and neck with the caress of a ghostly hand.

"Love!" The word was an expletive, spat out in a great gobbet of disgust that landed at John-Joe's feet. "Love! Sure, what would a guttersnipe like you know about love – you, that was dragged up without even a mother? Poets and artists and writers know about love. Saints and scholars know about love." Angrily McBride moved forward, till he was no more than an arm's length away. "St Paul knew about love.

Love is patient. That's what he said. Love is kind. *Kind!* Did you hear that, Brady? It does not insist on its own way. That's what St Paul said about love. What you felt for my daughter was nothing like love. When you hauled her into a murky corner and defiled her innocence with your filthy hands, there was nothing patient about your actions, was there, boy? When you covered her innocent mouth with yours and filled her belly with your bastard seed, where was the kindness? Eh? There wasn't any! There was only you insisting on your own way. So don't you snivel to me about love, when all your type know about is lust. Lust! Carnal lust! One of the seven deadly sins!"

Terrified, John-Joe quailed back as little whiskey-flecked drops of spittle flew from the doctor's mouth and a sudden flash of silver moonlight showed up the red glint of madness in his eyes.

"But you'll not get away with it. As God is my witness. Or the devil will do just as well. No one's dragging my daughter down into the cesspit, spoiling her innocence and blighting her chances of a good life. I had high hopes for her. Do you hear me? High hopes. And I'll see you and all belonging to you dead and six feet under, before I'll see you draw her down into the mire with you." Despite the alcohol he had clearly consumed, his hand was rock-steady as raising the gun till it was on a level with John-Joe's temple he deliberately twisted it so that the metal bit cold, hard and menacing into the yielding flesh.

Shaking with fear, John-Joe felt himself lose all control of his bladder and a warm trickle of urine roll down his legs. Holding his hands up in surrender, he heard his voice come out sounding strangely far away, almost as if it belonged to someone else. "L-listen, Dr McBride, I know what we did was wrong and that we should have waited. But one thing led to another – ye – ye know how it is. We just got carried away." Even as the words left his mouth, he realised that far from making the situation better, he was simply digging his own grave. Still, fuelled by a mixture of terror and nerves, the words kept on coming, tripping over themselves in their haste to convince, succeeding only in infuriating the doctor further. "B–but that's not to say I don't love Bernie. B–because I do. I love her with all my heart and soul. And I respect her. Honest to God, I do. That's why we're going to England – to – to make a new life for ourselves. A fresh start. Her, me and the baby."

"One thing led to another, and you just got carried away!" Maniacally, the doctor began to laugh, his voice rampaging obscenely through the woods startling birds and small animals from their sleep and sending them into a panic of flutterings and chirpings. "One thing led to another and *you* couldn't stop yourself. *You* couldn't stop yourself from defiling my daughter and dragging her down into the gutter with you. Because you *love* her so much! And *respect* her so much! Well, Brady, if that's your definition of love and respect, the pair of us are singing from different hymn sheets." Pausing for a moment, he hawked deeply and spat on the ground. "As for going to England – you can get that idea right out of your head, because the only place you're going, my lad, is straight to hell!" Baring his teeth in the rictus of a grin, his eyes never wavered from John-Joe's. "So you'd better start saying your prayers."

High above, well hidden amongst the branches of a horse-chestnut tree, a poacher, who had taken refuge upon their approach, gazed down in horror as, below, young John-Joe Brady made a sudden bolt for his life and Dr McBride, cold and clinical as one of his own instruments, curled his finger round the trigger, turned and calmly shot him in the back. Then, walking over to the prone body, he kicked it savagely, and without a backward look spun round and walked briskly away. A few moments later there was the spluttering cough of a car starting up on the main road, the hurried squeal of tyres as it accelerated away, and then silence, deep and profound, falling over the Copse like a shroud. The birds and animals went back to sleep and soon only the moon kept vigil, shining its spotlight on the young man lying inert on the ground, a growing dark stain seeping into the ground around him. When he was certain the coast was clear, the poacher climbed down.

Sergeant O'Shea's initial inclination upon O'Leary's barging into the police station and dripping what he immediately took to be pheasant's blood all over the floor, had been to bang him in a cell and charge him with poaching. An hour later, watching the still form of John-Joe Brady being bundled into an ambulance, he was mighty glad he had decided to take his wild-eyed, garbled story seriously. Puffing out his chest importantly, he drifted into daydream mode. A case of this magnitude didn't come along often and if he played his cards right he might just get promoted out of this godforsaken place, maybe up to Dublin even. Yes, Dublin! He fancied that, up amongst the big boys, holding his own. He could just see himself, plain clothes, of course, flanking the President, the envy of his peers, carrying himself with just the right amount of gravitas. 'There goes O'Shea,' they'd say. 'The President's right-hand man!' Giving himself a little shake, he reluctantly turned towards the business in hand.

"Right, men! It's time to visit the good doctor, I think." Importantly, he heaved a body more corpulent than it had a right to be into the only motor vehicle his division possessed, leaving his men to follow on bicycles, Shanks's mare or whatever mode of transportation they could find. "Tis a nasty business, Jim!" he remarked with satisfaction to his second-in-command, who also doubled as driver. "Didn't I always say there was something fishy about McBride? It's all in the eyebrows, see?" Jim shook his head, indicating that he didn't in the least see. Sergeant O'Shea shifted beside him, so that his backside squealed against the polished leather and reaching back into the dim and distant past began, much to his second's bewilderment, to intone a rhyme he had learned at his mother's knee. *"Beware of the man whose eyebrows meet, for in his heart there lies deceit."* Backside and leather squealed again. "Now do you see?"

"Oh, I do, I do!" the driver assured him for fear that the Sergeant would rhyme at him again. *"Beware of the man –* oh, that's a good one all right! *For in his heart –* Jaysus!" Startled he broke off as the headlights picked out the white, spectral form of a young woman running straight down the middle of the road towards them. "Tis the banshee!" Jumping on the brakes, he brought the car to a screeching halt only inches away from the wildly waving wraith bearing down upon them.

"Yerrah, catch yourself on, man!" Scathing, the police sergeant dug his companion hard in the ribs, though truth to tell his own heart was beating a little more rapidly than was its wont. "'Tis only the young McBride one! What's her name? Breda? No, Bernie!"

Desperately the girl clawed at the car door as it skidded to a stop. "Oh, help me! Please! Help me. Daddy's lost his mind and is trying to kill me. Ooh, quick let me in. *Please*! Let me in." Scrabbling all the while at the door handle, she glanced frantically back over her shoulder for signs that she was being pursued, almost losing her balance as the door swung suddenly open and she tumbled in.

"Shush now. You're all right!" Valiantly removing his jacket, Sergeant O'Shea twisted round and handed it to her, as dressed only in some sort of a long white shift thing that was saturated by the rain, she sat sobbing and shaking like a leaf, trying to make herself as small as possible in the back of the car. "No one's going to harm you. Do you hear me? It would take some man to get past me and Jim here, so it would. Not even the bould Fionn Mac Cumhaill could get past the two of us. Isn't that right, Jim?" As Jim nodded in an unconvinced kind of way, the policeman patted her on the knee. "So you can rest assured on that score. Now," he took a deep breath, "what's all this about your father?"

Pulling the jacket tightly about her shoulders, the girl strove hard to speak against the chattering of her teeth. "It's the baby, see?" Thanks to the poacher,

---

Emily Sage

Sergeant O'Shea *did* see. "He wants to take it out of me, and I'm so frightened."

"What?" Shaken to the core, Sergeant O'Shea rocked back, his eyes almost starting from his head. "Abort it, do you mean? Sure that's a sin! That goes against the whole of the Catholic Church. He wouldn't do that."

"He would." The young woman nodded frantically, tears mingling with the rain on her skin. "He did it to Mammy. That's how she died! And now he wants to do it to me, too."

"What! Ah, no love," Sergeant O'Shea shook his head in denial. "You've got it all wrong. Your mother died from a miscarriage, God rest her soul. Don't I remember it well? We were all stunned by it. Such a lovely woman, too. As lovely a woman as could be found anywhere in all of Ireland. It was tragic. Tragic, what happened to her. But then miscarriages are not that uncommon. Even though they have penicillin now," he added irrelevantly.

"Listen to me!" Bernie's eyes glittered with anger, the words issuing from between her lips in a series of small explosions. "She did not have a miscarriage. *He* killed her taking the baby out of her, because it wasn't his." Her face contorted, became at once both frightened and defiant. "She had an affair, you see!" Furiously she knuckled her eyes. "He went mad when he found out, and when she told him about the

Sunshine & Shadows

baby, he was fit to be tied. He ranted and raved and demanded to know who the father was. But she didn't tell him. She didn't tell anyone. It was a secret she carried to her grave." She jerked her head in the direction from which she had run. "I'm telling you, Sergeant O'Shea, he killed her all right, and now he wants to kill me." Terrified, her voice crescendoed into the wail of the frightened child who, mopping feverishly at her mother's brow, had tried in vain to bargain with death. But death had held all the winning cards and gradually her mother's face had taken on the bleached white of the sheets, and the sheets had turned rust-red with her blood. "I'm not going back inside. I'm not! I'm not! You can't make me!"

Without being asked, the driver started up the engine again, nosing the big black Anglia towards McBride's house as, way out of his depth, the sergeant attempted to soothe the terrified girl.

"Shush now." More shaken than he would admit to, he struggled to keep his voice level. "Nobody is going to make you do anything you don't want to do. You just stay in the car with Jim there, while I go and have a word with your father!"

Hesitantly the policeman climbed out of the car, praying that he would still make Dublin. A situation like this was a first for him. Petty thieves, drunks, lunatics even, were all in a day's work, but murdering doctors, now that was a horse of a different colour. Still, he thought, adjusting his peaked hat, there was nothing for it but to bite the bullet – he wished immediately that he had stumbled upon a happier figure of speech. Turning his back on the occupants of the car, he sketched a furtive Sign of the Cross, approached the door and rapped tentatively with the smart, brass knocker shaped like a Celtic harp. To his surprise and dismay it opened almost immediately to reveal the doctor, dressing-gowned and possessed both of a glass of port and a superior attitude guaranteed to get right up the sergeant's nose.

"Ah, Sergeant O'Shea." He raised his glass in a mock salute. "And to what do I owe the honour? Is it business or just a social call?"

Relieved to see there was no sign of a gun about the other man's person, the policeman took a step forward. "I would have thought, sir, that you might have been expecting me."

"Expecting you?" The doctor's face took on a puzzled expression, then cleared as he spied his daughter's white face peering fearfully through the window of the police car outside. "Ah, I see. Bernie!" He gave an exaggerated sigh. "Thanks for bringing her back. I hope she didn't put you to too much trouble." Shrugging his shoulders, he smiled at Sergeant O'Shea in an all-boys-together sort of way. "Women, eh! We had a bit of an argument earlier –

nothing serious, but the next thing I know she's ranting and raving and racing off into the night like a madwoman." He took a sip of his drink. "Ah well, fathers and daughters, you know how it is."

"No, I don't know how it is, Dr McBride." Taking off his hat, the sergeant made a big production out of scratching his head. "The Good Lord never blessed me with children of my own. So, why don't you tell me how it is and why a father would let his daughter run off in her shift on a night like this while he stayed safe by his fire with a glass in his hand? Oh, and while you're about it, maybe you can fill me in John-Joe Brady as well."

"John-Joe Brady?" If the doctor was rattled, he certainly didn't show it. Instead his brow corrugated into a frown of contemplation. "John-Joe Brady. That's Dick Brady's son, isn't it?" He gave a little shake of his head. "The poor man whose wife ran out on him years ago and left him with John-Joe and a couple of young lasses too. Well, what about him?"

Oh, he was cool customer right enough, Sergeant O'Shea thought, watching the little pantomime. You had to admire the gall of the man, standing there all got up like Little Lord Fauntleroy's father and making out like he was innocent and pure as the driven snow.

"What about him? Oh, what about him indeed!" The bit, rather than the bullet, between his teeth, the policeman moved swiftly in for the kill. "Now don't play me for a fool, McBride! I was in long trousers before ever you'd graduated from your mother's knee. There was a witness, see? A poacher! Maybe you know him? Goes by the name of O'Leary." The sergeant almost began to enjoy himself, as the other man's face paled perceptibly beneath the light from the lantern hanging over the door and he staggered a little uncertainly on his feet. "And there he was, hidden up a tree in Friar's Copse – tonight." With impeccable timing, he delivered his *coup de grace*. "Heard everything, so he did! Aye, and saw everything too, right down to you pulling the trigger and lashing out at the poor lad with your boot as you walked away!"

"Well now, Sergeant O'Shea, is that all the ammunition you've got in your armoury?" Making a swift recovery, the doctor laughed, the scornful laugh of a man who is sure of his place in society, the kind of laugh that wrong-footed Sergeant O'Shea and reduced him in his own mind to the lowly position of raw recruit. "Do you mean to tell me you'd take the word of some common thief, who was probably three sheets to the wind anyway, if my experience of O'Leary is anything to go by, over mine?" The doctor shook his head as if he could hardly believe it. "I can assure you, Sergeant O'Shea, I have been indoors all evening writing up my notes and nowhere near Friar's Copse." Assuming an expression of even greater hauteur, he shooed his free hand at the policeman. "Now, be off with you, man, before I lose my temper altogether and have you drummed out of the force as a disgrace to your uniform. By God, but it's a sad day, that has the constabulary turning up at my doorstep making wild accusations."

"I'll do better than take O'Leary's word, McBride." Remarkably, because his immediate instinct was to smash the other man in the mouth, the sergeant managed to keep his composure. "How about if I take young Brady's word? Because, he's not dead, you know. Even though you shot him in the back like the yellow-bellied coward you are. He's not dead." He batted his hat against his thigh. It gave him something to do with his hands and prevented him from striking out. "And staying on the subject of words, what about your daughter's word – or would you make a liar out of her as well? You see, Bernie maintains you tried to kill her. In fact," he paused for dramatic effect, "she said that you had already killed her mother. *Killed . . . her . . . mother*"! He repeated the last words, drawing them out slowly and with emphasis. "Now I don't have to tell you, that that's a very serious charge. Because that would be murder. *Murder!*" Replacing his hat, he began to use his fingers as an abacus, ticking off the charges one by one. "Now let's see, so far, that's one charge of murder we have and one, *two* charges of *attempted* murder, one of which has resulted in grievous bodily harm. And, of course, if young Brady dies, that would be, oh glory be, *two* charges of murder!" Menacing, he brought his face close to the other's, could smell a mixture of port-wine and fear emanating off him in waves. "So what do you have to say to that? Eh? What have you got to say to that?"

All pretence suddenly falling away, Dr McBride's face twisted into a mask of such savagery, such hatred, that the sergeant stepped hastily back and felt for his baton. "I say, I should have stayed there and finished the job! I should have stayed there and finished him off like the dog he is!" He jerked his chin towards the police car where his daughter sat, the white moon of her face pressed eerily against the window. "He got my daughter pregnant, Sergeant. Pregnant! Like she was some little trollop he picked up! And for that he had to pay the price." Slipping from his hand, the glass shattered on the ground, the contents pooling in a patch of ruby blood at their feet. "And the wages of sin, Sergeant O'Shea, shall be death!"

"And what about poor Bernie? Your own daughter. Was she destined to pay the wages of sin, as well?"

"No! No! No!" Violently, the doctor shook his

head from side to side. "I never wanted to harm my daughter. I only wanted to save her, to make her pure again, to give her back her life, her future. That *he* snatched away." The fury went out of his face, was replaced by an expression of enormous sadness that pleated his face into folds, adding ten years to his age. "And the only way I could do that was to kill him and to take that – that *thing* out of her." Wryly his lip curled. "I suppose you could say, I was doing a Canute on it, Sergeant. I was trying to turn back the tide."

"That *thing*?" Neither knowing or caring who the hell Canute was, the sergeant stared at him in disgust. "That *thing*? By which you mean the baby, I suppose."

Unapologetic, the doctor stared unblinkingly back. "Yes, that *thing*. That *thing* that was going to blight her life. That aberration that should never have been. That *thing* that was forced on her by that scum, Brady." He drew a deep ragged breath. "Before God, I'm glad I shot the bastard."

Behind them a faint click signalled the opening of the car door. There was a faint stirring of grass beneath bare feet, the sighing of a white robe trailing wetly across the ground and a moment later Bernie's stood there, looking from one to the other.

"Shot?" she asked fearfully. "Who's shot? What are you talking about?" And then as the terrible truth dawned, her mouth opened in a scream. "Oh, no, not John-Joe! Oh, God no, not John-Joe!" Grabbing hold of Sergeant O'Shea's lapels, she shook him till his teeth rattled. "Please! Please! Please! Tell me it's not John-Joe!"

"I'm sorry, Bernie." Awkwardly, the policeman held her away. "He was shot earlier this evening. Gunned down like a dog in Friar's Copse. I'm afraid it's too early yet to say whether he'll make it. He's lost an awful lot of blood."

"No! No! He can't die!" She wailed. "We're going to England tomorrow! To start a new life!"

Passing a weary hand across his brow, Sergeant O'Shea patted her gently on the arm. "I'm sorry, love, but poor John-Joe won't be going anywhere tomorrow." Pityingly he watched as, turning aside, she vomited into the grass, heaving and retching until her stomach could take no more and she fell to her knees, his heavy tunic slipping from her shoulders.

"Aw, Bernie . . ." All the arrogance gone out of him, the doctor moved to her side, sank to his own knees and attempted to draw her into his arms. "I did it for you, love. Don't you see? I did it for you!"

Lashing out, Bernie clawed at him, her nails scoring deep red tracks all down his face. "Get away from me!" Her voice was filled with hate. "I hate you! Do you hear me? I hate you! I hate you for what you did to John-Joe and for what you did to me!" She spat straight into his eyes, watched dispassionately as the spittle mingled with the rain, rolling down his cheeks like tears. "And I *hate* you for what you did to Mammy."

Not even attempting to wipe his face, he pleaded for understanding. "That was an accident, Bernie. A mistake. I never wanted to hurt your mother. I worshipped the ground she walked on."

"Oh, don't give me that!" Scrabbling to her feet, Bernie snarled down at him, her lips peeled back, teeth bared as if she would rip him to pieces like a she-wolf. "You hectored and bullied her every day of your married life. Don't make the mistake of thinking I was too young to remember. I remember it all. Everything: the shouting, the slaps, the way you disapproved of everything from the way she spoke to the way she dressed. You had more of a kind word for your old dog than you had for her. Small wonder if she sought comfort in someone else's arms." Her mouth twisted. "I only hope to God she enjoyed it."

Penitent, he stayed on his knees before her, a far cry from the proud and lofty figure of only a few minutes earlier. "Anything I did, Bernie, I did for love. For love of your mother. For love of you." He held out his hands, palms up, almost in supplication. "I did it for love, Bernie. Don't condemn me for that."

"And that makes it all right, does it?" Bernie

recoiled as from a venomous snake as he shuffled towards her. "Couple any crime in the world along with the word love and that somehow makes it all right, does it? Well, I've got news for you, Father, it doesn't." And then to his utter mortification, she quoted the words of St Paul at him, the very words he, himself, had quoted earlier at young Brady out there in Friar's Copse, with the rain beating a tattoo on the trees and ground and the wind lamenting in the branches. "Love is kind. *Kind!* What you did wasn't kind. What you did was wicked and evil and I only hope and pray you get what's coming to you. I hope and pray you rot in jail for the rest of your miserable life!"

Gratefully conscious of the sounds of reinforcements arriving, Sergeant O'Shea gruffly cleared his throat and, placing his hands on Bernie's shoulders, gently moved her to one side. "I think you'd better accompany me to the station, Dr McBride." Rummaging in his pockets he produced a pair of handcuffs, with a flourish, much as a magician might produce a dove, but jumping to his feet, the doctor nimbly side-stepped him, dashed into the house and slammed the door behind him.

"I'll accompany no man!" he called. "My account is to my Maker and only unto Him!"

Sergeant O'Shea was quick to understand the implication of that statement. "Now look here,

McBride," futilely he hammered on the door, "don't go doing anything stupid! I'm sure we can sort everything out down at the station. You wouldn't want to leave your daughter with a worse legacy than she's got to bear already, would you? And little Majella?" For the first time he remembered the doctor's youngest daughter. What age was she? Ten? Eleven? She must be in her bed. Pray God she would stay sleeping soundly and be spared these horrors.

A few moments later, the sharp report of a revolver discharged its deadly load, for a second time that night.

CHAPTER 16

Eileen couldn't seem to settle as she waited for John-Joe to open the latch and let himself in as he always did. An apple-tart, baked in his honour, and a batch of scones stood cooling on the table. She had made extra knowing he might be grateful for a bite to eat on the long journey ahead of him the following day and guessing that his sisters and father would be far too upset to think of such matters. Picking up on her mood, Larkin rose from his favourite place under the dresser and went to stand by the door where he commenced whimpering and scratching at the doorframe.

"What in the name of God is ailing you?" Paddy asked, leaving down a book he was reading and rising to open the door, only for the dog to scuttle back under the dresser again like Beelzebub himself was after him.

"The same thing that's ailing me, I suppose," Eileen answered for him. "I just can't seem to settle, Paddy. What do you think is keeping John-Joe?"

"Yerrah, he'll be taking his leave down in O'Dwyer's no doubt, and finding it hard to get away." Paddy was sarcastic. "Sure the only time they want to know you round here is when they're getting shut of you."

Gazing out the rain-spattered window, eyes trying to penetrate the thick, damp, darkness, Eileen shook her head. "No! There's something wrong. I've got a feeling . . ." Her gaze veered across the room. "And so has Larkin, haven't you, boy?" Whimpering his agreement, Larkin's tail swished back and forth, thumping against the floor like a half-hearted metronome.

Knowing better than to dismiss Eileen's 'feelings', Paddy threw her an anxious look. Over the years he had come both to respect and fear them. It was a known fact that some people had an extra sense, and he had no doubt but that Eileen was one of them. Sure hadn't she one of her feelings the night her own mother died, as hale and hearty a woman as ever drew breath and who to all intents and purposes seemed as sprightly as a spring chicken. He remembered how, unable to sleep that night, she had got up and walked the floor, stopping every now and again in front of the picture of the Sacred Heart with the little red lamp burning in front of it. At half-past five she had stopped her pacing, and with the tears streaming down her face had turned to him. "Mammy's dead!" she'd said and a chill had curled itself all the way from the roots of his hair down along his spine. Within an hour, Father Clarke called round and confirmed the news.

She'd been restless the day Liam died too, had been out of sorts for a whole week beforehand.

"Something's going to happen," she'd told him more than once. "I feel like there's a big black cloud pressing down on me and it'll only lift when whatever it is passes." Tragically, the big, black cloud had heralded the death of their only son. And now Eileen had yet another of her 'feelings'.

"Dear God," Paddy whispered, his own gaze straying over to the Sacred Heart, "let her be wrong this time. Please, let her be wrong!"

Not five minutes later, when there was a knock at the door, Paddy knew, with a sinking of his heart, that his wife was right yet again.

"Come in, Sergeant O'Shea." Eileen had the door open while the policeman's hand was still raised. The words fuelled with anxiety tumbled out of her. "It's John-Joe, isn't it? Something has happened to him. I know something must have happened to him, because we were expecting him ages ago." She held out her hands, let them drop helplessly again. "And it's not like him to be late, is it, Paddy? It's just not like him."

Wishing he was anywhere else but there, the sergeant cleared his throat. "Yes, I'm afraid it is about the lad, Mrs McNab."

Stepping back, Eileen ushered him in, though part of her wanted to push him back out again and slam the door, as if by so doing she could negate the bad news so clearly written over his face.

It wasn't so very long ago, the guard mused, as he refused the chair Eileen automatically pulled out, that he had been called upon to witness the couple's heartbreak and grief at the death of their young son under the wheels of Devlin's truck. Now, the thankless bitch that was Fate had placed him in almost identical circumstances, and all thoughts of Dublin and promotion were very far away as with every word he uttered, he watched the life drain from their eyes till only a flat grey vista of hopelessness remained. Outside, in sudden fury, the rain whipped itself into a frenzy and the wind gathered breath, howling in jealous competition and frightening the children from their bed. Now they stood peering around the curtain, perfectly still, three little ghosts, gazing with anxious faces at the little tableau of adults gathered there.

"What's wrong, Mammy?" Mollie plucked nervously at the sleeve of her nightdress. "Why's Sergeant O'Shea here? Is something wrong?"

Unable to answer, Eileen gazed on her eldest daughter as she stood with the light of the oil-lamp picking out the filaments of sun Paddy swore were caught in her hair. Mutely she held out her arms in a gesture that took in all three girls, who immediately ran into their protective circle. Then slowly, falteringly, she told them about John-Joe.

"He's not dead," she repeated at the end, more to convince herself than them. "He's not dead, but he's in a bad way. So we must all pray very hard for a miracle."

"I hate John-Joe!" Rose announced loudly into the shocked void Eileen's voice had left behind. "He said he was only practising on that McBride one, till I was grown up!" A great tear slid like a silver snail-track down her cheeks. "He'll never marry me now, Mammy, will he?"

"Don't be stupid –" Daisy began, then stopped abruptly, quelled by a look from her mother.

"I don't know, pet," Eileen said softly, stroking a black curl away the little girl's brow. "It's in God's hands now. Like I said, we can only pray."

In the wake of the tragedy everybody was very kind,

both to John-Joe's father and sisters and to the McNabs. Neighbours rallied round with offers of lifts to the hospital or whatever help they could give and Paddy and Eileen thanked them, whilst guiltily wishing that they would all just go away and leave them in peace.

The 'incident' was reported in all the newspapers, even the big nationals. Sergeant O'Shea had his picture taken and was on the front of the *Irish Independent*. Rumour had it that he was in line for a big promotion, maybe even up to Dublin, and the local begrudgers declared that there was "no houlding him any more" and "sure he doesn't recognise the sow now, and he the runt of the litter".

From behind her window, Coral Devlin watched sadly, wishing she too could do something to help, knowing better than to offer, especially as this new tragedy would undoubtedly have brought back all the old reminders of little Liam. Especially if John-Joe died.

And ever more frequently she brooded on the choices she had made that had brought her to this pass . . .

CHAPTER SEVENTEEN

"Gone? What do you mean, gone?" Aghast, Coral eyed the young nurse who, a blanket clutched in her hands, stood eying her curiously by the empty bed.

"Exactly what I said. He's gone, and bloody good riddance is what I say." Tossing the blanket to the floor, she energetically began yanking the remaining covers off. "Talk about difficult. Some people have no gratitude. I wasn't sorry to see the back of him, I can tell you."

"Well, some people are better at giving orders than taking them," Coral remarked, feeling compelled to defend Mick Devlin from this tight-lipped young woman oozing disapproval from her every pore. "And I expect it's not easy lying helpless in bed all day, when you've been used to calling the shots."

"Lying in bed all day? Just give me the chance!" Slyly her eyes played over Coral. "I've seen you before, haven't I? Up on Cavell, working with all those old geriatrics?" She shuddered, gave a little grimace. "I don't know how you do it."

"Somebody has to," Coral struggled to keep her voice calm. "Besides, being old is not a crime. But, being heartless – now, that should be made a hanging offence."

The other woman bridled. "Oooh, listen to you, Miss Lah-di-dah. So who died and made you the Lady of the Lamp?" Mocking, she nodded towards the empty bed. "Not that old Flo would have approved of you fraternising with the male patients. By all accounts she was dead set against that kind of thing."

Annoyed, Coral bit her lip. "I'm not fraternising with anybody. Mick Devlin is a friend of mine. That's all." Even to herself, the words sounded weak and unconvincing, butterflies without wings, and as if to underscore her own disbelief, the other nurse gave a disparaging snort.

"Hmmph! Obviously not such a good friend that he told you he was discharging himself. Against doctor's orders too!" Reaching into a large laundry basket to one side of her, she pulled out a freshly laundered sheet, unfolded it and threw it across the bed, then lay half across it, lifted one corner of the mattress and tucked the sheet underneath. Straightening up, she smoothed the bed with clockwise sweeps of her palm. "Mind you, he was a popular one with the ladies, though I can't for the life of me understand why. Now me, I like my men biddable. That one was far too into having his own way. You just had to look at him to know that life with him would be more snakes than ladders." Making her way to the other end of the bed, she went through the same routine again, lifting a corner of the mattress, slipping the sheet underneath, then straightening and smoothing, in a series of flawlessly orchestrated movements. "Still, each to their own and like I said, he was a popular one for the ladies, especially, it seems, the ones from Cavell ward." She tossed her head at Coral. "That's right, there was another one of your lot down earlier. Seems like you might have competition."

Her heart suddenly beating hammer and tongs, Coral tried hard to sound casual. "Oh really? Who was that, do you know?"

"No idea. She had red hair, though. And she was a bit overweight – you know the type – behind a reinforced door when the looks were given out." Stepping back, the nurse admired her handiwork, tugged at a rogue wrinkle, picked up the pillow and plumped it vigorously. "Sounded to me like they were having some sort of quarrel, a lover's tiff maybe. In any case, there was a bit of a heated discussion, voices raised and all that, and no sooner had she left than he upped and went too – discharged himself without so much as a by your leave. And, like I said before, good bloody riddance to bad rubbish!" She looked pointedly at Coral. "Now unless there's something else I can help you with, *some* of us have work to be getting on with!"

"Oh, yes, of course. Sorry!" Frowning, Coral turned way. Noreen! It could only have been Noreen. But what on earth had they argued about? And why on earth hadn't she said anything about it? Well, there was only one way to find out and that was to ask her.

Noreen was in the sluice room cleaning bedpans, a punishment assigned to her by Matron for being in gross dereliction of her duties earlier and disappearing unauthorised from the ward. Not that she seemed the least bit bothered, Coral observed cynically, coming quietly in behind her, as humming some tune off the radio she scrubbed and scoured, dried and polished, lining the bedpans up on the shelf above the sink like china ornaments on a Welsh dresser.

"Oh!" She gave a little jump as she became aware of Coral's presence and, for a moment, Coral fancied she saw just the merest flicker of something in her eyes. Wariness? Guilt? "How long have you been standing there?"

"Not long," Coral said, forcing herself to stay calm although inside she was seething with barely suppressed anger. How dare she stand there looking as if butter wouldn't melt in her mouth when, undoubtedly, she had been the cause of Mick discharging himself from the hospital? Wrinkling her nose against the strong smell of disinfectant, she gestured vaguely. "So, you're on bedpan duty. How come?"

Shrugging, Noreen picked up another pan and flushed the noxious contents down the toilet. "Why not me? As Matron says, we can't all be Queen Elizabeth sitting above in her palace with servants waiting on her hand and foot. Somebody has to play donkey."

"Yes, but it's usually an auxiliary unless, of course, Matron is punishing you for something." She raised an eyebrow. "So, is Matron punishing you? Come on, Noreen, spit it out. What have you done?"

It seemed to Coral that the other girl flushed a little, her already naturally high colour turning a darker pink that contrasted ill with the orange freckles spattering her face. "Nothing, really. I left the ward for a few minutes, if you must know, and herself wasn't too pleased. It's no big deal."

"Why?" Coral moved closer, the better to look into Noreen's eyes, because eyes, she'd heard, were the windows to the soul and she needed to know the truth, even knowing as she did that the truth would hurt. "Why did you leave the ward? Where did you go?"

With a nervous laugh, totally out of character for her, Noreen clicked her heels together and placed one soapy finger horizontally between her upper lip and nose to simulate Hitler's moustache. *"Gott in Himmel, Fräulein!* So many questions!"

Coral didn't laugh. "Where did you go?" she asked again in a deliberately measured way, and this time there was no mistaking the cold steel coating each word.

"Oh, I think you already know." Noreen immediately dropped the clowning. "Why else would you be standing there with a face on you like a slapped backside?"

A sick rage beginning to build inside her, Coral ignored the insult. "You're right. I do know. So what happened? What did you say that would make a seriously injured man discharge himself from hospital?" Her hands clenched themselves into claws. "If anything happens to him, it'll be on your conscience, you know."

"I'll sleep easy," Noreen snapped. "Besides, bad things don't happen to the likes of him. If I've said it once, I've said it a hundred times: the devil looks after his own. That Mick Devlin has a charmed life and will see us all down."

"Oh, come on, Noreen!" Coral's eyes flashed fire.

"What exactly did you say to him? Tell me . . . please!"

With a deep sigh, the other woman picked up a towel, dried her hands on it, then tossed it to one side. "Fine, have it your way! But I want you to bear in mind that whatever I did, I did for you. For your own good. Because, when it comes to Mick Devlin, you're blind, deaf and dumb and, if that's what love does to you, I'd sooner take the veil and seclude myself in a convent for the rest of my life."

"Oh, cut the sermon, Noreen! What happened?"

"I told him you were already engaged to be married." Hand on hips, Noreen went into battle stance. "I told him you had a lovely fella that was crazy about you and that you were crazy about." Defiant, her chin came up. "I said he shouldn't mistake your kindness for interest and that he was becoming an embarrassment and a nuisance and that you couldn't wait to see the back of him." She gave a satisfied nod. "And, of course, his pride couldn't take that. Honest to God, I've never seen anyone's face change so much in a split second. He looked like he'd been shot."

"Oh, Lord!" As the full effects of Noreen's words sank home, Coral felt her head start to spin and her pulse to race. "You didn't, Noreen! Please tell me you didn't!" She could hear the panic in her own voice.

"I did." Unrepentant, Noreen turned back to the bedpans, picked one up and threw it into the sink with a clatter. "And do you know what, it's a measure of how low the man is that he didn't even wait to check it from your own lips. Oh, no, as soon as his dignity took a knock, he was up from his bed like Lazarus and bolting for the door. And good bloody riddance to him!" she snarled, echoing the words of the other nurse.

Distraught, Coral drew a hand through her hair, pushing the hat balanced on it to a rakish angle guaranteed to bring the full brunt of Matron's wrath down around her ears. "I don't understand what you've got against him. I really don't." She spread her hands in appeal. "Okay, so he's a tough businessman who might not always watch his P's and Q's when it comes to his workmen. And yes, more seriously, he was involved in a road accident. But he's not the first and he won't be the last, and I'm sure he never set out deliberately to harm that little child. Neither of those things makes him a bad person, Noreen." She narrowed her eyes. "There must be more to this than you're letting on."

"Believe what you want!" Exasperated, Noreen hunched her shoulders. "Just don't come running to me when you're supping sorrow with a long spoon. That's all."

"Oh, leave the old sayings to your granny!" Coral snapped. "They're beginning to bore me. Just tell me where he's gone."

"How the hell would I know? Back to Ireland, I expect. He's probably catching the boat train to

Fishguard, as we speak. Hey, where are you going?" she yelled, as spinning on her heel suddenly, Coral dashed out of the room, almost flooring Matron as she came thundering along to find the source of the raised voices.

Reaching out, she grabbed Coral by the arm as she flew by, jerking her to a halt. "And just where do you think you're tearing off to, madam, with a whole ward full of patients waiting?"

"To get married," Coral yelled, fighting her way clear with difficulty and pelting off down the corridor. "To get married. Oh, and here, you can keep this! It might scare the sheep where I'm going!" Pausing for a moment, she pulled off her cap, and tossed it back over her shoulder, like a bride with her wedding bouquet.

"I don't know why I bother," Matron said, turning to Noreen in disgust. "You spend all your time training them up and just when they get to the stage where they might actually be a bit of use, they throw it all up to go off to be unpaid servants to some useless article of a man!" Clicking her teeth, she raked Noreen with a look. "Thank God, we're not all born beauties or there'd be nobody left to run the hospitals."

"Thank God, indeed!" Noreen agreed, returning the look with interest. "At least we can all rest easy, knowing the future is safe in your hands, Matron."

CHAPTER EIGHTEEN

"Will he be all right, doctor?" Anxious, Eileen scanned the doctor's face as he emerged from the hospital room. Behind her, John-Joe's father Dick, his sisters Nuala and Mary and Bernie McBride huddled white-faced on the benches that lined the corridor. "He will live, won't he?"

His face seamed with tiredness, the doctor bent a look that encompassed them all. "It's early days yet, but let's just say he's holding his own." Checking his watch, he frowned at the time. "He's young and he's strong and those two things alone give him a fighting chance."

"Can we see him?" Dick asked, his own eyes glazed both with exhaustion and grief and looking as if he had aged a good twenty years overnight.

"Just for a minute," the doctor agreed. "But you'll

have to take it in turns and be very very quiet. He needs peace and quiet now and plenty of it." His gaze veered over to where Bernie was sobbing uncontrollably, her face buried in her cupped hands. "So none of that carry-on, young lady. I know you're upset, but crying won't do any good at this stage. You'll have to be brave now. Do you hear me?"

"She'll be fine." Eileen put her arms around the weeping girl. "You go first, Dick, and then you two girls." She nodded at Mary and Nuala. "And mind what the doctor said. He's not to be disturbed. There now," she turned her attention to Bernie. "Calm down, love. All that upset is not good for the baby."

"I can't help it!" Bernie turned a face tragic in its grief to her. "I love him, Mrs McNab. I really love him and if – if he dies, I don't know how I'll bear it."

"Now listen here to me, Bernie." Taking a handkerchief out of her handbag, Eileen held it to the girl's nose, letting her blow into it as if she was a young child. "John-Joe will be okay. I've got a good feeling about it. Like the doctor said, he's young and he's strong and added to that he's got a family who worship the ground he walks on, not to mention you and the baby." Taking strength from her own words, she gave a watery smile. "So you see, everything will be all right." Reaching out, she gently patted Bernie's still-flat stomach. "And before you know it, John-Joe will be up and about and running around playing football with this little one here."

"Do you really think so?" Behind her tears, Bernie's face lit up, highlighting the fragile beauty that had so ensnared John-Joe, the creamy skin and expressive eyes of a shade somewhere between lilac and lavender and the full soft, almost childish mouth that trembled as she spoke to Eileen. "Oh, I do hope you're right." Shyly, she touched her own stomach. "More than anything, I want this little one to have a proper father. Someone to play with him and tell him stories and kiss him better when he falls over and grazes his knee. I want him to have a father who'll say his prayers with him at night and who'll be happy to leave a light on if he's scared and chase the ghosties out from under the bed and from inside the wardrobe." Intent on her vision, she nodded fervently. "I want him to have a father who'll tell him how special he is every single day of his life and who won't criticise him for the slightest little thing and make him feel a failure." She drew in her breath on a sob. "And I never, never want my child to be frightened of his own father!"

"The way you and your sister were?" Eileen's own eyes misted over. "It's true what they say about no one knowing what goes on behind closed doors. If you'd asked anyone on the street they would have told you how it was common knowledge that Oscar

McBride treasured his daughters. No one had the slightest idea you two were anything other than a pair of spoilt little princesses."

Bernie's eyes hardened. "I don't think my father ever really knew the true meaning of the word 'love', Mrs McNab. He never loved us. He controlled us. He *owned* us, body and soul, like you might own a slave or a poor mute animal. Oh, he kept us fed and watered and well clothed, come to that. But that wasn't out of love. That was because to do otherwise would have reflected badly on him and his place in the community." She dipped her head. "Do you know, I think it was a happy release for my mother when she died, because she was the complete opposite to him. He was hard and cold and she was soft and loving with a reckless streak that he tried to beat out of her." Her voice softened, became sad. "I remember so many things about her, lovely things, like the day she took us out for a picnic in the countryside and we wandered into that old graveyard just outside Oughterard." She wrinkled her brow. "Do you know the one, Mrs McNab? There's a little hill with an old grey church on top. It's in ruins now, of course, and so is most of the graveyard. There's hardly a headstone standing and it's hard to read those that are because the letters have either been eroded by the years or the lichen has laid claim and dug in." She gave herself a little shake. "Anyway, there was one grave, way over to one side, well away from all the rest and it had chains around it. Do you know what that means?"

Eileen nodded. "I think so. Was it a suicide?"

Bernie nodded. "Yes. Yes, it was and they had buried the poor thing on unconsecrated ground because suicide is a sin and they thought she didn't deserve to be buried with the others." A frown gathered between Bernie's eyes. "And as if that wasn't bad enough, they put chains around her grave too to show that her soul was forever shackled and would never find peace." Her chin came up. "But my mother didn't believe that. She said it was all rubbish and that if someone was desperate enough to take their own life, then it was sympathy and understanding that was called for and not condemnation. She said God was all-loving and all-forgiving and there was no way he'd condone that kind of carry on. And then she ripped the chains out of their moorings – it was easy, they were all rusted and corroded – and she flung them as far away as she could. I can still see it all as plain, as plain in my head. 'Fly free,' she said to the poor soul in the grave. 'Off you go, now, and meet your Maker. And when you get there, tell him Laura McBride said hello!' And, honest to God, Mrs McNab, didn't a shaft of sunlight appear out of nowhere and slant straight across the grave, like a ladder of light leading directly to the heavens above." Already in a heightened state of emotion, the tears gathered in her eyes and rolled down her cheeks. "That's what she was like, my mother. Like a wild pony, completely untameable." Like a child, she knuckled at her eyes. "And it comforts me to know that though he might have broken her body, he never ever managed to break her spirit!"

"And it's plain that spirit lives on in you." Moved, Eileen took the girl's hand and encased it between her own. "You'll make a very good mother, Bernie. Whatever you have, son or daughter, you'll always do what's right by them, because you have that rare thing called compassion, and a loving heart." She smiled, and patted the back of Bernie's hand. "Father Clarke once told me that God has a plan for us all. He said it was a bit like a jigsaw puzzle. At first the pieces are all over the place and it just looks like a mess. But then, one by one and bit by bit, the pieces all slot neatly into place and God's plan becomes clear. And do you know what, Bernie, I think God planned for you and John-Joe to be together, even if at first sight it looked like a right mess to the rest of us." Wryly, she smiled and pulled Bernie to her feet. "Now, come on, let's go in and see him. Come on." She gave a little tug, as Bernie hung back, a strange expression on her face.

"Will they put chains around my father's grave,

Mrs McBride? Will his soul be forever shackled and condemned to hell?" Her face twisted into bitter folds. "I hope they do. I hope he rots in hell. I hope he suffers the tortures of the damned because if anyone deserves it, he does."

Gently, Eileen pulled her to one side, as a couple of nurses brushed past, their voices light and gossipy, in stark contrast to that of Bernie's, so laden with pain. "You don't mean that, Bernie. Whatever he was, he was still your father and no one is one hundred per cent bad. In his own way, your father, God help him, created his own hell, for he killed or drove away the very things he loved the most and paid with the only thing he had left – his life."

"And my mother paid with her life too, and John-Joe almost paid with his, so don't ask me to forgive him. I can't!" Tears spilled over and rained down Bernie's face. Furious, she dashed them away. "And I don't know how you can."

Tears stood in Eileen's own eyes. "I'm not saying I forgive him and no one knows better than me that there's some things you can't forgive. But remember what your mother said. If someone is desperate enough to take their own life, then it's sympathy and understanding that's called for and not condemnation. I don't think your father was a well man, Bernie, and that's the truth."

Sparks shot from Bernie's eyes. "I don't care. Do

you hear me? I don't care if he was sick. I don't care that he's dead. The only thing I care about now is that John-Joe gets better and we have a chance to be a proper family."

"Let him, or her, who is without sin cast the first stone." Father Clarke fixed the little knot of people gathered in the church with a steely eye. "Or, let me put it another way – if you live in a glasshouse, think carefully before throwing stones." He leaned a little forward, his hands gripping the sides of the pulpit, the knuckles bone-white against the ruddiness of his skin. "So, if any of you are inclined to pull rank over that poor man in the box down there," his chin jerked to indicate the large wooden coffin placed on a trestle in front of the altar, "think again. Because *all* of you – aye, that's right – *all* of you are living on borrowed time." Curling his hand into a fist, he brought it down with a thwack." And one day, make no mistake, *all* of you will be called upon to make your own account to God. So, before any of you go getting ideas above your station, *walk* a mile in that poor man's shoes. *Spend* a day locked in his head, along with his thoughts and worries and anxieties! *Spend* a night tossing and turning and wrestling with the agonies of his soul. Then and only then will any of you have earned the right to act as judge and jury.

Then and only then will any of you have earned the right to stand up puffing with pride and boast that *you* are the better person." He brought his fist down a second time. "And remember this if you remember nothing else. When you were sick, or when your wives or children were sick, who did you turn to? Who was it dished out the potions and pills that cured your aches and pains? Who was it who came out all hours of the day and night to help with a difficult birth, say, or to ease the passage of a loved one out of the world? Who was it that listened to your gripes and groans and moans?" The fist came down a third and final time. "Dr McBride, that's who!" Belligerent, his glance bounced along the rows of seats, softened as it lingered on the bent heads of Bernie and her young sister, Majella. "None of us has any say in the hand of cards life deals us. Some of us get more Jacks than Aces and all we can do is play the best game we know how. Sometimes we hit a winning streak and for a while we're on top of the world, king of the castle, Mr and Mrs Invincible. That's all it hangs on, be very clear about that, the turn of a card. In a split second, in the blink of an eye, your whole life can change – you can go from winner to loser, from victor to vanquished." In summation, Father Clarke dropped his voice, which somehow made his message seem all the more powerful. "There you have it now, all done and dusted. Stand up him, or her, who is without sin and let's all have a good look at you. But when you pick up that stone, when you turn it over in your hand and take aim, when you raise your arm high above your head and cast it from you, be careful, be very careful that it doesn't come flying straight back and smite the head from your shoulders!"

Bernie sat next to her sister on an old gravestone some distance away from their father's newly dug grave, watching the small procession of mourners making their way out of the graveyard.

"I can't forgive him, Madge." Idly, she picked up a daisy and twisted the head off, picked up another, twirled it between her fingers. "I don't care what Father Clarke says – he was a bad man, an evil man."

"He told me stories," Majella said quietly, hunched over and spent from crying in the church. "At night when he tucked me into bed, he told me stories." A sad smile of remembrance curved her lips. "And he sang me songs, too." Brokenly, she began to sing the words to an old ballad: *"Mellow the moonlight to shine is beginning . . .".*

Beside her, Bernie bent her head and wept and, for the first time since his death, she was weeping for her father and nobody else.

CHAPTER NINETEEN

The sky was a deep blue canvas with nothing to mar its perfection but for the odd stroke of almost transparent strata, where some unseen celestial artist had dipped his brush in a pallet of cloud and trailed it experimentally across the heavens. From some hidden nook a blackbird sang its heart out, as butterflies, red admirals and cabbage whites, unfazed by the heat of the early afternoon, chased each other in ridiculous polkas across the air. For early May, it was unseasonably and uncomfortably hot, and the grass by the roadside, a lush green from the April rains, was already beginning to take on the desiccated stalky brown more usually seen in autumn.

In the cab of his lorry, Mick Devlin sweated uncomfortably. Rolling his shirt sleeves up and the windows down had made no difference at all and the mingled smells of overly hot leather and petrol fumes combined to turn his stomach and add to the anger he already felt. A wasp flew in, dive-bombed his face and, impatient, he batted it away. It was true what they said – if you want something done, do it yourself! But when it came to a whole building project, you needed men, good men, to help you out. And that's what you paid them for. Not to hang around all day talking nonsense which, judging from the lack of progress on the Bracken Lodge Estate, is apparently all they were doing. Gombeens all!

Disgusted, he rummaged around on the dashboard, picked up a packet of cigarettes and drew one out with his teeth. The building works should have been all but completed by now. Instead they were way behind and he was losing money hand over fist. Keeping one hand on the steering wheel, he managed with the other to strike a match and light up, drawing the comforting smoke deep down into his lungs, then blowing it out again in a blue-tinged swirl.

He hadn't been happy sacking the foreman at this late stage in the game, but Billy McDermott had only himself to blame. Mick had trusted him and Billy had broken that trust, because who the hell could he rely on to crack the whip in his absence, if not the foreman? He inhaled again, deeply. A bad foreman was like the bad apple in a barrel. He could spoil the lot. And, in this case, did!

Stepping on the accelerator, Mick Devlin pushed the lorry up the winding Galway roads, slewing past little patchwork fields filled with crops of the selfsame stones that enclosed them in a hotchpotch of higgledy-piggledy walls, then, brakes squealing, climbing higher as the road both curved and narrowed.

"To hell or to Connaught!" Cromwell was reputed to have said when he banished the Irish people from their arable rich lands and sent them wailing into the black West, where the land was as inhospitable as the stormy Atlantic sea battering at its shores. And the scorching heat certainly made it seem hellish today. As the sweat trickled down his brow and into his eyes, he raised a hand to wipe it away and it was then that he lost control, the vehicle veered up onto the bank and his life and the lives of many others changed forever.

"Excuse me," came a female voice. A hand on his shoulder shook him gently awake. "Are you all right? Only you were moaning and groaning and I thought you might be in pain."

"Wha-at?" Disoriented Mick Devlin struggled awake to find himself gazing into the anxious face of a complete stranger. "Oh, no. No, I'm fine." He smiled a little shakily, gestured round the train carriage. "Just a bit of a nightmare, that's all. Probably the motion." He could see by the woman's face that she didn't believe him, but maybe she was relieved not to have to get involved, because returning the ghost of a smile, she sank quickly back in her own seat.

"Well, if you're sure." She picked up a magazine. He recognised it as the *Sacred Heart Messenger*.

"I am." He nodded firmly. "But thanks for your concern." Picking up his own newspaper, he buried his head in the sports section, but the print blurred and danced before his eyes and his fingers trembled on the edges. After a while, he gave up all pretence at reading and sat gazing out the window, till night fell and it was too dark to see any more. After a while, his eyes closed.

He knew he'd hit something. But what? A fox? A rabbit? Dazed and with the blood gushing from where he'd banged his forehead against the steering wheel, Mick Devlin climbed slowly out, staggering a little on the incline as he made his way round to the front of the lorry. At first it was difficult to see anything, but then as he blinked the blood clear of his eyes he saw the little red-haired boy, his lower half pinioned beneath one of the front wheels, a butterfly net still clutched in his hand. He had no idea how long he stood there, or when the little crowd of people drawn from God-knows-where on this remote country road started to gather, their voices shocked and muted like a swarm of bees humming on the periphery of his consciousness.

Only when a woman started screaming and screaming did the paralysis that had turned him to stone loosen its grip and he collapsed to his knees by her side. "I'm sorry," he choked out the words. "I'm sorry." But her sorrow, all consuming, had no ears for his words, and unheard by anyone else they turned back on themselves and lodged deep within his own heart.

When the inquest into young McNab's death was over, Mick Devlin took off to England, or ran off to England as many a person put it, leaving a new foreman in charge of his business. Never mind that the coroner had ruled it to be an accident. Other people knew better, especially Billy McDermott who swore left, right and centre that Devlin had been as drunk as a lord that day and if anyone remembered that the foreman had received his walking papers a few hours before the tragedy, no one had bothered to say so.

Moving like an itinerant from county to county, for several months, Mick Devlin worked his way up the coast of England, trying hard to escape the memories that filled his every waking moment, drinking and gambling with fair-weather friends, carousing far into the night, every night, in a vain attempt to stave off the sleep that would eventually claim his tired body and allow the nightmares to come. Over and over they played in his head like a cinematic reel, sometimes starting right at the very beginning, sometimes part-way through and once more he would find himself in the sweat-soaked cab of his lorry, winding his way up narrow roads on his way to a destiny he could not change, or already past that point and standing helplessly looking down on the mangled body of little Liam McNab, or standing by a newly-dug grave, the profound silence of death disturbed only by the raucous taunting of a crow somewhere in the background. At other times, he would see himself on his knees beside a woman, her red hair switching about her shoulders although on that fateful day there hadn't been the breath of a breeze, her mouth opened cavernously in a red scream that seemed to echo round and round his head, till he thought it would burst right open. And once, terrifyingly, the nightmare had transported him into the body of another man, a man demented, half-running, half-staggering down the road, a road that seemed to go on and on with no end in sight, his hands held out imploring to the sky. "Why?" he'd screamed, and the sound was that of a soul in the bowels of hell. *"Whyyy?"* And the man's sorrow had built and risen up, drowning him from the inside out, so that when he woke up his bedclothes were saturated and he was tearing at his own neck in a desperate quest for air.

Then at last he reached London.

He noticed her immediately she came into the Galtymore, a slender girl in a cerise dress with a cloud of shining hair that rippled like molten gold round her shoulders. Laughing, as her friend pulled her through the doorway, her eyes, the velvet of black-eyed Susans, danced over the crowd jostling on the dance floor and over him, lingering not more than an instant, yet shocking him with their intensity as if they could see into his very soul, a thought that sent him cringing like a whipped cur back against the wall. But he didn't stay there long. Instead, like a plant that is hopelessly attracted to the sun, he left the shadows and sought her out again. On second sight, he saw that she was even more beautiful. Beautiful in a way that had nothing to do with her face or her eyes or her hair. He didn't need to know her to know that. Like the sun, goodness and purity shone out of her, a halo of pure light arcing about the room. Was it any wonder her dancing partners smiled and acted like they were the luckiest men in the world? They were and, good God, how he wanted to be one of them! How he wanted to tear them all apart! But, if she was all light and goodness, then he was all darkness and secrets. Even when, attracted by his lingering stare, she flicked him a half-amused, half-quizzical smile anyone else might have taken as an invitation, he found he couldn't ford the gulf that, in his own mind, had opened inseparably between them. When eventually she left the dance floor and disappeared into the powder room with a girl he recognised, with a sinking of the heart, as Billy McDermott's daughter, he went back to the guest-house where he was staying, gathered up his belongings and sat on the side of the bed. When morning came, it found him queuing for the boat train.

Back in Ireland once more, he immersed himself in the business, working all day every day to the point of exhaustion and halfway into the night. He slept in the clothes he stood up in. Sometimes in the cab of his lorry. Sometimes on the floor of a half-built building without even a roof to keep out the wind and the rain. Rarely in his own bed. Forgetting to eat, he grew gaunt and hollow-eyed and the dreams came more frequently, more vivid than ever; the woman screaming, the man, imploring, running down the street " *Why! Whyy!*" The child, dead beneath the wheels of his truck. Only when he thought of her, the dark-eyed angel, did he feel anything like peace and it was this that brought him back once more to London and Fate that landed him in the very hospital in which she was a nurse. The irony of it didn't escape him. A train accident had brought him to her and now another train was taking him away. This time, though, he was never coming back! There was no reason to, as Noreen McDermott had more than made plain, her eyes narrowed, her voice full of spite.

"Coral's engaged to a lovely man. A decent man. A respectable man. Crazy about her, he is. Worships the ground she walks on! And she's crazy about him too." Deliberately, she'd pushed against the bedstead, causing a red-hot shaft of pain to rocket through him. "They're planning to get wed soon. A big white wedding which even you with all your ill-gotten gain couldn't match. Five hundred guests is what I heard. So, why don't you shift your backside out of here, Devlin, because she's only playing with you!" With a short bark of humourless laughter, she'd pushed viciously against the bed again, causing him to cry out and a nurse at the far side of the room to look inquiringly up from her duties. "Oh, we don't half have a good laugh about what a big eejit you are. The whole hospital's laughing. Do you really think the likes of Coral Browne would really be interested in you, when she can get any man she sets her mind on?" She clicked her fingers. "You might be Mr Big

Fish back in Galway. You might be able to hire and
fire as the mood takes you and condemn
hardworking men like my father to the scrapheap,
but don't cod yourself, Devlin. Over here, you're
nothing. Nothing at all!" And the pain that had gone
through his body was as nothing compared to the
pain caused by her words.

Jerking awake again, Mick felt his heart beating
nineteen to the dozen and the woman opposite once
more watching him with concern.

"Terrible journey, isn't it?" She held out a packet
of sandwiches. They were crudely cut with some sort
of pink filling – bacon, he guessed. "Here, you look
like you could use something to eat. You're very pale
if you don't mind me saying so."

"I'm all right." He waved the packet away, his
stomach revolting at the sight. "Just a bit tired.
You're right, though. This journey seems to go on
forever and then in the heel of the hunt we have the
boat to contend with too."

"Aye, sheer Purgatory," the woman agreed,
"especially if the sea is kicking up rough, like."
Leaning forward, she scrutinised his face. "Look, I
don't mean to be nosey, but are you sure you're all
right?"

"Well, to be honest," he told her, in the hopes that

she might take the hint and leave him alone, "I've just come out of hospital and it's left me feeling a bit weak and tired. That's why I keep nodding off."

"Oh," she looked wise, "I thought something was up. Gallstones, was it? I remember when an aunt of mine had gallstones . . . "

Wearily, Mick Devlin leaned back and let her words wash over him, unsurprised to find she was still chattering away as the train finally rattled to a halt.

"So, don't eat the fat off the bacon if you can avoid it at all." Standing up, she reached up to the luggage rail above, and pulled down a shabby brown suitcase tied around with string. "And look after yourself. And say the rosary. And goodbye and God bless you."

"And you." Automatically making the correct response, he sat back to wait for the train to empty. The boat wouldn't leave for another hour and besides he was in no hurry. What matter if he reached Ireland today, tomorrow or the next day? What matter if he never reached it at all!

CHAPTER TWENTY

John-Joe was in a wheelchair. Depressed, he told Eileen he wished he'd died, earning himself a sharp rebuke.

"How dare you, John-Joe Brady!" Incensed, Eileen stared down at him. "How dare you talk like that when God has been good enough to spare you your life!"

"What life?" Scowling, John-Joe wrestled the heavy chair till it was positioned directly facing the hospital window. Outside he could see his three nieces playing with Larkin, running round and round, batting their hands in front of their mouths, whooping like Red Indians, amusing some of the patients, disturbing others. Sitting on the ground, beneath an old ash tree, he could see Bernie watching them, her knees pulled up almost to her chest, her beautiful hair fanning gently around her face, an open book face down on the grass beside her. In a little while, she wouldn't be able to sit like that any more. "I'm only half a man now, Aunty Eileen, with only half a life. What good am I to anyone?" Angry, he gestured towards Bernie. "What good am I to her, or to the baby? God, but she must curse the day I crossed her path!"

"Listen, John-Joe," Eileen's voice softened, as she stood behind him, studying the curve of his bent head. "I'm not saying it's going to be easy. It's not. It'll be a tough old climb. But you'll make it. The doctors didn't say there was no hope, which means there must be some and that's the rock you've got to cling to. You're going to have to dig deep inside you and dredge up every reserve of strength you've got and when you run out, you've got to pray for more, because soon you'll have a wife and child depending on you."

"I will not!" John-Joe gritted his teeth. "I'm not going to marry her, Aunty Eileen. I've no right to. Not now, and so I'm going to set her free. Sure how can I ask a young woman with all her life before her to tie herself to this?" Viciously, he brought his fist down on one of his useless legs.

"So you'd sooner set her adrift." Eileen's face darkened. "Her and the baby with neither kith nor kin, apart from young Majella, who's only a mere child. You'd sooner cast her out into a world that has no place for unwed mothers and that treats them worse than lepers. Is that it? Could you really bear to see her ending up in one of those Magdalen Homes for unmarried mothers, working her poor hands to the bone washing other people's dirty laundry, with even her name taken away from her? And what about your poor innocent little baby? Could you really bear for your flesh and blood to end up in an orphanage? Or what it if it's adopted? You won't know the first thing about the people who take it away. You won't know if they're good or bad. You won't even know where they live. For all you know the poor little thing could end up at the far side of the world. Shame on you, John-Joe! Shame on you for turning your back on someone who loves you with all her heart!"

John-Joe spun back around, his fury giving him strength. "Don't twist things, Aunty Eileen. You know that's the last thing I want. But what right have I got to love her now?" Bitter, he compressed his lips to a thin hard line. "I can't even dress myself. Isn't one baby enough for her to contend with? Anyway, Bernie's beautiful and before long she'll meet another man, a strong man with two good legs on him who can offer her a better life than me."

"And what if I don't want another man?" Unnoticed, Bernie had left her place under the tree and now she stood at the doorway, the muscles in her face working angrily. "I thought you loved me, John-Joe," her hand dropped to her stomach, "and our child."

"I do." Anguished, he wheeled himself across the room, as Eileen turned discreetly away, waving her hand distractedly at her three little daughters as they caught sight of her through the window and raised their own small hands in salutation. "I love you with all my heart and with all my soul, but look at me, Bernie. *Really* look at me! Is this what you want to land yourself with?" A sob caught in his throat. Manfully he suppressed it. "Don't you see, I'm not the man you fell in love with? That John-Joe Brady was a different man entirely. That John-Joe Brady could have made a life for us all." He shrugged despairingly. "What the hell can I do?"

"You can marry me. Like you promised." Bernie stuck her chin out. "You can be a husband to me and a father to our child. I didn't fall in love with your legs, John-Joe. I fell in love with you. *All* of you! And soon, I would have vowed to love, honour and obey you. In sickness and in health. Did you hear that? In sickness and in health. And I would have kept those vows and been happy to do so." Impassioned, she dropped to her knees, and reaching up took his face between her hands. "I still want to make those vows, John-Joe. I still want to marry you. I want to be with you always, till death do us part."

Gently prising her hands away, John-Joe brought them to his lips and kissed each of her fingers, his eyes bright, his voice husky. "Do you mean that, Bernie? Because if you do, I promise I'll move mountains to walk again and one day, as God's my judge, I'll make you glad you married me."

"I know you will." Leaning forward, Bernie covered his mouth with hers as, unnoticed, Eileen slipped quietly away.

Benedict Kiely was very kind after John-Joe's accident, sending word round with Bridget that Eileen was to take off as much time as she liked and on no account to attempt to come back before she was ready.

"That's very kind of him," Eileen said, as she poured Bridget a cup of tea.

"Kind bedamned!" Bridget shook her head scathingly. "It's just that he knows he'll never get anyone as good as you again, so he does."

Chuckling at the young woman's show of support, Eileen wished vainly once more that it was she who had caught John-Joe's eye, although to be fair she was becoming quite attached to Bernie. Still, life would have been far less complicated. "Be careful now, Bridget, or you'll fill me that full of my own importance that I'll turn into a second Madame

Bovary." Taking a sip of tea, she put down the cup and added a drop more milk. "Speaking of which, how is Her Ladyship these days? Bridget?" she repeated, as Bridget became suddenly engrossed in the contents of her own cup, staring intently into the beige bubbles massed along the edge, with all the intensity of a gypsy divining the future. "Bridget?" Her voice pierced her own ears. "Is something the matter?"

Sighing as if she had finally made a life-or-death decision, Bridget pushed her mug away, the spoon clinking against its enamel side, in a miniature death-toll that smote fear into Eileen's heart. "I don't know if I'm doing the right thing by telling you this, Eileen," she began hesitantly, the dark look in her eyes showing that what she was about to divulge was something which had caused her many a sleepless night. "You remember the day John-Joe called into the shop?"

Eileen nodded. She was unlikely ever to forget. "Go on!" she encouraged.

"Well, when you were talking to him, the quare one sent me out of the shop on a message. She said I was to run across to the chemist's and pick up a prescription she'd ordered." Candid eyes sought Eileen's. "Only there *was* no prescription and when I came back she had her ear glued to the door listening to yourself and your nephew." As Eileen made to interject, Bridget stopped her with a wave of her hand. "Anyway, later that evening I was going to the pictures with my friend, when who should I spy but your woman coming out of Dr McBride's with a smirk on her face the size of a saucer and not five minutes later McBride himself nearly mows the pair of us down tearing off some place in his car." Bridget's voice trailed off. "That's the gospel truth, Eileen," she said, after a moment, "and she's been going around as quiet as a mouse ever since and with a face as yellow as a windy cur."

As Eileen made the connection, she felt a sick rage begin to bubble in the pit of her stomach. Angrily she jumped to her feet, knocking her chair to the floor in her haste. "Oh my God! The bitch! So it was her who betrayed him to McBride! It all makes sense now all right. How else did McBride know where to waylay him?" Her voice rose anguished. "Why, Bridget? Why did she do that to an innocent boy who never did anybody a day's harm in his life?"

Bridget's voice was grim. "I don't know, Eileen. Sheer badness, I suppose – that and the fact that she's been eaten up with jealousy since the first day you started, especially as Mr Kiely thinks the sun, moon and stars shine out of you! Sure isn't it common knowledge that she's been setting her cap at him for years!" Gently she righted the chair, and persuaded Eileen back into it. "Mind you, I doubt, nasty piece of work though she is, that even she intended for matters to go as far as they did."

Eileen bowed her head. "So John-Joe, my lovely John-Joe is above in the Regional fighting for his life, all on account of some small-minded bitch's jealousy!"

"It would seem that way all right," Bridget agreed sadly.

"Well, the tide'll come in for that one too. You mark my words, Bridget." Eileen dashed a tear from her eye. "The tide'll come in for that one too. And I pray to Jesus Christ and all the saints that when it does, I'll be there, standing on the shore – watching it!"

As it happened, Bridget, taking it upon herself to acquaint Mr Kiely with the grisly speculation behind the wounding of Eileen's nephew, was instrumental in bringing the tide in for Madame Bovary, who found herself instantly dismissed and shortly after disappeared from the area.

When, eventually, Eileen felt able to return to work, it was to find herself elevated to the position of manageress.

"I don't know, Mr Kiely," she'd remonstrated upon his giving her the news, his face beet-red and shiny with pleasure. "I feel somehow like I'm profiting from John-Joe's misfortune. And that's wrong, Mr Kiely. It wouldn't sit well with me."

Mr Kiely stood firm. "You can put that notion right out of you head, Eileen," he assured her. "This was in the pipeline well before any of that unfortunate business happened at all. I had it in mind to transfer Madame Bovary to one of the other branches and have you take over here." Sincerity oozed from every pore. "So, will you be my new manageress? You'd be doing me a huge favour. Kiely's needs someone of your integrity. You're good with the staff and customers alike and you really know your stuff when it comes to the merchandise. So, come on, what do you say?"

Smiling the first real smile since John-Joe was attacked, Eileen nodded. "I say, thank you very much, Mr Kiely, and I'll try my hardest not to be a disappointment to you."

Returning her smile, Benedict Kiely grasped both her hands between his. "Eileen, I'm nothing if not confident that you'll be an unqualified success." With a playful wink, which other women might have misconstrued but Eileen knew to be completely without guile, he shooed her out of his office. "Now run along with you – there's a shop out there that won't manage itself."

"Janey!" Bridget was delighted with the news. "I was terrified he was going to get some other old bag in to replace herself. And you know the old saying, better the devil you know . . ."

"Well, I hope you're not referring to me as an old bag!" Eileen laughed. "Or the devil!"

Bridget picked up the banter. "What? Call Marie-Antoinette an old bag and risk getting my head chopped off. Do you think I'm stone mad?"

"I'll tell you what," Eileen said, when the two women had finished laughing, "there'll be no more Clarisses and Marie-Antoinettes round here. From now on it's plain old Bridget and Eileen. And that," she announced firmly and with relish, "is my first managerial decision."

CHAPTER TWENTY-ONE

"Can I have a new frock too, Mammy?" Tugging at her mother's hand, Rose turned a pleading face upwards.

"Of course you can and not one made by me either, but brand-new from a shop." Automatically, Eileen tucked a stray strand of hair behind the little girl's ear. "We can't have you making a show of us at John-Joe's wedding, now can we?" Satisfied, a smile curved her lips as she thought of the vanload of lovely dresses Kiely's had recently taken delivery of. Just right for a summer wedding. "I might even treat myself while I'm at it." And maybe she'd get a straw hat, she mused, not too wide at the brim. Simply trimmed with maybe an artificial flower or even a real one. Some fat pink rosebuds from the bush that stood on Liam's grave would be ideal. That way she'd feel like she was taking a part of him with her too.

"Can mine be red?" Daisy asked, slicing through the thought and, as usual, dashing any flights of fancy her mother might be having against the cold rocks of reality. "A big red frock, with a big spotty bow at the back and a white lace collar like that one Mary Jane O'Mahony wore to Mass last week." Breathless with excitement, she elbowed Rose out of the way in order to better harangue her mother. "And – and a big frilly underskirt?"

Laughing, Eileen drew the line. "No, Daisy. It's traditional for bridesmaids to be dressed the same and Bernie wants you all to wear sky blue – won't that be lovely? Think how well it'll match all those nice big bruises you got on your leg from falling out of that tree last week."

Non-committal, Daisy kicked idly at the ground with the toe of her shoe, still reluctant to let go entirely of her dream. "But what about the frilly underskirt? Couldn't I just have that? Annie Oakley has one and I won't even ask for a shotgun."

"God, you're a desperate case!" Laughing, Eileen chucked her under the chin. "No, Daisy. No frilly underskirt. Definitely not. But it'll be a lovely frock all the same, I promise. And I'm going to weave fresh flowers into your hair and make you each a little posy to carry."

"Oh no, not ringlets again!" Mollie, who up to this point had stayed uncharacteristically silent, gave a theatrical groan at the thoughts of the torture her mother routinely inflicted on their heads. "I hate ringlets. They give me a headache and I can't sleep at night with all those little knots poking into my scalp."

"I'm afraid so," Eileen grinned, "but as I've said time and time again, you have to suffer for style, Mollie. Now off with you to bed. All of you." She wagged a stern finger, but her eyes were merry. "And no fighting, mind! I'm in a good mood tonight so don't go spoiling it." And it was true, she reflected as in various states of joy or disgruntlement they trooped off behind the curtain, she *was* in a good mood. With every day, John-Joe was improving, all credit to Bernie who had the knack of geeing him up whenever he felt down. He still couldn't walk, though, although the doctors had managed to get him standing between two rail things and he'd started to feel the odd tingling sensation in his legs which, apparently, could mean that the feeling was coming back into them. Eileen prayed to Almighty God that it was so, because the sight of him, reduced to a mere shell of his former self, made her want to alternately weep and lash out in despair.

Going out of the cottage, she stood for a while gazing down at the Atlantic which, as always, seemed to reflect her mood. This evening it was calm, mirror-still with just little rills of silver water running in over the strand and dissolving into a white piping of lace of the kind you might find edging a bride's veil. Modestly drawing the evening clouds over itself, the sun had already begun its nightly pilgrimage, prompting Eileen to recall a conversation recently overhead between her husband and Mollie which couldn't but bring a smile to her lips.

"Where does the sun go at night, Daddy? Does it get drowned in the sea and is it a new sun that takes its place the next morning?"

"No, no, not at all, Mollie. It's the same old sun all over the world. In fact isn't it a great thing entirely to think that the sun you saw today is the same sun the Eskimos see when they come out of their igloos for a bit of fishing, and it's the same sun the elephants see when they're mooching through the long grasses in Africa and, believe it or not, it's the same sun the dinosaurs saw all those years ago before they became extinct. We're all seeing the same sun, only at different times. It doesn't get drowned at all, even though it looks that way to you and me when we see it fizzing and bobbing in the sea and setting the waves on fire. The truth is, Moll, it's merely slipping over the side of the world, the bit they call the horizon, and making its way down to Australia, the way the kangaroos and koalas can have a fair crack at it too . . ."

"And then those fellas with the bones through their noses can come out and throw their boomerangs too, I suppose, because they wouldn't be able to aim very well in the dark."

"Exactly!" Paddy said. "Exactly! That's it in a nutshell. And talking about the sun, did I ever tell you about that foreign fella, Icarus, and the way he flew too close to it and it melted all the wax in his feathers and sent him toppling to earth?"

And there, Eileen had left them, father and his daughter, two bent heads, one dark, the other as golden-red as the setting sun she was so interested in, sharing an intimacy that belonged to no one else but themselves.

Drawing her cardigan around her, more out of habit than because she was cold, Eileen stood a while longer before realising that she was no longer quite alone. With a sideways glance, she saw that Coral Devlin had also come out of her own house and was standing quietly a little way off to one side, in silent contemplation of the sea too. In the half-light, with her hair hanging loose around her shoulders, and her perfect creamy face partially in shadow, she reminded Eileen for a fleeting moment of the Madonna, some kind of long robe thing she was wearing adding to the illusion. There was an air of tranquillity about her, a sense of calm, which Eileen recognised at once, having felt it four times herself just before the birth of each of her children. Sensing Eileen's eyes on her, she turned slightly and for a moment their eyes locked across the distance, meeting silently in almost perfect communication, before suddenly confused and angry, Eileen turned on her heel and stomped stiff-backed inside her house.

Moving swiftly over to the dresser, she scrabbled about on top till her fingers closed on Liam's old gumboot. Her world had no place for Coral Devlin. No place for her husband, No place for her child. Tearing the brown paper off with shaking fingers, she pressed the little boot almost violently against her cheek, the good mood of earlier quickly dispelled by the tears that were never far from the surface.

Outside the sun gave a final salute, then graceful in defeat slipped over the edge of the world, leaving the silver-crowned moon and his army of stars to come and lay siege to the sky.

When Paddy came home from a late night at O'Dwyer's, he found her asleep in an armchair, the boot still clutched in her hand and Larkin curled loyally into a ball at her feet. Quietly retracing his steps, he went back out again, returning a few hours later to find Liam's gumboot tidied away and Eileen sound asleep in bed. Climbing quietly in beside her, he slid a protective arm around her waist, as outside the sea washed up in a gentle lullaby against the shore.

"I love you, Eileen McNab," he mouthed against the softness of her hair. "I love you."

"Hold still a minute, will you." Her mouth filled with pins, Eileen tugged at a length of white lace she was fashioning around Bernie McBride's waist. "Hmm, that's it. What do you think, girls?" Obediently, Mollie and her sisters dropped the playing cards they were building houses with and came over for a look.

"It's nice." Truculently, Daisy eyed the half-made garment. "But why is she having a frilly underskirt and I'm not?"

"Because, Bernie's the bride, dummy," Mollie grinned, sticking out her tongue and waggling her fingers in her ears in a way guaranteed to start a fight. "And you're not!"

"Now you stop that, Mollie," her mother warned. "I need all my concentration here. What do you think, Rose?"

"Beautiful!" Rose's small mouth formed an 'o' of wonder. "Bernie looks like a fairy princess. You do, Bernie. You look like Snow White. And you know I hated you because John-Joe said he was going to marry me and now he's marrying you instead – well,

I don't any more." Slyly her eyes slid towards Daisy. "I'm going to marry Kevin Keithley instead."

Taking a leaf out of Mollie's book, Daisy extended her tongue all the way to the roots. Not that she was bothered really. Kiss-curl was history, now that she had her eyes fixed on John Wayne.

"Aw, thanks, Rosie," Bernie winced as Eileen inadvertently stuck a pin in her leg. "I'd give you a hug, only your mother might kill me if I move a muscle."

"Hold still," Eileen said through gritted teeth, serving to emphasise what Bernie had just said. "I'm just about finished here. There!" Pulling the remaining pins out of her mouth, she replaced them in a small tin tobacco box. "Right, I'll tack that up tonight and it'll be ready in no time. And you," she said to Bernie's tummy, "slow down in there, will you, or I'll be worn out altering this frock for your mammy."

"Who are you talking to?" Puzzled, Rose exchanged glances with the equally puzzled Daisy, while Mollie stood slyly by, the superior look of one who has been let in on a secret on her face. "Who are you talking to, Mammy? Is there someone in Bernie's belly?"

Mentally kicking herself for being so careless around the younger two, Eileen got to her feet, one hand held dramatically to the small of her back. "Ah, don't mind me," she said. "It's all this kneeling. It's addled my brain."

"Kneeling down too long will do that to you all right," Bernie concurred, feeling a quick flash of shame that Eileen had to lie to protect the youngsters' innocence.

"Oh it will," Paddy agreed, arriving home right on cue, and seamlessly picking up the conversation. "Do you know I knew a woman once, who, whenever she went to Mass, had to stay either standing up or sitting down. Why?" With a deep shrug, he seemed to ask the question of the four walls surrounding him and then of each of his three daughters, his head bouncing from one to the other. "Why? Because whenever she knelt down it sent her off her head, that's why, and she'd start spouting all sorts of nonsense and codology. Nursery rhymes and poems she learned at school and even, and this is Gospel truth, the whole of the American Proclamation of Independence. It caused considerable confusion and mayhem in the church I can tell you. The uproar was terrible." He rolled his eyes. "And once, during a wedding, didn't she confuse the priest so much that the poor man got all mixed up, took the vows and ended up marrying the bride himself. Mind you, I believe they lived very happily ever after all the same. Six children at the last count is what I heard, and twins expected any day now."

"Really, Daddy?" Eyes out on stalks and successfully diverted from the intriguing subject of Bernie's belly, the three young sisters, Mollie included, clustered round to hear more of this amazing woman, while Eileen seized on the opportunity to usher Bernie behind the curtain. Sitting on the edge of bed, she pulled the girl in front of her, grasping her wrists to keep her still.

"Now, Bernie, I'm sorry to have to ask you this, but is marrying John-Joe what you really want? I mean, is it what you want more than anything in the world because, if it's not, now is the time to say so. Not when you're marching down the aisle and certainly not after it." Eileen wagged her head earnestly. "Be very sure, when you say 'I do', that you mean it." She tightened her grip. "Weddings and wedding dresses and being able to write Missus in front of your name are all well and good, but let's face it, the pair of you are starting off under two handicaps most other young couples don't have: a baby on the way and a husband in a wheelchair. I'm not saying these things to put you off, Bernie, but it wouldn't be fair simply to paint a pretty picture and send you off totally unprepared for reality. Life can be hard. It can be damn hard!" She made a little moue. "I know I'm not your mother, and I'd never dream of trying to take that good woman's place, but I'd like to think that if ever one of my own daughters was in need, someone would step in and give them a bit of friendly advice. And I'm saying it for John-Joe's sake too."

"And I appreciate it, Mrs McNab. Honestly, I do." Gently pulling her hands free, Bernie indicated the length of white lace still pinned round her. "I appreciate this and everything you've done for me and I want you to know that I really, really, really love John-Joe and would never do anything to hurt him." Sitting down on the bed beside Eileen, she clasped her hands in front of her, bent slightly forward across them. "Oh, I won't pretend I don't wish things were different. Of course, I do. I wish we'd waited to have a child and I wish John-Joe wasn't in a wheelchair. I wish my mother wasn't dead and I wish my father – well, the least said as regards that, the better." With a deep sigh, her chin came up slightly. "But there's no turning the clock back. This little one *is* on the way. John-Joe *is* crippled. My mother *is* dead and my father has left nothing behind for Majella and me but a bucketful of mixed emotions. Still, we have the future, Mrs McNab. We have the future, John-Joe and me, blowing ahead of us like a white unmarked canvas sail in the wind, or a slate yet to be written on. And we're going to write on that slate together, the pair of us. We're going to write on it, our story." She half-turned then, smiled at Eileen. "Okay, so the beginning might be a bit shaky all right, but we're sure as hell going to have a happy ending." She smoothed a hand down her dress. "Snow White always has a happy ending."

Yes, but the handsome prince was always on black charger. A wheelchair didn't have quite the same ring to it, Eileen thought gloomily, as still caught up in his own imaginary fairy tale, Paddy's voice came drifting round the curtain.

"And one time, didn't the poor woman start spouting Greek. Pure classical Greek, I'm telling you, of the sort spoken by scholars and philosophers and men of learning. But sure, of course, nobody else could talk Greek and so, as far as they were concerned, 'twas all double Dutch."

CHAPTER TWENTY-TWO

The morning of the wedding dawned sunny, bright and clear, a good omen Eileen hoped for the day that lay before them. Chivvying the girls out of bed, she forced them to sit down and eat a bit of breakfast, though the excitement combined with her own anxiety totally destroyed their appetites.

"Can we get dressed now?" Mollie begged, pushing a half-eaten piece of bread and marmalade away from her. "I'll be sick if I eat any more." She screwed up her face. "I can feel it now in my tummy."

"And you'll be sick later if you don't," Eileen snapped, her nerves already in pre-wedding tatters. "Don't forget, you'll be a long time standing in church and an even longer time waiting for your dinner. The bellies will be tripping you up with the hunger before you get anywhere near a sandwich. You'll be sorry you didn't eat your breakfast then, all right."

"I don't care!" Mollie tossed her head, still bound up in a mass of curling rags. "I want to get dressed now. Besides, I hate marmalade. Why d'ye have to give us marmalade? I bet nobody else has rotten stinking marmalade."

"Oh, stop whining, Mollie." Harassed, Eileen ran about like a headless chicken. There were still a hundred and one things to be done before they even set out for the church and arguing with Mollie wasn't one of them. "Daisy. Rose. Eat up!"

"I am!" Daisy said spraying crumbs across the table and sending Rose into the kind of paroxysms that, in Eileen's experience, didn't take long to turn to tears. Despairingly she lashed out at Larkin who, never the brightest of animals, chose exactly that moment to try and wrestle her slipper from her foot. "Get off me, you big eejit! Haven't I enough to be doing without you getting in on the act?" Grabbing a teacloth, Eileen swished him around the ears sending him scuttling for cover to his favourite place under the dresser. "Honest to God, you've got me heart scalded, the lot of you."

"Don't be mean, Mammy." Sure enough, Rose's hysteria of only moments before wasn't long about turning to tears. "Larkin's only playing. I hate you,

336

so I do! You're the meanest, most horriblest, most awful mother in the whole world!"

Waving a weary hand, Eileen subsided onto the nearest chair. "Oh, away with you all and get dressed, then. I'm past caring. Really, I am. But mind you wash yourselves properly and, Daisy, remember you've got a neck on you, just like everyone else."

"Would you calm down, Eily." Already washed and dressed in the smart new suit Eileen had made for him specially for the wedding, Paddy looked up from the corner where he had wisely chosen to retreat with a book and a cigarette. "Fussing won't accomplish anything and the ceremony is not till twelve o'clock." He checked his watch. "It's only half-nine now and I've booked the taxi for half-eleven. So, you've got all the time in the world."

"That's easy for you to say," Eileen fretted. "Sure you've nobody to think of only yourself. Me, I've got to get everyone ready, including myself, *and* clean up all of this mess." Dramatically she made a great sweep of the room which, if the truth be told, would take all of five minutes to tidy.

Deliberately Paddy stubbed out his cigarette and laid his book to one side. "All right so. What would you like me to do? Just tell me and I'll do it. Nothing would give me greater pleasure."

"Nothing!" Pulling a distracted hand through her hair, Eileen raked him with a resentful look. "I don't

want you to do anything. Just go back to your book
and don't be annoying me."

"Well, don't say I didn't offer, that's all."

"And that let's you off the hook nicely, doesn't it?"
Despite herself, Eileen smiled. "Just don't go thinking
you've pulled a fast one on me, Paddy McNab, you
lazy article you! I see exactly what you're up to. Not
only are you not going to do anything to help me, but
you've actually managed to get my blessing to sit on
your backside and read your book."

"Ah, go way outta that!" Paddy feigned innocence.
"That's not the way of it at all." But it was and they
both knew it. And not five minutes later, while Eileen
huffed and puffed, running between the three girls,
her hat, which she had yet to trim, and the kitchen
sink, he was somewhere out on the stormy moors,
lost in the howling of the hounds of the Baskervilles.

As the McNabs' door opened and the three girls
tumbled out one after the other in a river of sky-blue
satin, Coral Devlin let her curtain twitch back into
place, careful to leave just enough for her to peek
through. Molly had been full of nothing but the
wedding lately, regaling Coral with tales of poor
John-Joe and his futile attempts to walk, the beautiful
Bernie who was going to be his bride, the lovely
bridesmaid dresses she and her sister were going to

wear and the big straw hat her mammy had got and which Mollie's father joked made her look like a pioneer from the Wild West and which made him sing 'Bringing In The Sheaves' in a funny voice. She was going to trim it with roses from Liam's grave, Mollie said, then wide-eyed, clapped her hand over her mouth in case that innocent statement had somehow managed to give Coral offence.

"Well, I think that's a lovely idea." Tears sprang to Coral's eyes. She was like that lately, weeping and wailing over the slightest little thing. Mick laughed and said it was the baby that was making her feel blue and after it was born she'd be as right as rain and back to her old self again. She sincerely hoped he was right, because it was no fun spending your life as a watering-can.

"Mammy said it'll be the next best thing to having Liam with her," Mollie continued, then twisting her little brow looked concerned. "Are you all right, Mrs Devlin?"

Brushing the tears away with the back of her hand, Coral nodded. "I'm fine, Mollie. I just have a bit of a draught in my eye, that's all. I think it's a blast from the window."

"Oh." Satisfied, Mollie continued talking, her excitement growing by the minute. "I wish you could come too. I know. Maybe you could come if you left your husband behind. I don't think Mammy would mind a bit. After all, it wasn't you that killed our Liam."

Coral gave a watery smile. "That's very kind of you, Mollie, but I don't think so. This day is just for your family and nearest and dearest and I hope you all have a wonderful time."

And now she stood, skulking behind her window, desperate to be included if only in some small way in the happy family picture unfolding outside the McNabs' house.

"Do I look all right?" Eileen was twirling for her husband and daughters, the full skirt of her pale lemon dress flying out about her knees, one hand firmly anchoring the straw, rose-trimmed bonnet in place. She was wearing high-heels, Coral noticed, white high-heels with delicate ankle straps that contrasted well with the American tan of her stockings and elongated her shapely legs.

"You look beautiful, love." Paddy's voice carried gruff, proud on the still air. "The Queen of Sheba herself has nothing on you."

"Oh, go on with you!" Throwing back her head, Eileen laughed delightedly, her generous mouth outlined with just the merest hint of pink lipstick.

"It's true," Paddy insisted. "Isn't it, girls?" And, catching her breath, from her vantage point behind the window, Coral had to concur with the ready babble of agreement. This Eileen McNab, with her buttermilk skin and fiery red hair the colour of burnt sycamore leaves peeking out from below her bonnet, was truly beautiful, and a far cry from the haunted-looking woman usually in evidence. It was also clear that she was the adored backbone of the family, and Coral, so far from her own family, couldn't but feel a little envious watching her neighbour's husband and children cluster round Eileen, each one clearly desperate to bask in the sunshine of her approval.

"Look, Mammy," Mollie pointed down the road to where an ancient motor car could be seen wending its way up the promontory, "here's the taxi coming now. Can I sit with the driver?"

"No, love." Eileen adjusted her bonnet. "Let your father sit up front. You sit in the back with me and your sisters."

For once, Mollie didn't argue, but joined in a jumping up and down game started by Daisy, the point of which was apparently to see who could jump highest and stay in the air for longest.

"Be careful you don't tread on your hems or dislodge your wreaths," Eileen warned, sighing with relief as the taxi drew to a rattling halt. If she could just get them to the church looking half-way decent. After that, she didn't much care, because children would be children and new dresses weren't half so much fun as jumping in the biggest muddiest puddle you could find.

After they had all gone, piling one after the other into the car, Coral stayed for a while, her nose pressed against the window, remembering her own wedding day. Her mother called it a hole-in-the-corner affair and trotted out the old line about marrying in haste and repenting at leisure, but none of it meant anything to Coral. She was marrying Mick Devlin, come hell or high water. And nobody and nothing was going to stop her.

CHAPTER TWENTY-THREE

She found him halfway down the empty train, eyes closed, the greyish hospital pallor of his skin thrown into stark relief by the midnight hue of his hair.

"Mick!" Bending down, she gently shook his shoulder. "Mick, wake up! It's me, Coral."

"Coral?" Eyes fluttering open in disbelief, he gawped at her, struggling up straighter in his seat. "Coral, is that really you? Puzzled, he blinked to bring her into sharper focus. "H-how? W-where?"

"I followed you." Brazenly and completely out of character, she brought her face down to his, and kissed him lingeringly, full on the mouth. "I almost broke my neck trying to catch the train. But I made it. By the skin of my teeth. And then it was so packed, I had to stay where I was till every one got off."

Shaking his head, he still found it hard to believe

the evidence of his eyes. One moment he was dreaming of her. The next she was standing there before him, large as life and twice as beautiful. "But I don't understand. Your friend said . . ."

"Sshhh!" She stilled his words with a gentle finger across the lips. "Noreen's no friend of mine. Not any more! And anything she told you was a pack of lies. I'm not engaged to anyone, Mick. I was never engaged to anyone." She looked hurt for a moment. "I'm surprised you listened to her, really I am. Did you not think to check with me, instead of skulking off like that?"

"But everything she said made perfect sense." Mick waved a disparaging hand. "I mean look at me and look at you. You could have any one, Coral, any one in the world. And what am I? Nothing but a big hulking Irish labourer. A man with blood on his hands. A child's blood."

"You're the man I love," Coral said quietly. "And nothing's going to change that." Hunkering down in front of him, she gazed solemnly up into his face. "And yes, I know all about the child. Noreen made a point of telling me. But as I told her, you're not the first man to have an accident and you won't be the last. I really don't know why she took it into her head to hate you so much. I suppose in some strange twisted way she thought she was protecting me."

"I sacked her father." Raising one of her hands to his mouth, Mick turned it over and gently kissed the palm. "He was one of my workmen, except he didn't do much work. I suppose it's only natural that she'd hold a grudge. In fairness, I'd probably do the same myself, blood being thicker than water."

"Aaah . . ." Coral set her mouth. "So that's what was behind it. I understand now. I suppose she was too proud to tell me. Still, I can't forgive her. She knew how much I loved you, yet she did everything in her power to keep us apart."

His eyes more alive than they'd ever been, Mick sat up even straighter. "I want to hear that again, Coral, what you just said. I want to hear you say you love me."

"I love you." Coral dimpled up at him. "I love you, Mick Devlin. Now what do you intend to do about it?"

"I intend," Mick said, his own face breaking out into a huge smile, "to make a decent woman out of you, Coral Browne. But not just yet!" Reaching down he pulled her up into his arms, letting go of her again only when a weary railway guard poked his head into the carriage, enquiring in a surly voice if they had no homes to go to.

"None at the moment," Mick told him, "but do you see this woman here? This princess? Well, I'm going to build her the house of her dreams anywhere in the whole wide world the fancy takes her, be that Timbuctoo or Outer Mongolia. Or even the moon!"

"Is that a fact?" Unimpressed, the guard, wielding a rolled-up timetable, ushered them from the carriage. "Well, I'm delighted for the pair of you, I'm sure, but I'd be even more delighted by the sight of my own bed. So come on now, left, right, stir your stumps."

Despite Mick's fears, Coral fell in love with Galway straight away. "But we don't have to live here," he told her, concerned that eventually she would miss the bright lights of London and go running back. "I meant what I said. We can live anywhere you like. Anywhere at all. I'll build you a palace, Coral, I swear. A Taj Mahal like that Indian prince built his bride. To show the world how much I love you."

Laughing, Coral trailed her fingers over the side of the little wooden boat Mick had sailed out into the middle of Galway Bay. "I don't want a palace, Mick. I just want to be with you, here in Galway, living an ordinary life because that's what will really make me feel like a queen." She pointed over to where a small thatched cottage stood sentinel high on an outcrop of rock at the far side of the bay, its white walls glistening like royal icing in the evening sun. "Do you see that little house? That's where I want to live, right up there, next to it? Oh, can we, Mick? It looks so pretty and appealing, like something out of a fairytale."

346

"If that's what you truly want," Mick said, playing for time, bending low over the oars so she couldn't see the shadow that passed suddenly over his face, or the little slick of perspiration that broke out all across his forehead and which had nothing to do with the exertion of rowing. "But why up there?" He tried to keep the sudden note of desperation from his voice. "I've hardly shown you anywhere yet. There's loads of places, far nicer. And there's no hurry on us to make up our minds, is there?"

Her face all lit up like a child's, Coral shrugged. "Oh, I don't know, Mick. There's just something about it that feels right. I know it sounds nonsensical, but somehow I've got a feeling we could be happy there. It's like it's calling to me."

"Coral . . ." How could he conjure up the horrors of the past on this bright and glorious day? How could he banish the joy and pleasure on her sweet face? Reaching for the oars, he expertly sculled the boat round and headed back to the shore.

"Well, Mick?" asked Coral eagerly.

"I can make enquiries about the land," he said, as calmly as he could, "but . . . dearest . . . don't set your heart on it – it could be more complicated than you think."

"But it is! It is set on it!" said Coral, turning for one last glimpse and thrilled to see a woman come out from the whitewashed cottage and stand, one hand shading her eyes, gazing out to the sea, loose tendrils of red hair blowing round her head like escaped sunbeams. "Oh, look, there's our new neighbour! Do you think she'll like us?"

"She'll like you, anyway," Mick said, carefully keeping his face averted and his voice light. "How could she not?" As for him, Eileen McNab already hated him with every fibre of his being.

Wasn't fate a bastard? What cruel chance had led Coral to fix on that spot? Was he never to escape reminders of his guilt? He had tell her! All he had to do was open his mouth and say: "Coral, that's the last place in the world I want to live. That woman is the mother of the child I killed. Don't ask me to live with the constant reminder of my sin on the doorstep. Don't ask them to live with it." And being the kind of woman she was, Coral would understand completely.

Yet, something other than his guilt kept him silent and prevented the words from coming. Another part of him, a deeper part of his psyche told him this was his Nemesis and something he could no more run away from than his own shadow. In order to move forward, in order to regain peace of mind, he first of all had to go back. He had to retrace his steps. Somehow, he had to try and make amends to the McNabs, whilst all the time knowing he could never change the past. And perhaps his dark-eyed angel had been sent to him to point the way? Perhaps she was fated to heal the terrible rift between him and the McNab family?

On fire with excitement and blissfully ignorant of her lover's thoughts, Coral, was already busy planning the kind of house they would build. A house of dreams, high above the Atlantic ocean, never for one moment realising that to build on dreams is to build on quicksand.

They married in a simple, civil ceremony back in London with few guests on Mick's side and just as few on Coral's. She wore a cream suit cinched in at the waist and clutched a small bunch of African violets in her hands. Her brother, Jason, reluctantly gave her away, while her mother, having been treated to Noreen's biased opinion of the groom, stood by and cried tears of real sorrow.

"There's no smoke without fire," she warned, taking Coral to one side in a last-ditch effort to persuade her not to go through with it. "Noreen wouldn't have said those things unless they were true and even if only part of it is true, that's bad enough. I'm begging you, Coral. Look around you. This is not what we wanted for you. This – this hole-in-the-corner affair that looks like you've got something to hide. You should have a church wedding, a vicar, a choir. Most of all you should have a good, kind, decent man who'll love and cherish you for the rest of your life. A man you can step out with and be proud of." She jerked her head to where Mick, guessing himself to be the not very favourable subject of their discourse, stood shuffling uncomfortably over to one side, a worried frown on his face.

Coral threw him a reassuring look. "Mick *is* good and kind and decent." Rebellious, she stuck out her chin. "And I am proud of him. And what's more he makes me happy, happier than I've ever been in my whole life. And he makes me feel complete, as though a final piece of the jigsaw has slotted into place." Pleading, she held her mother's eyes. "So, if you love me, Mother, truly love me, then you'll be happy for me too." Lifting her shoulders, she took a deep determined breath. "But one way or another, I'm going to marry Mick."

And because they did love her, and more than anything else they wanted her to be happy, Jason and her mother cast all their doubts to the back of their minds and smiled till their jaws ached.

CHAPTER TWENTY-FOUR

Bernie chose to be married in the little church in Salthill, which was packed to capacity as the car carrying Eileen and her family pulled up. And, because this was no ordinary wedding, there were scores of people lining up outside. Everyone knew the story of how the groom had been shot and crippled by the bride's father and how the doctor had later taken his own life. Some, true enough, came for a gawp and a gossip, but, in the main, most genuinely came to wish the young couple well.

Climbing out of the car, her long dress rucked up around her knees, Rosie looked around in amazement. "What are all those people doing here, Mammy? I hope they haven't come for the wedding, because there won't be near enough sandwiches to go round."

"Yeah, and they needn't think they're getting any of mine." Sticking out a lugubrious lip that went ill with her bridesmaid's outfit, Daisy glared at the crowds, earning a sharp rebuke from her mother.

"Take that scowl off your face at once, Daisy, and don't be so ridiculous. Most of those people are only here to catch a glimpse of the bride and groom and as soon as they've seen what they came for, they'll be off home to their own houses. And their own dinners!"

"Well, that's all right then." Appeased, Daisy swapped her scowl for an unconvincing smile bordering on the beatific, stiffening with excitement as a large black Anglia, bedecked with a length of white ribbon, pulled up in front of the church. "Oh, look, Mammy, it's John-Joe!"

Eileen felt her eyes brim over as, jumping out of the far side, Dick rushed round and helped his son out of the car and into his wheelchair.

"Lord, John-Joe," she said, bending down to kiss his cheek and tuck one of Liam's rosebuds in his buttonhole, "that's one mighty suit you've got on. You look like a real film star in that, so you do. Bernie is going to be so proud." She winked. "Mind you, if I was twenty years younger and wasn't your aunt, I'd give that Bernie a run for her money, I'm telling you. I'd leave her standing at the starting post."

Suddenly overcome with shyness, John-Joe ducked his head. "Am I all right, Aunty Eileen? Really? I'd hate to let her down." Reaching out, he banged against the wheel of his chair. "It's bad enough that I have to lug this contraption around with me."

"Now listen here to me, John-Joe." Eileen dropped her voice so that only he could hear. "The only way you're going to let Bernie down is if you go around feeling sorry for yourself. No one's holding a big stick over her. She's choosing to marry you because she loves you. Whatever you do, remember that. Nothing else matters. Nothing at all. Now come on, it's time you were inside because she'll be here any minute and it wouldn't do to have the two of you bumping into each other outside the church." A chuckle entered her voice. "Besides, Paddy's already waiting for you in there and if you think your nerves are bad, you should see his! The poor man's a nervous wreck. Anyone would think it was himself that was getting married. Here, Dick," she motioned to her brother who was busy chatting to the crowds and receiving hearty congratulations in his capacity as father of the groom, "take John-Joe inside, will you? Bernie will be here at any minute."

Not five minutes later an escalating *oooh* from the crowds signalled the arrival of the bride in yet another Anglia, this one white, with pink ribbons and a garland of flowers draped across the bonnet.

"Oh, Mammy, doesn't she look beautiful?" Mollie whispered, as flanked by her younger sister, Majella, who was acting as chief bridesmaid, Bernie climbed gracefully out.

"Indeed she does." Appraising, Eileen's eyes ran over the dress she'd spent so much time making. White guipure lace over white satin. Simple and elegant, it had been a good choice. She tweaked her daughter's nose. "But you know what they say, Moll, all brides are beautiful on their wedding day. Even the ugly ones."

"Bernie's beautiful every day," Mollie said loyally, gazing in awe at the young woman swathed in white lace, her luscious blonde hair piled on top of her head and the simple short veil pinned at the top with one perfect pink rose.

Eileen had just noticed the rose. One of Liam's roses. But where was the lovely orange-blossom bridal wreath they had sent down from Clerys in Dublin? Rushing over to Bernie, she hugged her carefully, then holding her at arm's length fussed unnecessarily with the dress, tugging a fold here, a ribbon there.

"Oh, Bernie, Bernie, you look gorgeous! John-Joe's a lucky man, so he is." She dropped a kiss on the young woman's cheek, careful not to mark her with lipstick. "Thank God, the dress is perfect, even if I do say so myself. You'd have to go a long way to find a nicer one. But what on earth happened to your wreath? The Clerys wreath?"

Shyly, Bernie reached up and touched the rose. "The other one was lovely all right, but I just thought this was more appropriate. It makes me feel more like one of the family. I know how much you all loved Liam, and how much you miss him. So I'm wearing this in his honour."

"Thank you," Eileen said, almost too full to speak. "Thank you for that and you know, Bernie, we're very happy to have you as a member of the family." Quickly she drew a deep breath and composed herself. If ever there was a time to go blubbing, this wasn't it. "Now let's get you inside before poor old John-Joe think he's been jilted at the altar. God love him, he's already on tenterhooks as it is. Anyone would think he was facing the firing squad and not Father Clarke. Come on, girls!" Gathering the bridesmaids, who were busily engaged in acting the eejit and showing off before the crowds, she issued them with instructions. "Majella, you're chief bridesmaid, so you pick up Bernie's train." Grabbing the child's hands, she flipped them over and back. "I hope your hands are nice and clean and that your nails are clipped. Mollie! Mollie, get down off that fence and listen. You and Daisy walk side by side behind Majella and no pushing and shoving one another. Do you hear me? And you, Rosie, bring up

---

the rear – *walk* behind them," she clarified, seeing a look of pure puzzlement drape itself across her youngest daughter's face. "And remember all of you, I said *walk* – don't run! Go on then, off you all go, and good luck!" She blew a kiss, as from somewhere inside a creaky organ started up the Wedding March.

Much to Paddy's consternation, Eileen cried all through the wedding, sniffing like one possessed and dabbing furiously at her eyes as if they had done her some kind of mortal injury. At one point he felt compelled to lean over and remind her it was supposed to be a celebration and not a funeral, only to be met with a withering look. Like most women, there was nothing Eileen McNab enjoyed more than a good cry at a wedding. When the time came for the young couple to take their vows, he thought she would go hysterical altogether, especially when, to everyone's surprise and delight, John-Joe was helped out of the wheelchair by his father, and standing tall, straight and proud, he slipped the ring on Bernie's finger. To be truthful, Paddy felt his own eyes well up at that point but, of course, that was down to a stray dust mote, he told himself, and nothing at all to do with the sentiment of the occasion.

"Well, you did it," he told John-Joe outside the church, bending down to give him a friendly puck on the arm, as Eileen fussed over a glowing Bernie and people gathered round to admire the ring. "You've had it now, me boy, all right. You're a lifer, like the rest of us. Everywhere you go now you'll have the ball and chain behind you. There won't be a moment's peace from morning till night."

"And there's nothing I'd like more," John-Joe beamed up at his uncle. "Besides, don't go codding me that you're not happy to be tied to Aunty Eileen's apron strings. I never saw a couple more suited, apart from myself and Bernie, of course."

Paddy tapped his nose. "Well, just don't go letting on to your Aunty Eileen. I like to keep her on her toes." A frown crossed his forehead. "Speaking of which, that was a great performance you put in there in the church. I didn't know you could stand for that long. I think some people thought they were witnessing a miracle."

"I'm getting stronger, Uncle Paddy," John-Joe confessed. "Slowly, mind, but at least there's some feeling coming back into my legs. It's too soon to say if I'll make a complete recovery, but while there's still hope, I'll pull out all the stops."

"See to it that you do," Paddy said. "After all, you're a family man now. You've got everything to live for."

"I know. And we've decided we're still going away, Uncle Paddy. Bernie thinks it'll be good for all of us to make a fresh start, including young Majella.

No matter how it goes, we'll always be objects of curiosity here. Galway is a very small pond. To the folks round here, I'll always be a bit of a freak, the fella who was shot by the mad doctor up in Friar's Copse, and Bernie and her sister will always carry the stigma of being the madman's daughters." He fiddled idly with his buttonhole. "We don't want any more reminders of that, Uncle Paddy. All we want now is to simply get on with our lives in the best way we can."

"I can understand that," Paddy said, "and for what it's worth, I think you're doing the right thing. England you're going to, is it?"

John-Joe nodded. "Bernie has contacts there. An aunt and an uncle. They've invited us to stay and that will do for starters. There's also the possibility of a job for me – a bit of clerical work is all, but it's a beginning and it'll do."

"Until you get on your feet?" Paddy said, and it was a loaded question.

"Exactly. Until I get on my feet." His mouth set in a straight determined line, John-Joe shook his uncle's hand. "Now, I think, I'd better lay claim to my wife, before she realises she's made a big mistake and runs for the hills."

"I doubt that," Paddy said, and there was real affection in his eyes. "In anyone's book, you're a blessing, John-Joe. I only wish Eileen and myself could have been on hand to help when the baby is born."

A roguish glint in his eye, John-Joe, fearful that he might disgrace himself and start sobbing like a girl, attempted to bring matters back to a less emotional footing. "I'll tell you what, Uncle Paddy, if it's a boy –" he paused as his uncle looked expectant, "I won't be calling him after you!" He grinned. "Actually, if it's a boy, Bernie has her heart set on Finn and if it's a girl, we've decided we'll call her Orla. So there you have it – Finn or Orla Brady."

"Well," Paddy joked, equally relieved at reverting to kind, "whatever you call it, just don't call it too early in the morning!"

CHAPTER TWENTY-FIVE

The pains took Coral Devlin by surprise. By all calculations the baby wasn't due for fully another month. Taking a deep breath, she ordered herself not to panic. It could be that this was just a practice-run and not the real thing at all. She'd read about contractions like these in a medical book. Apparently it was the body's way of rehearsing for what lay ahead. A sharp pain across her abdomen that brought her sobbing to her knees, such was its severity, rapidly disabused her of the notion that it was anything but the real thing. There was no doubt about it, the baby was starting and she was alone. With difficulty, and after several false starts, she managed to pull herself to her feet and lean heavily on the kitchen table for support. Mick had gone to a hurling match over the other side of Galway and wouldn't be home for hours yet and, judging from the rapidity with which the contractions were coming, there it would be minutes, rather than hours, before the baby came. Beads of perspiration, born both of labour and fear, broke out along her forehead.

"Somebody help me!" she prayed, pulling herself lumberingly across the room, in an effort to get to the window by the sink. Outside there was hope. Her only hope! Outside she could hear the McNab girls' high-pitched rhythmic voices chanting a skipping-rhyme.

> *"Granny in the kitchen,*
> *Doing a bit of stitching,*
> *In came a burglar*
> *And knocked Granny out!*
> *How many hours*
> *Was she knocked out?"*

Round went the rope in a progressively quicker series of wide arcs.

"One o'clock, two o'clock, three o'clock . . ."

Suddenly distracted into stepping on the rope Rose pointed to Devlin's window, where Coral, white as a ghost, had suddenly appeared, her arms waving up and down as though she were drowning and desperate to attract attention.

"Look! Something's wrong with Mrs Devlin!"

As both her sisters whipped round to look, they saw Coral slowly crumple from view.

"Go and get Mammy!" Mollie yelled, anxiety making her voice shrill, all her instincts screaming that there was something terribly wrong with Coral. "Just do it!" she snapped as Daisy got that mutinous look on her face that betokened an argument. Then, wings on her heels, she raced towards the Devlins' house. Bursting in through the back door, she made directly for the kitchen and the groaning she could hear coming from inside.

"What is it, Coral? Is it the baby? Don't worry. It'll be all right," she crooned, dropping to the floor, where the young woman lay, her face contorted in pain, her body arching in a series of convulsions over which she appeared to have no control whatsoever. "Daisy's gone to get Mammy. She'll take care of you. Now, you just hold on there and I'll be back in a minute with a nice cool cloth for your forehead."

"Thanks . . . Mollie," Coral ground out the words with difficulty as the young girl returned a few seconds later, a damp cloth in her hands.

"There now," Molly said soothingly, mopping at Coral's feverish temples. "Isn't that better?" Anxiously she threw a glance at the doorway. What in God's name was keeping her mother? Despite the bad blood between the two families, never for one moment did Mollie doubt that her mother would come. And come she did, only seconds later, armed with clean cloths, and towels and goodness knows what else. A quick assessing glance showed her how things stood with her neighbour.

"You'll have to help me, Mollie," she said baldly, getting down on her knees and palpating Coral's stomach.

"Me?" Appalled, Mollie's eyes flew to her mother's. "You want me to help?"

Eileen nodded briskly. "Yes, you! Now look, there's nothing to worry about. You just bring me whatever I ask for, and myself, Mrs Devlin here and nature will do the rest. You two – outside and play!" she ordered, as Daisy and Rose poked curious heads around the door.

"'Snot fair, Mollie has all the fun!" Daisy whined, retreating nevertheless under the gimlet glare of her mother.

"This little one seems to be in a fierce hurry altogether, Moll. Babies are like that, you know – especially first babies. They keep to their own schedule, some coming early, some coming late, but none arriving on time. A bit like a CIE bus, I always think. Now you run and fetch a blanket. I don't think we'd better move her, not at this late stage. But we'll make you as comfortable as we can, eh?" Brightly she smiled down at her neighbour, the first smile that she'd ever given her, she realised guiltily. "You'll be all right, alannah." Gently she smoothed the sweat-soaked, blonde hair back from the young woman's brow. "Sure aren't you only doing what generations of women have always done?" Gratefully, Coral Devlin squeezed her fingers, shrieking as another great contraction turned her insides to molten lava. "Look, breathe like this," Eileen instructed, demonstrating a series of quick, short pants. "It makes it easier. You have to learn to go with the pains, ride them like a wave." Gently her hand pressed down on the other woman's swollen abdomen, experience telling her that it wouldn't be all that long before Coral needed to push. This would not be the first baby she delivered. As a child, Eileen had often assisted her own mother, who had been in great demand both as a midwife and a layer-out of the dead. Now, she sent up a swift prayer of thanks for the knowledge gained, whilst guiltily resenting finding herself landed in this position. If only the child hadn't been in such a hurry to be born, there would have been time to get Coral safely into hospital, but babies, like she said, came at their own pace and there was no arguing with that.

When the pains were coming one on top of the other with barely a second's respite between, Eileen gave the go-ahead. "All right, start to bear down now. That's it, push. Easy now." Her hands reached out, gentling the young woman as her back arced in agony and her screams put the heart across Mollie. "Just try and breathe like I showed you. Good! Good girl! That's the business. You're doing great."

Her eyes like saucers and her heart going like the clappers, Mollie stood well back out of the way. She had seen her friend Delia Mackey's terrier give birth to a litter of pups once, but that was nothing like this. After a little bit of shifting about the place, Parsnip had simply dropped her pups and, in another minute or two, there she was, licking the faces off them. "Is she going to die, Mammy?" Mollie's eyes were anxious, her face white as a sheet, making the sprinkling of freckles round her nose stand out like an outbreak of the measles.

Flicking her own damp hair back from her forehead, Eileen threw her a quick glance. "Yerrah, indeed she is not! In a few minutes she'll think all her birthdays have come together and she won't remember a bit about the pain."

"Did you?" Coral asked, during a momentary respite, her voice weak as the mewing of a two-day-old kitten. "Did you think all your birthdays had come together?"

Eileen folded her lips firmly. "Yes. Yes, I did. With each and every one of them."

"It must be hard for you – " Her face creased in agony, Coral broke off mid-sentence, making a huge effort to ride a contraction out, just as Eileen had told her. She panted, struggling to speak. "It – it must be hard for you being here with me, when your son . . ."

"Shush, now," Eileen interrupted, pain, as always, lancing through her heart at the memory of Liam, but managing to keep her voice soft all the same. "Now is not the time for recriminations. Let's get this little one born and worry about everything else later. Eh?"

"Oh, Lord! Oh Jesus!" Coral Devlin gave a sudden scream of pure agony as a pain, worse than any that had gone before, seized her tired body in a vice-like grip. "Help me!" she begged, her eyes ranging wildly between Eileen and the terrified Mollie. "Please help me!"

"It's okay. It's okay. You're doing fine," Eileen's voice rose, encouragingly. "It'll all be over soon, I promise. Just keep pushing – that's it. Almost there, now. I can see the head starting to crown – just a little bit more effort now and we're in business!" Excitedly she beckoned Mollie nearer. "Look, Moll! Can you see the head?"

The joys of birth passing her completely by, the overwrought Mollie nodded, her eyes filling up with tears that cascaded over onto her cheeks.

Eileen laughed, jubilant as she was at every birth, as with a final heroic push from Coral, the rest of the baby slithered free. "Oh, a little boy! Wipe those tears away, Mollie McNab! Can't you see Coral's grand now?" Abruptly her laughter faded as she caught sight of the cord that had become twisted round the child's neck. Not wanting her young daughter to witness any complications and become more upset than she already was, she flapped her hand. "Quick, you run along now, Mollie, and put the kettle on. Mrs Devlin and myself will be gasping for a cup of tea in a minute."

Worn out to the point of exhaustion, but alerted by the note in Eileen's voice, Coral struggled to sit up. "What is it? Is something wrong? Mrs McNab?" Wide with anxiety, her eyes scanned Eileen's face. "Is something wrong with my baby? Tell me, please!"

"It's the cord," Eileen gasped. "It's twisted round his neck." This was serious. She'd seen it happen once or twice before and the unfortunate child, starved too long of oxygen, end up brain-damaged for life. Her fingers surprisingly steady, she worked quickly and deftly to disentangle the cord, sending up a swift prayer of thanks when, eventually, it came free of his windpipe. Then cutting and tying it off, she wiped the child's mouth and eyes and, patting his bottom, held him upside down, waiting for the cry that is the plaintive signal of all newborn life. Nothing happened.

"What's wrong? Why isn't he crying?" Beseechingly, Coral Devlin stared over to where Eileen had laid the baby down on the kitchen table and was now gently blowing into its mouth and pressing gently on its tiny chest. "Is he dead? Oh, please don't tell me he's dead!"

"No, thank God!" Eileen sighed in relief, as the baby's chest, a tiny bellows, began to rise and fall by itself. "But I won't pretend it wasn't a near thing." A tender smile lit up her face as, turning a rosy shade of pink, the baby gave a little snuffle. "Still, you're all right now, aren't you? You're hale and hearty and as gorgeous a piece of humanity as ever was born!" Wrapping him in a towel, she walked across and gently placed him on Coral's breast. "There, son," she said, "get acquainted with your mother." Then turning away, so that Coral couldn't see the tears standing in her eyes, she called loudly for Mollie. "Hurry up with that tea, Moll, would you, before the tongue dries up in me head!"

Cradling the baby close, Coral smiled down at him, her face serene and radiant as a Madonna. "Hello, Dominic Devlin," she said. "Pleased to meet you."

The talk in O'Dwyer's was all about how Devlin's wife had almost died giving birth to a premature baby and how, Eileen McNab, all credit to her, had laid aside her own grievances and stepped in to save them both. There was much shaking of heads and mutterings over pints of beer, and more than one man offered it as his opinion that it would have been poetic justice if she'd left them both to die.

After the birth of little Dominic, Coral found she wanted to go home. Becoming a mother made her long for her own, so it came as little surprise really when Devlin announced he was moving lock, stock and barrel and taking his wife and child back to England.

He stood on the McNabs' doorstep, 'with all the proudness gone out of him' as Paddy was to remark later to Eileen.

"I'm in your debt, Mrs McNab." Shuffling uncomfortably, his eyes scanned the tips of his boots. "If it wasn't for you, I would have lost them both." His voice broke. "I couldn't have borne that, you know. I wouldn't have wanted to go on living."

Eileen shook her head. "Not at all. I'm no hero. I only did what anyone would do, Mr. Devlin. No more. No less!"

"No!" Devlin's head came up at that, his face suffused with colour. "No, that's not true. You could have left them. After what I did to you and yours, you could have just left them. It says it in the Bible, doesn't it? An eye for an eye. A tooth for a tooth." His voice dropped, even as his eyes held hers. "And a son for a son!" His fist struck his chest, *mea culpa!* "But you didn't leave them. After all the pain. After all the sorrow I put you through. You still had the love, the humanity and courage to open up your heart and save my child. And when I look in his cradle, Mrs McNab, that's *my son* I see lying there. That's a part of me, my flesh and blood, and my heart fair breaks with love for him." He stepped back a pace, almost as if he was not worthy to stand too close to them. "Forgive me," he said. "Forgive me for taking your child away from you. As God is my judge, it was an accident and there isn't a day or a night that goes past when I don't think of him and wish I could turn back time. Forgive me for never having had the courage to approach you before, for never having had the courage to look you in the face and see the pain in your eyes – the pain put there by me. The truth is I tried often enough to steel myself, but my courage always failed me. Coward that I am, maybe I was hoping Coral and that little girl of yours, Mollie, could help me build some bridges, because, God help me, I didn't fully understand what I took away from you. I knew I had wounded you terribly but I didn't understand that I'd broken your hearts. I understand now." The words were simple, insufficient, but with their saying some of the pain went out of his neighbours' eyes.

Mollie was sad Coral was leaving. "Can I really come and visit you in London?" she asked for the umpteenth time. "Will you take me to see the Queen up at Buckingham Palace?"

Cradling the baby in her arms, Coral chuckled. "Well, you can certainly come and visit me. I'm not so sure about the Queen, though. I'm not sure how keen she is on visitors." She traced a soothing finger across the baby's face, as he made little snuffling noises and screwed up his face in search of his bottle. "Now, you've written down the address properly, haven't you?"

Scornfully, Mollie waved a ragged piece of paper under her nose. "Of course. Blossom Cottage, Totterdown, Tooting, I'll write every day. Well, maybe not *every* day," she amended craftily, "but most days."

"Excellent, it'll be good practice for you," Coral joked. "And I'll make sure to correct all the spellings and send them back to you."

"And send me back a box of chocolates too," Mollie replied, quick as always to take advantage, rather than umbrage.

"We'll see," Coral said, standing up and carefully supporting the baby's head as she heard her husband's car draw up outside. "Now give me a hand with my suitcases, will you? There's a good girl."

And so, only a few short months after Devlin and his wife had come to live opposite the McNabs', they moved out again. Mollie and her sisters, with a great show of importance, helped to load the removal van, trooping in and out of the house like a busy trio of army ants, till soon the house was an empty shell that echoed hollowly when the children cupped their hands round their mouths and called loudly in the empty rooms.

"The house," Devlin offered, closing the door behind him and not bothering to lock it. "It's yours if you want it . Or . . . I can send in the bulldozers."

"God bless you! Take care of little Dominic!" Eileen called a short time later as, flanked by her daughters, and with Paddy standing in the background, she waved them away on their new life.

"I will," Coral called, bending her lips to the baby's head and waving furiously back as the car bumped and nosed its way down the hill and out along the coast road. "I will."

"I'll miss Coral, Mammy." Mollie, her eyes full of unshed tears, confided when the car, a mere speck in the distance, rounded a corner and disappeared into forever.

"I know you will, alannah." Reaching out, Eileen cuddled her daughter's tousled head to her breast, smiling as she thought of all the little subterfuges poor Mollie had had to go through in order to visit

Coral, unaware that her mother had conspired all along.

Behind her, a sudden shout of pain from the Devlins' house brought her firmly back to the present, and another moment found herself and Mollie gazing down at a guilty but unrepentant Daisy who was lying crumpled on the floor at the bottom of the stairs.

"You're useless, Daisy McNab!" Mollie's voice was scornful. "Watch me!"

In less than a minute she had mounted the stairs, leaving her sisters open-mouthed in a mixture of envy and admiration, and her mother to scold, as expertly she whizzed side-saddle down the polished, wooden banisters.

"Don't coming running to me when you're killed stone dead, you three!" Eileen warned as Daisy and Rose with a great roar of excitement followed suit. "Just don't coming running to me, that's all."

Behind her, Paddy laughed.

Down on the coast road Coral was holding up the baby, so that he could have his first glimpse of the great Atlantic Ocean beating against the shore.

"Look, darling!" she crooned, as the grey-green waters capped with white seahorses swept gracefully, inevitably towards them. "The tide's come in."

EPILOGUE

Lifting her face to the sky, the young woman sniffed deeply of the fresh clean air.

"God, it's great to get out of London, isn't it? Great to be able to breathe properly for a change, instead of choking on stinking petrol fumes. Galway is like, so cool."

Grinning, her boyfriend threaded an arm through hers. "It certainly is!" he agreed. "One of my better ideas coming here, I think."

Playfully, she pucked him in the shoulder. "Huh! Don't get carried away just because you had one lousy little idea in your life –"

"That's one more lousy little idea than you ever had!" The riposte was swift. "That little going-in-search-of-our-roots speech I gave was brilliant. Imagine the fuss the folks would have kicked up if I'd said we were really coming over a dirty weekend and that history and visiting dry old ruins was the last thing on our minds!"

Laughing delightedly, she stood on tiptoe and planted a kiss on his lips. "Funny isn't it, how they still talk about Galway as 'home', when they must be living in England now for what, twenty, thirty, a hundred years?" Her mouth trembled a little. "And I wish they wouldn't, because it always seems to makes them so sad. Sad and happy at the same time – a funny mixture."

The boy waved a dismissive hand. "Oh, that's parents for you, although, admittedly, my dad doesn't talk all that much about when he was young. Personally, I think he's harbouring a deep dark secret, especially as when I said that once Mum shouted at me and Dad disappeared off down to the pub and didn't come back for hours. I never dared mention it again." Reaching out, his arm encircled her waist, drew her close into him. "Yet, they raised no objections when I said I was coming over here." He grinned. "Maybe they think I'll have some sort of Road-to-Damascus experience, *find* myself and come back a reformed character."

"Who knows, maybe you will." Pulling away, the girl started up the beach. "C'mon, Diesel's miles ahead of us, away up that hill. We'd better catch up with him before he disappears into the wilds and is lost forever."

Affecting a mock salute, the young man clicked his heels. "All right, boss! Whatever you say, boss." Turning their backs on the Altlantic Ocean, murky as a dusty emerald in the late evening sunshine, the young couple set off up the hill to where a black and white collie could be seen digging furiously beneath a pile of old stones.

"Gosh! Fancy living away up here," the girl said, as close up the rocks formed themselves into the ruins of an old cottage, with a bigger pile of ruins strewn over to one side. Standing for a moment, she gazed out across the sea, her hand acting as a visor, eyes slightly squinted against the chill breeze that had suddenly blown up, seemingly from nowhere. "Still, I must say, it's a wonderful view. You can see for miles." Dusting some loose clay off one of the bigger stones she sat down upon it, resting her chin on her hands. "I wonder what they were like? The family that lived here."

Shrugging, her boyfriend drew his anorak closer about his body. "Dunno. Ordinary, I suppose. Boring."

Suddenly impatient, the girl pulled idly at a bit of scutch grass. "Do you know what your problem is?"

"No." Plonking himself down beside her, coming close to knocking her off balance, he reached out and steadied her by the elbow. "But I suppose you're going to tell me."

"Right! You've no imagination."

"And you've too much of it."

Refusing to rise to his bait she transferred the blade into her mouth, gazing earnestly into the distance, a faraway look in her eyes. "No, seriously though, I wonder what their name was, if they had children, if they were happy?" A note of excitement entered her voice. "Hey, maybe it belonged to one of our relatives. I'm sure some of them used to live somewhere around here. Oh, I wish now I'd paid more attention to their stories when I was little!"

The boy raised a cynical eyebrow. "Maybe, but I doubt it. Galway is a big place and this beach stretches for miles. Still, whoever it was, you can bet your life they would definitely have been called Murphy, or McDonagh or Houlihan – something terribly Irish anyway living so far out in the sticks." He grinned wickedly. "As for kids, they'd have had a whole shedload, contraception not being an option back then and the nights being very, very cold. Oh, and I doubt if they had the sophisticated delights of TV, either. They'd have had to do something to keep themselves amused."

Chuckling, the girl dug him in the ribs. "God, you're an awful cynic! Where's your sense of romance?"

Pleased to hear the smile in her voice, he cuddled her close. He felt uncomfortable when she went all fey, something he put down to that mysterious condition called female hormones. "As for, were they happy? I expect they had their ups and downs just like anyone else. You know, into each life some rain must fall, and all that."

"Ah, I suppose you're right! I don't imagine we'll ever know anyway, though when I go home again, I might ask a few more questions and this time actually listen to the answers! All joking aside, I suppose we really should know where we came from." With the quicksilver change of temperament so much a prerogative of the young, she jumped to her feet, then stumbled back a bit, a little alarmed. "Oh, yeuch! Diesel's found something! What is it? Is it a rat?" In a panic she flapped her hand. "Keep it away from me. Please!"

The boy shook his head. "Calm down. It's just a smelly old gumboot. Look, he wants to play fetch. C'm'ere, fella!" With a whoop the young man wrested the boot from the dog's mouth, then darted away down the hill tossing his trophy aloft, with Diesel barking madly at his heels.

"Oi!" the girl called, jumping up and down and waving her arms. "Don't be mean, wait for me!" Without a backward glance at the cottage ruins, so lately the scene of her ruminations, she scrambled after them, giggling and squealing as she slipped and slid on the shale-covered strand.

Back and forth the gumboot flew between them, their voices rising and dipping on the clear evening air, echoes of other young voices that had risen with just the same careless *joie de vivre*, not all that many years before. Only when long shadows crept in from the west and mopped tentatively at the little pool of sunlight that was all that was left of the day, did they tire of their game.

"Leave that old boot now, Diesel!" the young man commanded, picking up a sharp stick and using the tip to mark out a large heart in the sand. "There," he remarked with satisfaction, finishing off with a flourish and a Cupid's arrow. "There's my sense of romance for you. Will that do?" Turning, he took the girl in his arms, nuzzling his face beneath her soft hair and dropping a series of small kisses on her neck.

"For the moment," she laughed, leaning into him and returning his kisses with gusto. "But," she jerked her head to where the waves were making heavy inroads onto the beach, "may I suggest we continue this back at the hotel, unless you want to end up with very wet feet. Or we could go for a late swim, if you like."

"I like your first idea far better." Eyes twinkling, he grabbed her by the hand, and broke into a trot. "So, come on, what are you waiting for?"

Abandoned, the gumboot lay on the beach, a

small black exclamation mark, patiently waiting for the sea to turn beachcomber and sweep it far out on the turning tide. Soon all that remained to show the young couple had ever been there at all was the rough-hewn heart carved into the sand.

POOLBEG

DON'T FORGET! VISIT OUR WEBSITE AT
WWW.POOLBEG.COM AND YOU WILL FIND
ALL YOUR FAVOURITE AUTHORS AVAILABLE
TO BUY. WATCH OUT FOR OUR SPECIAL
ONLINE OFFERS!

POOLBEG.COM – THE *IRISH* FOR BESTSELLERS!

Also published by Poolbeg.com

MARGARET KAINE
RING OF CLAY

It was almost certain that the stranger who had fathered her child would be a guest at her wedding . . .

A brilliant scholar, Beth Sherwin, born into a Catholic working-class family in the Potteries, in North Staffordshire, is devastated when at seventeen she becomes pregnant. The year is 1956 and to protect her loving mother Rose, she bears her secret alone, giving up her baby, Rosemary, for adoption.

Pursuing a career in marketing, she meets Michael, the elder son of the prestigious Rushton family. But she has to fight class prejudice, and the jealousy of her old enemy Ursula. When he asks her to marry him, she faces a dilemma. Dare she tell Michael her guilty secret and risk losing him?

Yet there is another threat to her happiness - her search for the identity of Rosemary's father is becoming an obsession ...

ISBN 1-84223-064-6

Also published by Poolbeg.com

MARGARET KAINE
ROSEMARY

The sequel to *Ring of Clay*

"She could still hear that tremulous young voice . . . hope began to flicker, slowly at first and then gathering momentum. Rosemary would be nineteen now, nineteen yesterday."

For three women – Rosemary, her mother Beth and grandmother Rose – a single phone call ends years of heartbreak and regret.

For Rosemary, alone and determined to find her roots, it is the end of a search begun when she first held her birth certificate, staring in bewilderment at the heading: Certified Copy of Entry from Adopted Children's Register.

But the end of one journey is the beginning of another – one which brings both romance and the nightmare truth about her conception. Rosemary has sprung from a tough soil: the clay of North Staffordshire where her ancestors have worked in The Potteries for generations. Yet will she have the strength to endure what she is about to discover?

ISBN 1-84223-082-4

Also published by Poolbeg.com

STILL WATERS RUN DEEP

NANCY ROSS

A scandal has broken – the secret mistress of Roderick
Macauley, MP, has just sold her diary to the
newspapers. He may have to resign.

Bridget, Macauley's daughter, sets off for Pondings,
the family home. Her only thought is to be with her
mother Duibhne in this crisis. But the political scandal
is just the tip of the iceberg. Other secrets are lurking
that will rock the family to the core.

Delphine Blake, reporter on *The Daily Graphic*,
stumbles upon an even more startling story – the truth
about the cool, beautiful Duibhne Macauley – or Lady
Duibhne Shannon, as she was formerly known.

As Duibhne's extraordinary story unfolds, we learn
that her serenity is like the polished, unruffled surface
of a lake, hiding powerful currents and sinister secrets
in its depths.

ISBN 1-84223-106-5

Also published by Poolbeg.com

THE
ENCHANTED
ISLAND

NANCY ROSS

*'It seemed to her that this short episode in her life had the
substance of a dream – a dream from which she feared she
must now awaken.'*

Christabel first meets Ambrose Silveridge at a dinner
party. The Silveridge name is synonymous with
immense wealth and generosity. But Christabel is
attracted to his striking good looks and how he
overshadows everyone else at the table.

After a whirlwind romance, Ambrose proposes, but
the forceful Lady Silveridge shows her displeasure at
her son's choice of wife. By marrying Christabel he
will lose his birthright. Christabel is enraged and her
angered response drives the couple apart.

Hurt and confused, she goes to stay with her Aunt
Bell on the tiny island, La Isla de la Fuga, the Island of
Escape. Among its inhabitants she finds friendship
and understanding and learns an intriguing tale of
love which endures against all odds.

Can the love between Christabel and Ambrose
overcome the obstacles in its path?

ISBN 1-84223-132-4